TELL ME HOW IT ENDS

TELL ME HOW IT ENDS
Copyright © 2023 Quinton Li
First published April 9 2023 by Quinton Li Editorial

All rights reserved. No part of this book may be used or reproduced in any manner whatsoever without written permission, except in the case of brief quotations embodied in critical articles or reviews. This book is a work of fiction. Names, characters, businesses, organisations, places, events and incidents are either the product of the author's imagination or are used fictitiously. Any resemblance to actual persons, living or dead, or locales is entirely coincidental.

Contact: **www.quintonli.com**

Cover Artist and Designer: Alex Patrascu (www.apatrascu.com)
Editor: B. K. Ntouris
Tarot Deck: Rider-Waite

ISBN: 978-0-6456815-0-5

 A catalogue record for this book is available from the National Library of Australia

TELL ME HOW IT ENDS
QUINTON LI

Book 1 of the Chaos in the Cards series

Dedication

To my best friend, Saiza

Thank you for always brainstorming with me, helping me create names and being there for my writing journey.

—

Content Warnings

This book contains references and themes to absent parent(s), alcohol consumption, anxiety, assault, drowning, emotional abuse, family-based trauma, fantasy racism and violence, hallucinations, hostages, imprisonment, kidnapping, occult, panic attacks and verbal abuse.

Please take care while reading. The depicted experiences do not reflect collective groups and are drawn from the personal experiences of the author.

Beware of typos. There may still be a few that made it into the final version. That could be owed to the author and ARC readers being human beings, and how we miss things sometimes. Have fun!

TELL ME HOW IT ENDS
TAKES PLACE IN
VESTIRR & EXCAVA
IN THE CONTINENT OF KYROSS

KINGDOM OF EXCAVA

EXCAVA CITY-STATE

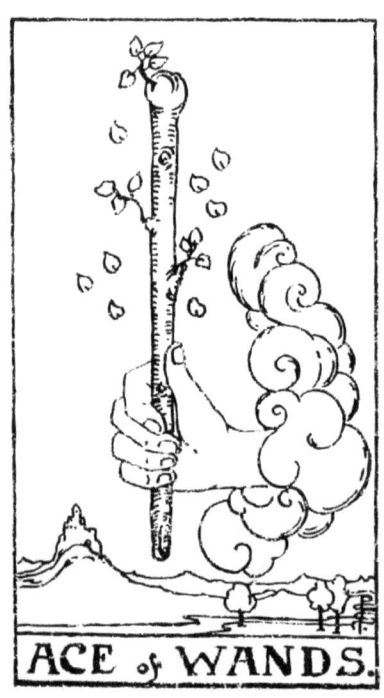

Chapter 1
Ace of Wands

With a flick of the wrist, an Ace of Clubs was tossed into the air and cheers erupted from a game table that stretched from one end of the hall to the other.

And just as quickly as the wave of celebration came, the crowd scrambled to swap those sitting and standing; the dealer gathering the deck of cards to pass around again. As patrons readied themselves for the next game, many held their chips close, and some even topped their stacks with jewellery, gems, and ingots.

Once the cards were dealt, they held their breaths. Iris, too, held her breath.

Her signature blue cloak flowed over her shoulders, and her pure white gloves covered any remaining skin. Her gaze was set on a single large clock that hung in the middle of an otherwise blank wall to the left of her and ticked by—she was counting every minute towards the end of her shift.

Both tension and glee rose as high as the ceilings of the Galacia Gambling House, the broad stone and wooden columns intersecting the game floor reminiscent of prize money, waged property, and the occasional family heirlooms which kept the atmosphere afloat. Iris had once heard an art gallery thrown into the pot—it wasn't pretty when the gallery owner had lost.

Cool glass clinked against a golden ring as she picked up her drink. She swirled its contents, the ice mostly melted by now, before taking a sip. Even in the middle of a reading, her eyes wandered in idle moments as her client took their time to reply.

In a moment, her focus snapped to the short, drunk woman before her, sobs and gushing filling her ears despite the drowning noise of conversation and clattering chips around them. With the constant wails of her client, who was a mess, Iris was glad she chose a glass of water over any alcohol that would worsen the headache she already had.

She had hardly placed the glass back down when the crying woman grasped her hand.

"He's just… he's just the worstest, Missus Galacia… just the worstest…" She cried even louder, throwing her head back. "But I love him! I love him…"

Iris grimaced on the inside. "Mrs Galacia is my mother. Call me Sybil." She pulled her hand away from the patron as gently as she could. "The cards and I have told you time and time again that unless you stand up to him, this isn't going to work out."

The woman sniffed, staring back at her. After so many readings she had done for this poor girl, she was praying to Ter and Mian the message would finally get through. At first, the patron's expression was unreadable, but then, a quiver of the lips later, she burst out crying again.

"Tell your cards I love him, though! He's made me feel like no one else ever before, he's not that bad, he can't be. I can't stand up to him… I can't…" And with that, the woman stood up, threw a handful of coins onto the table, hoisted up her long dress, and stumbled away from the booth into the mass of laughter, cries, and colour.

Iris let out a sigh of relief. That woman couldn't stand her partner, yet she wasn't able to confront him. She never quite understood the appeal of homemaking alongside a man who only valued his partner for just that, but it was a thought she never let settle.

Out of all her clients, this one was amongst the most annoying to deal with. The constant demand for readings from her was good for business, but bad for her patience. There were only so many times she could ask her cards the same question.

As the evening turned to night, the line to her booth waned. The pool of rich men asking about wealth, young women asking about love, and others seeking insight about wellness had dried.

She mentally noted there were a lack of caemi people by her booth that day, and barely any colourful animal ears and tails peeking over the crowd on the game floor. When she did spot them, they averted their gaze and went right for the front door, often being escorted. Perhaps it was a crucial trend she had to note in her reports.

Iris gathered the gold and silver coins strewn around her table and dropped them into her till. By the time a waiter made their rotation back to her side of the casino, a new glass of iced water was within arm's reach. Twenty-seven minutes to go.

Her gloved fingers nimbly picked up her tarot cards and did a simple round of overhand shuffling. She watched the cards as they flicked into her other hand, and once satisfied, gently placed the deck onto the cloth before her.

A ruckus formed from the other side of the gambling house—a usual occurrence whenever her younger sister was about to come to the stage. Dancing and singing were becoming more popular in these times alongside new-found travelling circuses and zoos. What the majority regarded as magic, yet another rising entertainment, was technically the blanket term for her tarot readings—mysterious cards that could tell the future and fortune of oneself.

Unfortunately, some didn't find them as novel as others.

A group of men and women bedazzled in jewels and donning animal furs strutted past her booth, the gold and ruby jingling obnoxiously. She couldn't help but wonder if they did that on purpose, to attract attention, submit others to their wealth. It was strange to see animal furs so naturally regarded as a sign of success.

The six of them sent sneers her way, which she was more than used to. These types never seemed to miss walking by her and exchanging shifty glances, only for one of them to either question her or do something of the nature.

A laugh came from one of the men, though it sounded more like a fit of coughs. "Have you heard? Yet another year in a row where the Galacias won't be attending the ball."

A glare was sent her way by another. "Oh, but when do we ever see them do more than dance for us and play with cards, all just to get a taste of our gold?"

Iris looked away, putting in no effort to keep her face expressionless. She had heard stories of thrill and scandal each year, usually for a week after the ball. Sometimes, other young people would come by to get readings about the events of the night. Though, it wasn't that she cared for the ball, as her mother would never let her go. It was an event only for the most successful, and the last Galacia to have gone was her father years ago.

It was more that these patrons wasted their time trying to chide her when she had a job to do, and they had money to spend. Simply fact and how things worked in the gambling house.

One lady in particular, who had been tightly grasping another woman's arm—and also didn't appear to know how to apply lipstick properly—stepped to the edge of her table. It was a moment later that the lady lazily pushed the pile of tarot cards over and laughed with her friends, and another moment later that she returned to her pack.

Ironic. Iris had watched the lady's wicked smile quiver as she knew something the others didn't. Perhaps this lady's childish performance was compensating for the fact she'd come to see Iris the previous day, inquiring about the one the lady was grasping the arm of.

People were, indeed, very strange.

Before she would proceed to her next client, she closed her eyes and took three deep breaths. From the bottom of her feet, even through her dark-coloured flats, she felt the ever-familiar carpeted floor beneath her, drew her energy and breath up, keeping her mind in the moment. Once she had reached the top of her being, she opened her eyes and took a final breath to complete the ritual. It was important for a businesswoman like her, who was constantly exposed to the everyday energies of her clients, to have a grounding technique to be at her best ability.

She monitored her surroundings, walls that had never seen an empty room boxing in the large casino formed by three stories. Hundreds of people populated the game floor, but nothing less was expected in the city of Vestirr, the trading capital of the continent where people were always carrying funds to play away.

While Iris didn't know the exact ongoings of the city outside of the gambling house, she grew up learning a busy house meant a busy town.

As she scanned a sea of tailcoats and gowns, an unusual speck stood out. It was a man, standing between game tables and marvelling at the tall architecture of the gambling house, as if he had never seen a building so grand.

Dirt and soot covered what looked like a thrown together outfit designed to imitate those around him—a ragged muslin shirt covered in a cheap coat. She continued observing the man from under her hood. He didn't look lost: his shoulders were held up with confidence and his expression barely wavered at those much better off around him.

Why would someone of his class be in an establishment such as this one—did he even have the money to spend? She had heard the house was accessible enough from the town square, large and flashy, with a clear path to the docks and foreign roads. Her mother had shown her a map once, saying to study the map was to study the 'physical market flow'. Had he only wandered in?

The man's gaze met hers out of nowhere, a hint of recognition flashing across his eyes in a fleeting moment. In a blink, he was staring at her cards splayed across the table. Perhaps he was a potential customer? She beckoned him over with a graceful wave.

"Wish to receive a reading, sir?"

The man immediately approached, then pulled out the chair on his side of the table. He took a seat with no prompting. "I would like that very much."

A moment passed as he looked at the table in front of him, small crystals decoratively sitting in a pile, a candle lit despite the bright lights provided by the gambling house's interior. The cloth covering the round table was detailed with gold patterns, complementing the purple.

"I am… quite interested to see what the future has in store. Although I do hope it won't be as dismal as that of the poor woman who ran off in tears a few minutes ago," he added with a bit of a laugh. The small smile his lips settled on illuminated the mood.

How curious… The way he spoke and carried himself greatly differed from how he was dressed. With such a posh tone, it was odd that he looked as if he had just finished working in a mine, or perhaps a factory, his dark hands yet to be cleaned from grease and his bushy hair unkempt.

The man must have noticed what she was thinking as he stiffened up, eyes darting away from her and his eyebrows furrowing. What was he hiding?

Nevertheless, Iris had a job to do, and the personal life of her clients only mattered in the context of her readings. "Of course, shall we begin?"

He looked back to her, the smile returning once again. "I'm looking forward to what your cards have to show me."

Iris hummed in response before giving a slight nod. "I doubt the cards will be as snappy towards you as with my previous client. They don't like repeating questions; I will say that much."

She quickly moved on, closing her eyes for a moment and taking a deep breath. The silky cloth of her cloak and gloves gently hugged her, her heartbeat growing louder in her ears. Despite her lack of vision, she could feel the man's intense stare.

She straightened her deck and opened her eyes. "Do you have a specific question, or would you like a general reading?"

He hesitated. Was he going over his life? Many found themselves unprepared when they met with her and the time came to ask a question, though she found a pattern in inquiries of literature, arts, and politics. Or perhaps he was thinking of his partner. It was common for some men to be worried if they had wives, as women were growing as a significant group in the working class.

"A general reading should be fine," he finally decided.

She nodded and started shuffling her cards. The rhythm of the cards coming together and the action of smoothing out the edges while shuffling filled her with a sense of joy, no matter how many times she did this very action.

"I just—I want to know if I'm headed down the right path, is all," he said with a hint of strain. "I'm sure you understand how frustrating it can be, not knowing whether you've made the right choices."

The last statement made her think. She wasn't one to make many choices in her everyday life, settling with her job at her mother's gambling house as a fortune teller. Every morning came with the same routine, same preparation, same time she would take a seat at her little table. She didn't understand how frustrating it was, because she never had to make the right or wrong choice.

She pursed her lips. "I completely understand," she lied.

The man gave an excited nod as he sat straighter in his chair and leaned forward. Iris didn't appreciate how close he was trying to get to her or the cards, and she instinctively shifted back. The way her expression faltered caught his attention, and she quickly regained her calm, professional appearance.

Under a murmur, she addressed the cards. "What is the path ahead of this man?"

Her shuffling seemed to go on for a while, the sound of the cards landing in her hand becoming rhythmic. The noise of the gambling house around her faded away as she closed her eyes and focused on the question.

In her mind, she could see a stream of mist forming in her palms and wrapping the cards, almost like they were weaving through to select the correct ones to answer the question and bringing them to be drawn at the top.

Like always, she could count the last three beats of the shuffle and the cards perfectly straightened in her hands with a satisfying toss.

Sound came rushing back to her ears, and she looked at the man before her. She held the deck out in one hand. "If you may, please cut the deck."

Her clients cutting the deck wasn't always necessary, and she relied on her instinct to tell her whether it mattered each time. She understood that, like the mist from her hands, she could imagine something similar coming from her client's hands to almost impart the cards with their essence.

He did as he was told and took a chunk of the cards, placing them on the table. Iris put the remainder of the deck on top. No matter where the client cut the deck, the cards she needed would be drawn.

She laid out three cards between them.

Seven of Cups. The Fool. Ten of Cups. All of them were upright.

"Interesting…" Her eyes hovered over the cards. "Two of three are cups. They are typically associated with matters of the heart, emotions, family, love. Those sorts of things."

She gently tapped the Seven of Cups and narrowed her eyes. "This card symbolises you have many options to choose from. With so many things going on, you must feel overwhelmed, unable to focus properly. Do not put more things on your plate than you can handle. There is no point only completing tasks halfway."

She glanced up and gave him a stare. He was as blank as a slate, no obvious reactions in response to her words. Maybe this was something he had already thought about, and the reading served as a confirmation.

The man tilted his head, really observing the card. It pictured a man's back, and seven golden cups being presented to him amongst the dark clouds. Multiple things resided in the cups, from a snake to a wreath to a tower. He pointed to the cup with the wreath.

"Is there a reason this cup has a skull symbol on it?"

It was an honest question, as the rest of the cups didn't have any markings. Normally, clients didn't notice the skull when drawing this card.

"The skull is a reminder we are mortal. The wreath can indicate receiving wealth and success, growth even. Symbols in tarot are open to interpretation, so there isn't only one meaning to this."

Iris took a breath and focused on the card, thinking about the skull in relation to the other cups. "What you perceive as a victory or triumph may be deemed as brutality, abuse of power and status, corruption, manipulation and greed by others."

The man blinked, processing the interpretation. Iris did find this meaning intriguing—it made sense that gaining something individually could mean taking it from others. A part of her wondered what it would signify for this client as someone who looked like he didn't have much himself.

"Does the order of the cards matter?" He took a long look at each card. Perhaps his understanding so far was patchy, but he was making an attempt to read what they were trying to say.

"Yes, actually. In this case, you can see it as the order of events or decisions happening. The Seven of Cups marks the beginning, where you will be presented with options to advance."

At this point, he remained silent with no more questions for now, but leaned in ever so slightly. Iris' hand moved to the middle card, The Fool.

"From the option you choose will come an opening, an adventure if you will. You are on the edge of an exciting, unexpected journey. This may require you to take a leap of faith. This card can indicate a literal adventure or seeing something in another way. Generally positive, but no adventure comes without reflection beforehand."

Iris paused to give the man a chance to ask questions. She was in no rush to finish this reading—a few more minutes with him was more money for her, after all—and it was less likely she would have to start a new reading just as her shift was ending.

"I see. I suppose such positive imagery on the card is a good sign?"

The Fool pictured on the card was posed in a relaxed, yet open manner, holding a bag on a stick while standing on the edge of a cliff. Not even giving her a chance to answer, the patron continued, "He appears to be standing in a dangerous spot, but he isn't frightened."

It was more a statement than a question, but Iris still answered, "If you look closely, The Fool is wearing two yellow shoes. On some cards, different characters are wearing mismatched shoes, which can indicate being unsteady on your feet."

"And so, this means he's balanced," the man mumbled.

"Correct."

The man nodded, mulling this over. Iris took this opportunity to observe the last card and gather her thoughts and interpretations. The reading for this client was looking bright in result, which meant her client could leave in a good mood rather than a crying mess.

"And the last card?" He peered at Iris in curiosity.

Her hand moved to the Ten of Cups. "True happiness and fulfilment are associated with this card. It points to family and friends who may bring positive energy and attract good things. Once you begin looking at things in a different light, you will notice an abundance of what you're searching for coming your way."

Iris tilted her head as something suddenly came to mind. "The cards say you're taking things too seriously." She pulled her hands back and folded them on the table. She was no stranger to saying that final sentence, as readings, even in love and career, came to that conclusion. Perhaps it went to show how serious people were these days, and why patrons enjoyed letting themselves go in the gambling house. "Any further questions, sir?"

For a moment, the man didn't say a word. He placed a hand on his chin and rubbed it thoughtfully. Iris watched him carefully, noticing his lips twitch as if he were biting the inside of his cheek.

"You say the cups represent matters of the heart," he said, glancing down at the cards on the table. "I assure you, I don't mean to challenge your reading, it's just... I am not a particularly emotional person and any positive ties with my family have been all but severed in recent years."

She raised her eyebrows at the sudden confession. If her words were to be taken literally, what he just said contradicted her reading, and she didn't want that. After all, her cards were always correct.

"I understand if you are unable to answer a question like this, but why might two cards of this nature have been drawn?" he added.

She wondered about the possibilities. It wasn't unfeasible that her readings were wrong, but she knew to not give up on a reading just like that. There were two possibilities—either this man was lying about something, or the interpretation was to be taken another way.

It was safer to go with the second option.

"Well, what I can offer you is..." she began quietly before nodding to herself. "... things change over time. Perhaps you just need to find the right people."

She tapped the cards. "They speak for the track ahead of you. You may experience some development. This leads to your question about family."

The man furrowed his eyebrows, perhaps coming to doubt the reading. It was unlikely he was going to leave without paying, but she wanted him to hold on a little while longer.

"Family doesn't always mean bloodlines." She placed a hand over her mouth as she continued musing. "Those around you who you care for, and would do anything for, are the ones you can consider family. As I said, your emotions may be tied to when you find the right people."

She had to admit these thoughts weren't her own and were only fabricated by clients over the years—who was she to speak of non-family bloodlines when she was so close to her own? In any case, she used her knowledge to her advantage at this moment.

"So they may as well be my family?" The man finished with a quizzical look.

"Is that something you have ever considered, sir?"

"I—" he began, then paused. A moment of thought.

Was his initial response to defend himself? Of course, the question was not an attack, but a prompt. She kept her gaze pinned on him, watching for any movement—even a twitch. Anything could give away his thoughts and hint to Iris what to say next.

"No," he finally said, looking uncertainly at the cards. "I don't suppose I have considered that."

His eyes darted back and forth between the spread before him. "I have much to think about, don't I?" he added, the frown he was wearing transforming into a pleasant smile.

She nodded in reply, closing her eyes in relief that the client didn't take her earlier comments about family the wrong way.

"You do indeed have much to think about. A lot can happen with a change of perspective, and I hope to see good things come of this reading." The corner of her lips slightly twitched, but nothing more.

A loud clatter filled her ears.

Her eyes widened as fast as she jumped in her chair. A large bag of coins sat on the table—much more than the actual cost of the reading. Surely, he wasn't seriously going to give her so much?

A few people turned their way at the sound, but caught her stare, her position recognised. Their heads spun back around to their games. Her narrowed eyes lingered for a moment before turning back to the bag.

The man gestured to it as if she hadn't noticed it already. "Thank you very much for your time. This has been most enlightening."

He was so casual to offer that much money. She imagined he was in a position where he needed it more, so why was he blowing it all on her reading? Instead of voicing her concern, she continued behaving in a professional fashion. Perhaps being paid so much over the actual cost of the reading meant she would receive more praise from her mother and siblings.

"It pleases me to hear you have gained something from this reading. I understand you have a curious mind, which is admirable."

Flattery. That's what she needed to hide any thoughts on all the money she had just received. She wondered how much was in the bag. Her hand swiped the bag off the table and behind her cloak before any prying eyes got ideas.

The man stood up to leave, but something seemed to stop him. He looked away for a brief moment, his mouth gaping slightly, as though he was trying to form what he wanted to say.

"Actually," he said, resting one hand on the back of the chair, "if you would permit me… can I offer you a piece of advice?"

Advice… she pursed her lips, then hummed in response. She leaned back in her chair and crossed her arms, quite suspicious of the offer but open to being entertained. "Go ahead, sir."

"Life can always be subject to change," he began slowly. "Just because something has always been a certain way doesn't mean you can't turn it on its head or turn your back on it altogether if you're so inclined. Believe me, I've been there. But no matter the circumstances, and no matter how little control one feels they have, one can always choose to take matters into their own hands."

As he said those words, her mind went to her cards. Her gloved hands had always been the ones handling the cards. She shuffled them everyday, laid them out as well. She analysed the cards and pulled them apart, studying them constantly for new meanings and interpretations.

She often handled the cards of those around her, but what if she were to handle the cards dealt to her? That small thought of perhaps even another tarot reader like her laying the cards for her, to read what that reader's cards may make of her, was a thought she used to entertain. Used to. She didn't have time for silly dreams, and she'd never admit it, but she wouldn't even follow her own advice despite her line of work, so why would she follow another reader's?

"The world is vast; the opportunities are even more so. Don't be afraid to seek them out if you feel the time is right." He reached into his pocket and took out another coin, flipping it off his hand towards her.

And at that moment, she caught it.

"Take care, Sybil," he said with a wink. "Best of luck to you." With that, he turned on his heel and headed towards the exit with no other business to attend to.

"Take care, sir," she mumbled in return.

This wasn't right, was it? Her work and purpose were here. This very building was all she needed, all she had. Her mother was raising her to be a successful businesswoman, just like her, and she couldn't do that by seeking out the world—especially not on her own. The last time she had thoughts like this was... years ago. She was a child. A child with eyes too wide for her own good.

It was out of line to consider leaving this place: she had a responsibility. Her mother would give her what was coming if she pursued what she was thinking of.

Her hands seemed to shake a little and she scrunched them into fists before lifting her right hand and staring at the coin in her palm.

It was the usual diameter and thickness, nothing peculiar about the weight. She held the coin closer to inspect the design.

On one face was a window, similarly shaped like a stained window in a temple. The other face was blank, just a smooth circle of gold. Her thumb ran over the window engraving.

Money was for profit and living. Living meant providing for the family, the business, and only the basics. Her profits were never for personal use, according to her older brother; she was simply earning back what she had lost, and anything more went to her mother. She would never in her life imagine a profit such as this. She could never consider using it for herself.

Who was that? was her final thought before she realised her shift was over.

Chapter 2
two of pentacles

Iris sat at her desk days after the event she referred to as the incident, for lack of a better term.

Although it wasn't her working hours, she shuffled through her papers to keep her hands occupied. Ever since that man had come in for a reading, she was having dreams of a short, cloaked figure with caemi ears, and crows had been landing on her windowsill. Varying in number, they were either silent for hours on end or they would caw until the sunset. Iris could only stare at them from her side of the glass.

Occasionally, the man reappeared in her mind, unprompted. Sometimes, she would dream of a small, dark room and a third person sitting inside. But neither was she familiar with where that room could be, nor did she ever see the person clearly.

She had attempted to drown away superstitious thoughts by focusing on her work. The constant stream of clients, having to keep an air of professionalism, watching the gamblers throw their money away only to come up to her and blame her, as if she had affected their odds against the house.

Her gaze hovered away from the papers she was working on, warm light falling onto the peculiar coin set to the side. The coin travelled with her to and from her room, to the bar, to her booth, and even to bed. She placed it on her table as well when she did readings. In the past few days, the energy around her felt low, but whenever she touched the coin, a spark ran through her.

It was easy to suspect that everything happening to her was related to this coin, but she had no way of proving it, so that thought was useless.

Usually, it was easy for her to move on after a client, no matter what the cards showed, but something about that reading resonated with her. When was the last time she had done something for fun, for herself? For as long as she could remember, she had been trapped in a constant cycle of working, eating, sleeping, and 'round again.

It hadn't dawned on her that she lived such a routine-based life until recently. Was this really all she had for the rest of her life? She was still very young, barely an adult, and other people her age indulged in the very topics she read about—love, adventure, wellbeing…

She slapped her cheeks gently. *What am I thinking? Why would one reading for a random man change anything?*

She took a sip of her drink. That was impossible, just as impossible as her cards being wrong. She huffed to herself and propped her elbow on the desk, her head lying in her palm. Even if she did want to leave, she had no way of doing so. Why would she leave her family, anyway?

"Thank you all for attending," her mother said.

Iris tapped her fingers against her knee and inhaled sharply. Something had to be wrong, for it was rare for her family to gather and meet like this.

By her side, her second brother was taking meeting notes. The rest of her siblings stared at their mother, waiting for her to continue. Based on the way they all sat in a stiff manner, hands either folded in their lap or resting on the table, and the uneasy silence that fell upon them, none of them were used to this situation.

"I assume there's an urgent matter on the agenda?" Fleur asked, neatening her high ponytail before her palms returned to their position. Ever since her sister was a baby, she had a bright and preppy personality, and her stage name fit her well because of her flowery nature and the way she danced.

With a curious mind and professional confidence, it wasn't unusual for the youngest sibling to ask all the questions. During inner monologues, Iris often praised her sister's ability to share her thoughts. True dialogue and conversations were for business only—a bedtime story repeated by their mother before they entered the business.

Her mother crossed her arms over her chest. "A very serious proposal sent out by Her Majesty, Queen Taelore."

The hair on Iris' arms stood at the name; the tension in the room was palpable. Her eyes went over to her mother's face. A frown with a clenched jaw—this wasn't going to be good.

"And what has Her Majesty requested, mother?" Her eldest brother spoke up with forced confidence, now that he stopped fiddling with the papers. He placed the stack of documents ahead of him with a quill on top. Even while nervous, Taelyn still played the part of his show name—Czar, the appointed heir of the gambling house.

The energy didn't so much shift as silence hung in the air. Although the queen had been coronated a mere year ago, there had been rumours about the plans she had in store for their entire continent. What she would follow through with was unpredictable.

"The letters were delivered a while ago," her mother stalled, tapping her fingers on the table. "I've taken time to think it over." There was a pause before her mother added, "As you're part of the business, it's time you knew instead of having to listen to the gossip and rumours of our patrons." She shot a look at each of them.

"That's why there's been more guards," Fleur blurted out.

Having pondered for a moment, Iris turned to face her sister, only to see everyone else was already giving her a look. More guards? She hadn't noticed that much of a difference, being at the back of the gambling house most of the time. She supposed her siblings were more aware of it as stage performers and bartenders, right at the centre of attention and in the busiest areas of the building.

"I'm sorry," Fleur quickly threw in an apology and rubbed her arm, her eyes darting between the siblings. "The increased number of guards was sudden, really. I didn't expect it when performing the other day."

Iris could only imagine what it was like for her sister. Fleur worked as a stage dancer where all eyes were on her, especially on her. More people would mean more pressure and expectations. Everyone had a standard to uphold in the Galacia Gambling House.

"Apology accepted. And you're correct, the guards are involved. They are close subjects of the queen, after all." Her mother pulled a folded piece of paper from the pile and opened it, her eyes scanning over the words.

Czar's trained expression was unmoved by the news. He shared many qualities such as that poker face with their mother. "There has also been a decrease of—"

"A decrease of caemi, yes. That is what we're here for," her mother finished, adding an exasperated sigh.

Iris furrowed her eyebrows and tilted her head, looking at her lap in thought. That would explain why there was less of a magical presence in the building lately, but she figured it was temporary. In passing, she heard stories and rumours of caemi patrons needing to move away from home, and some of the readings she did were in concern for caemi friends in particular, but she never really paid attention to race when it came to her work.

"What is the meaning of this?" The second eldest, Aldo, lifted his head from note-taking with a stern stare towards their mother. She never understood why he tried so hard to hold on to their eldest brother's mannerisms when he had a personality of his own. His studious nature resulted in him advancing in bookkeeping while also doing bartending.

"The queen is requesting caemi to be sent to Syriphia, and Kyross is to be occupied by senti only. Halfies as well, they're being taken away." Her mother rubbed her temple as she revealed the proposal.

Iris was worried about her mother. Usually, she only reacted this way in her disciplinary meetings, and she would keep a cool and collected demeanour in times of stress—which Iris looked highly upon.

Unfortunately, she was never one for politics, so such a drastic change taking place made no sense to her. She had never seen anything go wrong with caemi around, and she was usually at home working, so what happened outside didn't matter to her.

In the gambling house, caemi and senti got along despite their differences. Possessing magic and additional features, such as animal ears and tails, never affected business. Those who gambled in the Galacia Gambling House were serious about the game and never brought personal advantages into it. At the table, it didn't matter if you were caemi or senti.

"And so this must mean something for the business?" Czar spoke again, taking the lead.

Iris blinked. Right, even if she didn't understand the politics of the situation, she had a duty to fulfil in the business. This meeting was more than reading a letter. Caemi made up a large chunk of the gambling house's customers, which meant a downfall in profits if they were to leave. Now they'd have to work even harder.

"An inherent decrease in our patron base."

That Iris only just noticed. No wonder her till had been feeling lighter.

Her mother tapped her fingers on top of a pile of paperwork. Iris could tell her mother was thinking of possible solutions as she always had a habit of doing. She hoped to problem-solve as well as her mother one day.

She looked around as her siblings and mother discussed the consequences that would befall their gambling house and services, how their caemi patrons and performers would need to be replaced, how this would be a money loss for them.

And how was she going to contribute? She would look to her mother and tell her she would work on balancing her profits, having no concern of an entire species being driven out of their continent for a reason she didn't know. She would be made to forget caemi existed, and life would go on.

Wasn't that wrong? Or was she the one out of line? Her siblings didn't seem bothered by the world-changing issue, and her mother carried on with business. They were treating the situation as if a supplier had suddenly stopped selling to them, or transport ships were being delayed. Perhaps it wasn't something she was supposed to be concerned about; she was a senti.

"Sybil." Her mother leaned towards her, her hands together. Her stare was impaling—Iris almost felt the heat coming from it.

She snapped out of her thoughts and was thrown back into her chair.

"Yes, boss?" She quickly cleared her throat and regained her composure. Her mother was still her work superior, and she had to maintain a professional appearance.

"You haven't been contributing to the discussion. Would you care to share your thoughts?" Her mother's voice lowered as she spoke, like she was afraid of those downstairs on the game floor hearing her disappointment.

The room darkened, and her mind flickered to an image of cold metal wrapped around her wrists. Holding one of her forearms allowed the warmth of her palm to distract herself from the feeling. She attempted to gather her thoughts to form something worthwhile to share with her family, but she hadn't been following the discussion.

"Well, I think…" she began quietly.

"Speak up, young lady," her mother snapped.

Iris pursed her lips. Oh Ter, she didn't know what to do. If she admitted she wasn't listening, there was bound to be punishment involved. If she lied, her siblings would see right through her. Her breath started to quicken, and she looked to her siblings for any hints from their expressions or body language, but this wasn't like a reading. She had no answers.

She held in a sigh of defeat. It would be rude for her to express herself like that in front of her boss. "I wish to be excused for my inability to contribute. I apologise, mother."

She could feel her siblings cringe on either side of her. *How embarrassing*, they were probably thinking. *I thought she was better than this.*

Her boss exchanged looks with Czar before he chimed in. "Mother, it would be best to calm down and let Iris step out to gather her thoughts." He shot her a stern look, but sympathy swirled behind his eyes. It was a rare look that caught Iris' breath in her throat.

She wasn't given a moment to comment, though, as her mother waved a hand in her direction without turning her head. "You are excused from this meeting, but not from your actions. I will be having a private meeting with you tomorrow. I would hope you've formed a better answer by then."

Iris got up in an instant and nodded just as fast. A frown tugged her mouth and the hairs on the back of her neck stood. This wasn't it, right? She didn't know how close she was to receiving punishment, as her boss often kept how many strikes they had private. It felt like this was the last one. Her siblings must have been doing well enough to have no strikes at all.

She exited the room quickly, shutting the door behind her and almost clipping her cloak in the doorframe. She leaned against the hardwood and listened to the conversation continue as if she were never there.

It was miraculous how quickly her family could get back to talking about the business.

She paced back and forth in her room, a hand covering her mouth as her mind swirled. Her cloak made gentle woosh sounds, and her hood rested on her shoulders. For a moment, she paused, bringing her feet together and closing her eyes.

It wasn't an option to speak up about the issue to her mother tomorrow, that wasn't what she was asking for. Her mother needed her plan for her service, otherwise there were going to be consequences for her. It wasn't her place to talk about politics, which was something high-class patrons discussed amongst each other while drinking liqueur and making bets on dice.

The only solution was to continue focusing on the business. It had been fine all this time, so why make a change if she didn't have to?

Right? It wasn't like she received a bag of coins in hundreds the other day, met a mysterious man who spoke like he was a noble yet dressed like a peasant, felt the fluctuating magical presence in the building despite being a senti, and now an entire race was being removed from her continent.

Everything was going to be fine and remain the same. Things were normal, she just had to make sure she pleased her mother tomorrow to avoid any real confrontation.

A knock on the door interrupted her thoughts, and she quickly went to answer it, ensuring her composure was maintained. She was met by Czar smirking down at her.

"Ah, sister. It's good to see you."

Usually, when her siblings came to her door, they needed to collect something from her, but her papers weren't due until the next day. So why did her brother need her?

"Likewise. Are you here to collect papers?"

"You exhibited quite the display during the meeting." He leaned against the doorway while Iris kept a straight back with hands folded in front of her. "Very unlike you."

Her eyes looked to posture, then his eyes. Shoulders held back, slightly puffed chest. His eyes were narrowing and grin widening. It seemed like he knew something was off, but at the same time it felt like his presence was mocking her.

Before she could reply, he continued, "You know, it's okay if you're going to lose even more money. Tarot reading was never really a *thing*, hm?" He followed with a laugh, heavily contrasted with the look of pity he had spared her earlier.

Remarks like this weren't new to Iris, but she never knew how to respond to them so they would stop. She did believe her siblings contributed more to the family, and what they did asked for more talent, but she had always been drawn to tarot cards. She couldn't imagine herself not doing readings.

"I will try my best, like you and the others, to keep up my profits," Iris simply replied, keeping eye contact with her brother.

He only shrugged in response, moving to the next topic. "What do you have to say about the caemi?"

That was sudden, and she didn't have a response prepared. Why was her brother asking about this? She settled for an answer that didn't go into her thoughts too much.

"I don't concern myself with politics. I leave that to our mother and the patrons."

"Are you sure? You were thinking about something during that meeting."

Was he trying to provoke her, or did he have something he wanted to say? Was he purely wondering? Unfortunately, her brother wore a well-trained poker face that prevented her from figuring out the answer.

"I'm just… curious," Iris offered. She shifted her feet slightly, which she should've kept under control. It was a sign of nervousness her brother could pick up on.

"About?" he coaxed. His voice remained patient, which was reassuring. Perhaps he just wanted to talk instead of sticking to business matters.

How much detail could she share with her brother without affecting her image or wasting his time? Conversations with her siblings were usually short and focused, so she was unsure how far she could go.

"What are the caemi so involved in that they're being separated from us? I'm unsure of the queen's intentions, so I was thinking about it."

Her brother chuckled, leaving Iris confused. She didn't find any part of what she said funny. He shook his head and brushed his hair back before looking at her with a more serious expression than his previous reaction had led on.

"I don't see you finding anything out on your own any time soon, considering how little you know right now. Do you even pay attention to what people say around you?" He paused briefly, not leaving enough time for her to respond. "They attempted assassination, Iris. People tend to make big changes when their life is threatened."

Assassination. As in… caemi infiltrating the royal family castle and trying to kill the queen? It was obvious what it meant, and she wouldn't think to pose such a stupid question to her brother. But why would they do that? She supposed it was her own fault for not being informed enough or paying attention like her siblings did.

This explained why the queen would want to exclude the caemi from Kyross. The possibility of them trying to murder her again was risky for the queen, and so, to protect herself and her people, she chose to separate the races. Though part of her felt something was still off about the situation. Were all caemi out to overthrow the senti? How many were involved?

"I suppose it makes sense for this change to be happening," Iris replied, not revealing any deeper thoughts she had.

"Exactly. But we don't need to worry about any caemi coming in to attack us because of the queen's request. We will be carrying on business as usual, with additional campaigns to bring more customers."

She would have to discuss this tomorrow with her mother as well, so she could continue with her readings. "Thank you for informing me about the situation." She added a slight bow.

Her brother nodded in response. "Of course." There was a pause as he sucked air through his teeth. "There's something else important I've come here to tell you."

Her lips twisted into a frown. From how her brother was acting leading up to this important announcement, she had a feeling it wasn't good news. "What is it?"

"Tonight, I'll be leaving Vestirr to travel to the capital. The business guild is having a meeting about the recent changes, and the boss wants me to represent the house."

Iris was unsure what to reply. A sibling's absence wouldn't affect the Galacia Gambling house, since all of them had been trained not to rely on others both for their service and performance. But something was bothering her brother despite that, nervousness showing in how he glanced away.

"Congratulations." An empty celebration. Her eldest brother was growing to be the one to take over the business, but this didn't feel like a triumph.

"Thank you, Iris." An empty reply. It seemed like he also knew this conversation was purely business and nothing else.

"When will you return?" she blurted as he looked towards the doors of the other siblings' rooms. He had to announce the news to them as well.

"I may be away for a couple of months. I will be reporting back here by letter while I'm away."

"I see." Silence between them lingered. Business as usual, but the situation still called for serious guild meetings like this, where her brother had to be sent away.

Her brother cleared his throat and crossed his arms, his previous solemn expression turning to one more serious, a hint of mockery returning.

"And know I won't be telling the boss about this conversation about the caemi."

Iris blinked. A swift topic change, but she didn't consider the possibility he would reveal her ignorance about the situation to the boss, leaving an uneasy feeling in her stomach. But she had to trust her brother.

With no response, he gave Iris a wave and began to walk away to the next room before looking back briefly. "I hope you're not hiding anything, Iris."

She gulped. She didn't think she was, but that sentence made her doubt.

Chapter 3
three of Wands

Now that Iris knew about the caemi ban in Kyross, it was hard not to notice. The gambling house itself remained the same, with its illuminated hanging lights that made it hard to tell if it was day or night, the sweet smell of wine, or perhaps the fruity smell that was coming from the incense her mother lit, and occasionally, the scent of cigarette smoke.

Men, women, and others were gathered around tables in their well-tailored clothing and shoes that were only worn by people who could afford to enjoy the gambling house. Now that caemi weren't around anymore, the crowd lacked the diversity of colour.

While senti wore garments of expensive fabrics with the brooches or clips decorating their otherwise plain clothing, caemi fashion had advanced to accommodate the extra animal ears on top of their heads, as well as their tails. With so much focus on adapting the fabric came bedazzlement and basic yet elegant designs either embroidered with thread or sewn on with sequins and gems.

To put it simply, when looking around from her booth or the upstairs balcony that led to her family's rooms, the scene was duller than it used to be.

It wasn't supposed to bother her. After all, her brother told her business was going to run as usual and there was nothing to worry about. But that uneasy feeling from yesterday continued to grow, and the prospect that she should be doing more was eating away at her.

Iris sighed, fixing her gloves and straightening her cloak before gently picking up her cards. It was the middle of the day, and she was seated at her booth once again. Her routine dictated for her to take her position after breakfast, properly presented for potential customers. Aside from the lack of caemi, nothing else was out of the ordinary, as she gave readings throughout the day.

She idly scanned those seated at tables in front of her and travelling to and from the bar, recognising regular faces. Even if there was a new face, they were accompanied by someone she knew by how they dressed or their mannerisms.

While waiting for her next customer to arrive, Iris played with the cards in her hands. Perhaps she could use this chance to do a reading for herself—to refresh her mind for the readings to come. Although she knew that was just an excuse.

A reading was always useful when she was feeling off or needed advice for something. Tarot reading was what she was best at, and 'best at' was to a high standard as well. Her siblings' and mother's services and line of work were impressive, but she found a lot of success from her readings.

It wasn't only the future Iris could read, but past and present as well. She proved her talent to clients when they hadn't revealed anything about themselves, yet she could tell them specific details just by reading the cards.

She was able to pull whatever cards she needed at the very moment, no matter how many, and she always moderated the questions to be fit for a reading. Altogether, it was a perfect ritual for her.

It began with breathing. A deep inhale, hold, a steady exhale. Repeat. This was one of the keys to focusing properly. Not on anything in particular since, as a senti, she didn't use magic for what she did, but it developed the focus she needed to keep her train of thought going and have a keen eye for the symbols that jumped out at her to be interpreted.

Next was the shuffle. Despite starting slowly to ensure she wouldn't lose grip on the cards, she quickly formed a fast rhythm, the cards flying from one hand to the other. As she imagined the mist emerging from her palms and surrounding the cards, the background noise faded away.

For a brief moment, unease crept up on her, as if there was something coming towards her from the other side of the gambling house. It was on occasion while shuffling that these chills would be sent up her neck or through her hands, or an image that didn't make sense to her would appear in her head. Sometimes, she would reflect on them after a while and connect them to coincidences, but she often pulled herself back into shuffling and concentration.

Even if the cards weren't perfectly straight with every shuffle, a few sticking out, Iris never dropped a card. What would years of practice and dedication amount to if she dropped them?

At last, her hands came to a stop, and the fortune telling cards neatened with each gloved finger lining up their edges. The sound of chatter, music, jeering, and cheering returned around her. It was time for her to pull the top three cards off the deck. She laid each card on the table, but instead of placing them upside-down, like she did for patrons, she positioned them to face her.

Seven of Wands. Death. Reversed Strength.

For a moment, she could only stare at the cards. She hardly did readings for herself anymore, which was likely a good sign because it meant she didn't feel anxious as often, but it also involved her mother calling it a waste of her service. She didn't pay herself to read the cards.

One of the worries when it came to readings like this was that she would have to read the message not only for herself, but to herself. With the cards as a catalyst, she was driven to take her own advice.

She took another deep breath before she began, her eyes focusing on the first card.

"Seven of Wands," she spoke quietly, as if trying to keep the answer to her troubles to herself.

"Challenge coming my way, something to defend."

Her fingers traced over the drawing on the card, mulling over the potential interpretation. A man on top of a hill, armed with a wand and defending against six others. His shoes didn't match, suggesting he was caught unaware in his position. It wasn't a good sign. Her hand moved to cover her mouth as she went deeper into thought.

So what did this card mean for her? It was obvious the cards were depicting her as the man on the hill. She did agree she had an unsure stance on the situation, but the other six attacking wands were an additional symbol to unpack.

What was sticking out to her that she had to defend against? She supposed her mother was part of that side, but she was only doing what she had to—managing her business and ensuring her employees were doing the right thing.

Her brother had confronted her yesterday, but it hadn't been as threatening as she expected. He'd displayed friendly body language. Though he'd also mentioned reporting her to the boss at the end, albeit reassuring her he wouldn't tell them. But of all people, she found her family members the most difficult to read.

In this situation, Iris even considered herself to be an enemy. Usually, she wasn't concerned with the things happening outside her home, as they weren't affecting money or food supplies. Her mother always provided meals for her and her siblings, which she was grateful for.

This time, it concerned something much different from just coins and corn, this was about a population of people. She couldn't figure everything out without the help of her siblings or parents telling her, but they seemed to expect her to already know what was going on.

Iris pursed her lips, deciding to move onto the next card, which had the potential to reveal more answers. How the cards worked together was important to the reading and message to be shown to her.

"Death." Her voice was only a whisper as she examined the card, and its imagery ran through her mind.

The knight and horse depicted spared no one along their path. Not children nor servants of the divine. Yet, in the distance, the sun was rising. A new beginning whilst the old was being purged.

Whenever Iris pulled Death for a reading, it was usually met by an unwelcome look or sound coming from her client. Death for people meant the end, mortality, losing everything they had earned during their lifetime, and having to reside in the underworld for the remainder of their existence.

Contrary to common belief, Death could be interpreted more as a positive or neutral sign and had little to do with the despair people became consumed in after the mere appearance of the card. While people and surroundings were being destroyed by Death, it was an opening for new to replace the old. It was a reminder that because Death wasn't exclusive, belongings and people had to be appreciated while they were around.

Considering it was the middle card after the Seven of Wands, she assumed it meant that whether she won or lost the battle against the other wands, Death would be upon them to purge something and introduce a new light, as symbolised by the sunrise.

It made her wary to think over the possibilities. All of them meant dealing with confrontation, challenges, and something new. It meant her normal, everyday routine was going to change.

But what could be coming? Her mother would be meeting with her today, but there was nothing else she could imagine appearing or getting in the way.

The reading so far was only leaving her more confused than before. Her cards were leading her towards change, perhaps renewal, but she didn't need anything different from what she had right now, nor did she want anything to change. Everything was perfect as it was.

"Reversed Strength." Iris pushed those thoughts away as she moved on to the last card. "Inner strength—"

"Perhaps to do with self-doubt as well. What do you think?" a voice spoke.

Iris jumped in her seat, snapping her head towards the voice. Behind her stood a short, cloaked figure, the hood lifted and blocking most of their face.

Whoever this was, what were they doing behind her, and how did they know about this card? Someone mysterious like this was the last thing she needed on her path to making things normal again. Yet, it made her curious. What were the chances she was coming across another tarot reader?

"You must be wondering how I knew that, right?"

She could hear the grin in their voice, as if they were proud of themself for catching her off guard.

"I've never met anyone else who did readings," Iris replied, restraining any excitement she had about the situation.

They chuckled; Iris wasn't able to tell if they were a boy or girl. "Unfortunately, today's not your lucky day, Sybil."

The cloaked person went around to the client's side, tracing their hand along the edge of the table and feeling the cloth. They pulled out the chair and took a seat, leaning in with one elbow placed beside the crystals and resting their chin on their hand.

Iris held her breath. So they weren't a reader like her, but it still didn't answer how they knew anything about the card. They also knew who she was. Either way, why would she trust this random person?

"I'm not a reader myself, but I do know of someone who is," they finally revealed.

So there were more people like her, although she supposed she was never going to meet any of them unless they came to see her at the gambling house. The thought sent a pang of sadness through her, but she didn't have to show them that.

"Interesting, that would explain how you knew a potential interpretation."

Iris couldn't tell the person's expression as they looked at the three cards laid out between them. They gave her a small nod.

"The reading seems rather accurate, don't you think?" The grin could be heard in their voice once again.

She didn't know what they were talking about or how they could make that judgement about her. The reading was for her eyes only, not for potential clients to view. It was simply a way to pass time before she had to serve a patron. At least, that was what she told herself.

"Pay no attention to these." Iris swiftly gathered the cards on the table and shuffled them back into the deck. "Would you like a reading?"

"I'm not here for a reading, actually," they replied with no hesitation. "I'm here for you, Sybil."

They lifted their hands and pulled back their hood, revealing the appearance of a normal, young senti. She watched as their short black hair popped out from under the hood, and she expected their eyes to be navy based on a feeling, but as they lowered their hands, brown eyes were revealed. Iris brushed it off as the light playing tricks on her.

"My name is Marin Boudreau," they began, pulling back the sleeves of their cloak to adjust their shirt cuffs underneath. "I need your help."

Iris stared at the young senti in front of her, tilting her head. If they didn't want a reading, how would she be able to help them? She racked her mind for any other potential reasons they would be specifically after her, but nothing came to mind.

"I don't understand. I can only offer readings as a service. You may want to talk to my boss or the other employees if you're after something else." Iris straightened her cards, noticing a few patrons were beginning to gather near her table for readings. There were less than usual, as expected. No caemi.

Marin shook their head, then glanced around. "There's too many people here. We need to go somewhere quiet so I can explain." They held their hand out to take Iris'.

She immediately retracted her hands to her lap, furrowing her eyebrows. "I'm not going anywhere with you. I have a business to run, which means you need to leave."

While she wanted to believe the matter was serious, it definitely didn't concern her. She didn't have relations with anyone outside her family, so Marin must have had the wrong person or had the wrong idea.

"Please, if you could just listen—"

"Unless you're paying for a reading, I'll be serving the next customer."

Marin frowned, shoving their hand into a cloak pocket and dropping a handful of coins onto the table. "Is it just money you're after?" they asked, no grin or snarkiness to their question.

Iris flinched at the coins and the sudden change in tone and expression. They didn't seem like a dangerous person, but she had a feeling they were more insistent than they led on.

At this point, she was unsure how to proceed. They were willing to pay for her time, but they weren't after what she was offering. She couldn't leave her booth either, with customers waiting and her mother threatening to pull her away for a meeting at any moment.

"It needs to be in exchange for a reading. This isn't a good time for other matters," Iris offered, only eyeing the coins but not picking them up. As much as she didn't really care about helping Marin, she was curious. They seemed so sure they had the right person.

"I'm a little short on my time here," Marin answered, gathering the coins and returning them to their pocket. She supposed they wouldn't be receiving a reading today. "We'll have to do this another way."

Iris tried to guess what they were thinking, but movement from the corner of her eye caught her attention and broke her focus. If Marin, with their cryptic sentences and urgency, didn't already faze her natural routine, then seeing her mother tread down the stairs and walk towards her surely did.

She gulped, looking between Marin and her mother. She tried her best to show respect by keeping her attention to her boss, but part of her wished she could go back to what she was doing with Marin, even if it slightly frustrated her to be so curious.

Having a private meeting with the boss under the circumstances she was in from yesterday was bad. Her siblings typically got praise from their meetings, but Iris could never do as much as them to receive the same. Now it was time to face her boss in shame.

Marin seemed to notice the tensions rising as they swiftly put their hood up. They flashed a smile at Iris before getting up.

"You'll be seeing me again soon."

And they disappeared into the crowd as Iris was left to face her mother alone.

Chapter 4
four of cups

Disapproval was usually painted on her mother's face when she was looking over Iris' records. This time was no exception.

Iris could only describe her experience sitting in her mother's office as cold, threatening, and draining. She could be sitting for minutes or hours, depending on how long her mother wanted to keep her there, sitting and waiting. Cold and threatened. Drained.

She could never work out why she felt this way sitting in this room. It was part of her house, after all. Maybe it was the dim lights, which made her wonder how her mother worked in here. Or perhaps the way the curtains were drawn and only the silhouettes of the trees outside could be seen.

She was also starting to feel it on the gambling floor as well, which made it even more odd to her—that looming feeling like she was always being watched but ignored at the same time.

"There are areas for improvement," her mother began as she always did. There were always areas for improvement in her line of work, apparently. "Caemi have been absent from the gambling house for a while now. You should have already been substituting for this loss."

"I didn't know of the caemi situation until yesterday, mother," Iris blurted in an attempt to explain herself. While she looked up to her mother's ability to maintain a business and loved her, she knew she didn't have time for her excuses.

"Did you not hear me? They have been absent for days, maybe even weeks. How am I to call you a proper businesswoman under the Galacia family if you cannot keep up?"

Iris held her breath as her mother continued to throw questions at her. She couldn't bring herself to meet her eyes, and so she stared at her mother's jet black hair, cut so sharply above her shoulders that it reminded Iris of knives. There was not much she could say or do to stop her mother, not that she was considering it—her mother was only trying to bring out the best in her for the sake of the family.

"It's your responsibility to know about these things. Do you know how much strain this brings on the company? How about on me, Iris? You need to think about these things if you want to be successful."

Iris nodded. She needed to be better. She had to do more to help her boss and the business. Her mother worked so hard to get here in life, and there was no lack in reminder that it wasn't easy moving from the other side of the world as a young lady in search for a better life for her future family. Her readings were never enough compared to what everyone else did.

"My patience is thinning, and you know how patient I have been with you. I've been trying to let you do this, but it's just not working anymore. I'm not having you become like your father, running off and doing something that won't amount to anything in life."

It was many years ago when Iris had come across tarot cards, incidentally gifted to her by a young caemi who had sneaked by the guards—as a family member, she could peruse the gambling floor as she pleased as a child, but other children were caught by the collar and dragged away. While it wasn't long before her companion for a day was taken away, she would never forget the stories she was told of tarot readers travelling the world and telling the most important people of events to come. At the same time, she wished she remembered that caemi's name to thank them one day... if she didn't forget all of them by then.

It was also many years ago when Iris had finally mustered the courage to ask her mother if she could make the tarot reading her part in the business. The idea was met with debate, but she was lucky for interest to soar when she started at 12 years old. Such novelty led her success for years as she improved. But nowadays, she had to work harder to maintain her place.

In the middle of her mother's ramble, a crow cawed outside of the office window. Her mother snapped at her to pay attention, but another crow landed on the windowsill. Of course, the curtain was in the way, so she could only see their shapes, but it was almost like they were staring at her.

A few more crows gathered and cawed, wonder rising within her. The cloaked figure—Marin Boudreau, the crows, the cawing, the dreams. Everything that had been happening up to this point since she'd received that strange coin. Why did it all make her so curious?

Lost in her thoughts, she stared at the window until her mother suddenly grabbed her face. Ter, her mother was angry. If the flaring nostrils weren't enough to tell, her twisted frown certainly did.

"How disrespectful can you get? You're so ungrateful for my help, why do I even try anymore?"

Iris rubbed her chin as her mother let go of her and marched towards the window. The pain was sharp, but fortunately short lasting.

Her mother pulled back the curtains and threw open the windows, the crows scattering from the commotion and sunrays filtering into the room that highlighted her mother's golden complexion and Iris' paler hands.

"They're just stupid birds, Iris." Her mother whipped back around and glared at her. "Is this what you wanted? To make your mother upset?"

Iris opened her mouth to answer, but there was nothing to say. Her stomach turned and her heart pounded. She didn't want to stay here longer than she needed to, and her mother's yelling just made it worse.

"Listen to me now, girl." Her mother pinched the bridge of her nose, sighing. "I have had enough of your attitude. This is my house, my enterprise, my investment. You will do as I say if you want to remain part of this legacy. I did not become a Galacia to see this family fail. You will present me with profits by the end of this week and show me what it means to be my daughter."

She straightened her back, and it took all of her remaining courage to speak up. "How much would you like me to earn, mother?"

"I hoped your mind was capable enough to work this out, but since you clearly can't, I will be setting a minimum of a thousand coins. You stain my name with your incompetence, Sybil. Do better."

Her heart stopped at the amount given, but she made herself stand up and bow down to her waist. Her position was on the line, and her position was all she had. "Of course, mother."

With a final sigh, she was dismissed. "Get out of my office."

A wave of relief washed over Iris as she shut her mother's door behind her. She was never so happy to hear the shouts and clamouring of those enjoying the gambling floor below.

Earning the funds her mother wanted was at the top of her priorities, and her mother had kindly given her a goal to achieve. The meeting revealed how little she was doing to support the family—she couldn't imagine how disappointed her siblings were in her.

Her mother and siblings considered tarot to be a waste of time and insisted her learning a new skill would help her reputation, but no matter how much they warned her of losses and disinterest, she couldn't make herself let go. If she was going to be the best businesswoman she could be, she would find a way to make it work. Hopefully, her family would share the same sentiment someday.

As she neared her bedroom, she scouted the area to see if anyone was watching her. The last thing she wanted was for someone to see her coming from her mother's office. With a quick skip into her room and a spin to turn the lock, she leaned against the door and breathed deeply. At least she had a start with the coins she stored away.

With silence confirming her solitude, she moved to her bookcase propped against the wall and reached into it. Worksheets, documents, and papers her mother assigned to her over the years squished her hands between the books.

She shimmied a short pile of books from their place and steadied them against her chest, then placed them onto the desk. The empty space revealed a visible but narrowly outlined square on the wall.

She held her breath and pushed the square in—it moved with little resistance. A small compartment was disclosed and within it sat the very coin pouch she kept for herself, hidden away from the eyes of others.

Admittedly, her brothers would know of the compartment, as they were the ones who'd showed it to her when they were kids.

They told her it was good for hiding chocolate from their mother, though it always ended up melting.

It had been years since then, so she didn't have to worry as much about her brothers snooping.

She nursed the pouch in her left hand and opened it with the other. She had already counted the coins after her shift ended the other day, and it came to a few hundred coins. Plenty more than she'd ever had for herself, but not enough to show her mother.

Now that she had a use for the coins, it wouldn't hurt to recount them just to make sure she knew what she had. With a few hundred, it would save a significant amount of effort for the larger goal.

The coins were stacked in piles of ten, indeed coming to a few hundred in her grasp. As she counted, her heartbeat quickened. This was the first time a customer had paid so much, and she knew it would never happen again. Apart from working longer hours, the goal her mother proposed was starting to seem impossible.

She carefully placed each tower of coins into the pouch again when her hand froze at the sound of footsteps a short distance away. Unfamiliar footsteps. They didn't belong to her family.

She couldn't risk anyone discovering her stash of money. The trouble she would be in was not worth it. They would accuse her of being a thief, and that would be enough to lose her position in the Galacia Gambling House.

Instead of picking up the coins with care, she held the opening of the pouch at the edge of the table and used her arm to slide as many coins as possible at once. A few missed the bag and fell to the carpeted floor, but there was no time to mind them. Tightening the drawstring, she stuffed it back into the wall, covered the compartment, and pushed the books back into place.

Letting out a sigh of relief, she stumbled back into her desk chair, now being met with silence. She remained still for a few moments more, and nothing came of it. Was she just imagining things?

A frown twitched at her lips. Had she just wasted her time panicking? But then, the doorknob started to turn. The hairs on the back of her neck stood on end as she stared at the locked door. If her siblings wanted to come in, they would knock or call out before entering. Even if they didn't know she was in her room, why would they be trying to get in?

The knob started shaking, and it only got more aggressive as seconds passed by.

"Hello? Did you need something?" It came out blunter than she wanted, but her mind drew a blank for what to say.

There was no response and only more shaking of the doorknob until… it stopped.

A solid thud came from the other side of the door, which suddenly swung open. A short, hooded figure emerged with a satisfied chuckle.

"Marin?" Iris yelled, but it sounded more like an exasperated yelp. What in Ter's name was this senti doing upstairs, and in her room? "How did you get up here?"

Aside from that question, Iris was at a loss for words. Security was meant to stop anyone from climbing upstairs so, unless the senti got past the guards somehow, they weren't supposed to be up here.

The senti ignored the question, walking up to her and lowering their hood. Their expression remained stern and serious despite the chuckle they just had. "Iris Galacia," they started.

She flinched. How did they know her name? Her surname, Galacia, came from the name of the gambling house, but her first name was only known by her family members—even they mostly called her Sybil.

"I need you to come with me."

"What do you want from me?" She had half a mind to run out of her room and call the guards on Marin.

They hesitated, moving their jaw in their hand. "Is this a good place to talk?"

The way they kept avoiding her questions made her more suspicious, but she could tell that if she wanted anything out of this trespassing senti, she would have to play along for now.

"The gambling house is far too busy at any time of day. We're better off staying on this floor instead of trying to combat the crowd." The only place she could think of was the room they were standing in. This didn't come without concerns being, for one, letting a stranger stay in her room, and two, what if her family members caught her talking to said stranger up here?

Marin nodded. "There are way too many guards at the main entrance, anyway." Before saying anything else, they walked over to the desk and took a seat backwards so they could still see Iris while resting their elbows on top of the chair's back.

Iris eyed the other senti, taking a seat on the bed herself and keeping her distance. She noted Marin was surprisingly comfortable walking into a room they didn't own, which was weird, but not exactly wrong of them.

"With the caemi ban, that is a given," Iris replied. "Not that I could say much, I only found out about it yesterday." It still made her feel guilty to have been so negligent.

Part of her wished her siblings would've told her about it, but she had to be independent if she wanted to be successful. That's what her mother told her.

"At least you know about it now. I'm sure these guards are also armed with anti-caemi charms or something magically manufactured. Wouldn't put it past the Excava royal family," Marin mumbled on.

Iris cleared her throat, watching as the senti got distracted in their thoughts. "An explanation? You know my name, found my booth, now you're in my room. I want to know what you want with me and how you managed to get in here. You should probably use the most of this time, Marin."

Once again, her words were left unanswered as the senti stood up and walked over to her bookcase. They eyed a row of her books that hid her compartment. She held her breath, not wanting to raise any suspicion, but her efforts proved useless when Marin removed the books, worked out the compartment, and returned to their seat with her bag of coins.

"How did you know it was there?" She stood up and held her hand out to take it back. She thought the hiding spot was clever, but apparently not.

"Oh, I didn't." They chuckled, dropping the bag onto her palm and complying with her silent request. "I wanted to see if you have anything useful in there. This will definitely help."

"So, you're trying to rob me?" With the money back in her hands, she went to sit down with the bag by her side. What did they mean by 'help'?

"No, of course not." They waved their hand back and forth. "You know I would've done that already if I wanted to."

So they had a bit of a smart-ass attitude as well. It wasn't unexpected from what Marin had demonstrated so far, but she was tempted to move past her professional demeanour to let her frustrations out. Their confidence and smug look were sickening.

"Earlier, I heard your siblings chatting in the corridor. They talk more than you think. They just threw names out while I was trying to find you, and I figured it out."

She raised her eyebrows. Why would her siblings be talking about her?

"And how did you find me?"

"In which instance? The first time, I followed people going to visit 'Sybil' and you were just sitting there doing a reading for yourself. The second time, well…" They looked away as their cheeks became tinted red. "I wasn't allowed to go upstairs, so I went outside and climbed the side of the building. No one was really watching, and I kinda had to look for which room you were in. Rolled into someone else's room first, but it was empty, so I just made my way around to this one. The only locked room."

"Ter, you went through so much trouble to track me down. You're fortunate I'm not making you leave right now—I don't typically converse with strangers outside of work."

Marin stifled a laugh, which made her a little concerned. There was nothing funny about what she said, and she didn't like where this was going. Once the young senti recovered, they went to adjust the cuffs of their sleeves. "When I leave, you're coming with me." A nonchalant response.

She furrowed her eyebrows, giving the senti a quizzical look. "What are you talking about? I am not involving myself with you, especially after you broke into my home."

Their lips scrunched into a frown, disappointment painting their face. "You—" They stood up suddenly, but paused for a moment before sitting down again. "This is your home? It's a gambling house, for Mian's sake. What kind of home is that?"

"Well, I have a room right here, don't I?" Iris huffed, but didn't let their question get the best of her. She had to maintain her appearance.

"It must suck to live here. There's always smoke everywhere and people drinking alcohol. You can see stains on the carpet. There's no windows except up here, what's up with that?" Marin began to ramble again, but stopped to take a breath.

"I've lived here all my life. The smoke isn't a bother anymore and alcohol is the norm. The cleaning may be lacking, but it's always so busy. And it's not like it affects my room. It's nice here, with my family."

Seven of Wands came to mind. Was it related to this conversation and her having to defend her home against this stranger? It could also relate to Reversed Strength as a moment of doubt being sowed by another and having to work through it.

Marin moved their jaw again, their eyes moving from left to right, as though they were choosing their next words. "Honestly, it's hard to believe you think this is normal. It's like you've never left the place or something."

They laughed, but Iris was confused. Why was that funny?

"You're right. I've never left the Galacia Gambling House. If I have, I don't remember when."

The short senti gasped, followed by a coughing fit. "What do you—*cough*—mean you've—*cough cough*—never left?" They looked up at Iris with wide eyes.

"I mean exactly what I said. I've never needed to go outside, so I haven't. My business is here." Quite literally at that. Her days were packed with work, which meant there was no time to go outside.

"Really?" Disbelief washed over Marin's face. "Or are you just not allowed to?"

"I don't see how that's relevant."

Whether she was 'allowed to' or not didn't matter. While her mother never let her go outside and told her to stay inside to work, it came from a place of logic and care. She was to be raised in her mother's interest if she was going to be successful.

Marin ran their hand over their face with a groan of frustration. "Listen. Now isn't the time to debate this because we're literally getting nowhere. I'll explain why I'm here."

Iris leaned forward in anticipation. This explanation was long awaiting ever since Marin first appeared behind her. She was ready to get her answers, then make them leave so she could figure out what she would do about her mother.

The short senti took a moment to gather their thoughts before looking at Iris with a solemn look. "I need your help to rescue my friend."

Chapter 5
five of swords

"What—" Her mind took a turn, not expecting such an upfront request from the stranger.

"Let me continue, Iris." Marin held their hand up, then brought it to their chin. "With all this caemi stuff going on, she got caught up in an arrest."

"So she's a caemi?"

"Yes, but why does that matter?" They raised an eyebrow.

"I suppose it doesn't? Just that the queen said…" She glanced away. She didn't know much about what the queen said.

"She was arrested for no reason. She was just minding her own business. That's enough to prove she didn't deserve it." The senti gestured with wide waves of their arms, evidently passionate about their friend's arrest. "Anyway, she's trapped in the capital. You've figured out she's a caemi. Clever enough to work out why I need to rescue her?"

In all honesty, Iris had no idea. It wasn't her business to know what happened to caemi after they were caught. Were they just taken home? Were they brought before the queen?

"I don't quite know, but I imagine there has to be a reason if you're so serious about it."

"Of course I'm serious. The queen hates caemi. We need to rescue Kalaya from the prison they're keeping her in and make sure she can get home safely. I am not leaving her in the hands of Excavan royalty." Some sputtering and stuttering followed before they gathered the rest of their words. "Haven't you heard? They'll kill caemi who refuse to be questioned. It's rigged. They have nothing to reveal, and Kalaya is innocent."

Iris held her hands up. "I'm not going to get involved in this. It sounds like a problem you need to deal with. Even if I came along, I'm just a tarot reader. My cards don't exactly rescue people."

Marin perked up and pointed to her. "I'm sure that merits to something. Listen, she's the one who told me to come to you. She didn't tell me why or what you could do, but she's like you."

"Like me? What do you mean?" Sometimes, she thought about meeting others like her before bed, being sent to sleep with a dream of getting to know a fellow tarot reader. Having someone like her for a client one day—someone she could relate to and talk to—was wishful thinking. She would never admit it, though. Never to her family.

"She does the card stuff, like you. Remember how I mentioned knowing someone? It's her. She does other things, too. I'm sure you'd want to meet her, right?"

A well of joy rose inside of her, and she was fighting off a wide smile. A chance to meet someone who read tarot cards—was this too good to be true? Despite her excitement, she tried her best to contain herself.

"Perhaps. To meet someone else like me would be..." She was at a loss for words, and she couldn't help a small smile peek through. "It appeals to me."

Marin clapped, sharing the excitement. "Yeah? So you have to come with me. She needs us to find her, and I'm sure when we do, she'll tell you why she insisted for me to come to you, and you guys can talk about your cards and whatever. It'll be great."

Iris was almost inclined to agree on the spot before she remembered her mission for the week. Right. The business and her mother needed the money. She couldn't go.

"Unfortunately not," she said, fighting back a frown, though she couldn't help the sinking feeling in her chest.

"What?" Marin shouted. They were disappointed again; she could feel it. "I mean, why can't you? It's a win-win situation for both of us."

Iris brought her hands into her lap and folded them. "I have something to do this week. My mother needs to see profits from my work, and I can't do that if I'm not here."

"Hm, that doesn't sound very fun," Marin murmured, but got up from their seat. She watched as the senti rubbed their hands together before taking a seat beside her. "Look, we'll be back in no time, and I'll pay you for your troubles."

They grabbed the pouch of coins and held it up by the neck. "You see this bag? I will… triple this amount! I'll pay you four times as much if I must! We'll need some for the trip itself, so I'll throw in extra. We just need to travel to Excava Kingdom, across the sea, one city over, basically. After we get my friend back, you guys talk for a while, we'll send her on her way, then I'll equip you, with your profits and supplies. Then all it takes is a short trip on a safe ship back here. How about that?"

Iris was left speechless. Just earlier, she was struggling to wrap her head around the thought of earning so much money in so little time, and now her solution was being presented to her.

Her brother did tell her the trip was only a few days, with the meeting being what would keep him there. Would the business be alright for a few days without her? Her siblings would still be here, as well as her mother, who always knew what to do.

If she helped Marin with what they needed, she could meet their friend and learn more about what she loved to do. It could help her with her business! It was a business learning experience as well as a profitable adventure.

But could she really rely on this random stranger to pay her the money she needed?

"How can I trust you? We've only just met."

They placed a hand on their chin in thought. "I'm going to be honest, Iris, we don't have time for trust games before you say yes. I couldn't have known about the tarot cards without my friend, and you said you want to meet her. You also need the money. I don't think you have a choice, do you?"

She didn't want to admit Marin's words made sense to her and, even if they didn't, she would try her best to make sense of them to justify her leaving. If she let this chance go, she would be alone in making the money she needed and she would miss the opportunity to meet their friend.

"I suppose you're right. It's only fitting towards what I need, and I will be back as soon as possible." Iris nodded, maintaining an expressionless face, but internally going over the thought of the trip ahead.

"Exactly!" Marin placed a hand on top of Iris' shoulder, which caught her by surprise, but she was too focused on meeting another tarot reader to scold them for it. They got up with a stretch. "Let's go."

Wait. "Right now?" Iris asked. She looked around her room. Didn't she have to pack before going?

"Of course. We can't waste any more time. There's a lot we need to do before we can get to Excava. I've already spent some time explaining the situation."

Now it was Iris' turn to grab their shoulder, holding them in place. "I think you're going too fast, we need to devise a way out of here."

Marin gasped. "You're right!"

Iris shook her head, but just as she thought Marin was finally slowing down, they diverted their attention to her closet, rummaging through it and dragging out a suitcase.

"Here, you can bring this." They unzipped it and started throwing her clothes into the bag, topping it with the bag of coins. "Get your tarot cards as well. Have to keep them safe, right?"

"Yes…" She felt her pocket to confirm the stack of cards was still in there, safely stored in the velvet pouch she made for it. "I'm going to be asking you more questions along the way. Don't forget that."

"I expect questions, but as long as we're moving, I'll answer them. Now… can't we go back the way I came? We can just climb out the window."

"Climb out the window? I will most certainly not be doing that. We're two stories high!" Iris followed Marin around the room as they walked to the window and peered out of it.

"How about we just use the front door? No climbing needed; we just walk right out." They made their way to the door and grabbed the handle, only for it to fall to the ground. "Oops."

Iris gasped, a frown settling on her lips. "What did you do?"

Marin looked away. "I may have broken the lock, and the doorknob….*sss*."

She opened her mouth to say something, but there wasn't much she could do about it now. Amongst other things, it was going to be something to deal with when she was back. Telling her mother about leaving was the right thing to do. However, her mother would be against her taking this journey, and it was the only way she was going to earn the money she needed.

"We can't go out the front, they will see me leaving and I'm not supposed to go anywhere. Especially not with a stranger such as yourself."

"They being who? The guards?"

"The guards and…" Well, she would've said her siblings, though they worked on the other side of the house. Would they really notice her leaving with how crowded the gambling floor was? "They would question me, under my mother's orders."

"Okay, we need a distraction, then. If we can do that, the guards will move away from the door, and we can get out without them knowing." Marin walked over to the desk now, leaving the doorknob on the floor. Iris couldn't help but stare at it for a moment. "How do you cause a scene amongst a group of gamblers?"

She turned her attention to Marin, who started rummaging through her things. A group of gamblers, huh? Being around gamblers for her whole life had its perks, and one of them was knowing nothing instilled anger in them more than discovering a cheater.

As a worker of the house, she was often approached with accusations about the house rigging the games in their favour, to ensure more money came to the house than back to the patrons. While they never had evidence to confirm their claims, it didn't stop them from wanting the money they gambled away back.

Somehow, if they could feed the gamblers evidence of cheating, sowing the seeds of discourse amongst the crowd, the guards would get involved.

Iris snapped back to reality. "Is there a mirror in there?" She caught Marin scattering a variety of items from writing tools to make-up brushes all over her desk. "You really don't have to do that."

"Got one!" Marin triumphantly turned to her with a small hand-held mirror sitting in their hands.

"Right…" She walked over and took the mirror. "I think we can use this to our advantage."

"In what way?" Marin tilted their head, sliding everything else on the desk back into the drawer they came from. She didn't appreciate how careless they were being, but then again, she didn't use these things very often.

"Gamblers don't want to be cheated out of their money. If we make it seem like someone is cheating... even the house, we can cause enough commotion for the guards to leave their post."

"Isn't this your family business, though?" Marin went back to pull something out of the drawer and placed it on the table. It was a ball of yarn.

"Well, yes..." She didn't consider that. "But it'll be okay. The guards can handle the situation, and my mother is very clever as well. She can handle it."

"Of course." Marin held their hand out to take the mirror back and grabbed the end of the yarn, tying the two together. "I can see what you're going for with the mirror. It's a cheat to seeing other people's cards, correct?"

"That's exactly it." Surprise surrounded her words.

"If we find a high spot to dangle the mirror, we can catch people's attention. At least, the plan is for the gamblers to focus on the mirror rather than whoever's set the contraption up."

Iris was certain this would work. The entire perimeter of the second floor could be used since they had an open view of the gambling floor and also a banister to hide behind in case people looked for them.

"We can definitely do it from outside my door. We just need to be careful of anyone seeing us." Especially one of her siblings or her mother.

The plan to ride on the emotional highs and lows of the gamblers was piecing together. By letting the mirror drop amongst the tables but preventing it from seeming like a coincidence by keeping the mirror in their control, it would construct lies in the minds of those below.

From there, well, she didn't know what would happen, but she hoped it would bring enough attention to the guards around the house to move them and let Marin and her leave without them noticing.

"Alright, let's do it then." Marin held up the completed contraption, the ball of yarn securely attached to the small mirror. "This should be enough to reach the lower floor."

Iris nodded; it was time to leave. She patted her pocket a final time to make sure her deck was still there and glanced at the suitcase on the floor. Would this be enough to leave with? She didn't have many belongings, did she?

With the plan in mind, she pushed that thought away. Right now, her focus would be staying attentive with Marin, not only for the guards but for the short senti themself.

"I don't like that I trust you," Iris blurted as Marin walked over to her broken door and worked out how to open it. "Your appearance makes sense alongside my reading, but I've never met you before."

"Tarot is a funny thing to trust, isn't it?" They turned to her and smiled. They were right.

Marin picked up the suitcase, two straps in a loop on one side which fit around their arms and let the suitcase rest on their back. "I'll let you have the pleasure of walking without the suitcase. I'm putting you through this trouble, anyway."

Iris blinked—how could they carry such a heavy suitcase on their back? She didn't really know what to say except, "Thank you."

Marin crouched down, peering between the banister spindles at the buzzing floor below. Iris joined them, sitting on her knees instead as to not stretch her dress. Every day she would walk past this railing, and every day she would glance over blurred faces in a sea of bodies. They were just customers, nothing more. That's what her mother had told her.

A few patrons leaned their chairs back, peeling the wallpaper with the edge of their seats. Some carelessly left remnants of fancy finger foods on the carpet and let their drinks spill just to call for new ones. There was a lot to see from up here, and a lot to be upset about—the costs of cleaning up after their customers came from the family's earnings.

Amongst the chatter and playing, beverages were being shaken at the bar. As to what the drinks were, or who the bartenders were, she didn't know. She just knew it was more fun to watch them making drinks when caemi were around to create a sparkly, magical show out of it.

"Alright, here's what we'll do," Marin said, wrapping some of the yarn around their hand. "I'll be the one to lower the mirror, and you can be the lookout. Once the pot starts boiling… that's when we go."

She looked between the mirror and the gamblers below. She didn't see any pots anywhere. "What pot? How will I know when we should go?"

They shrugged before letting the mirror drop through the spindles. "Oh, you'll know."

The mirror dangled down gradually, short jumps in between as Marin adjusted their grip on the yarn. Their idea of a distraction was barely breaking the concentration amongst the people—it was their money on the line, after all. No one looked up, and the games continued as normal. They needed more if they wanted the plan to go accordingly.

Iris hummed in thought, staring at the string. Her eyes trailed along it, and the lights hanging from the ceiling caught her attention. They were warm, efficiently brightened the house, and were at a similar height to the mirror.

"Just hanging the mirror won't do. Shake it up and down and catch the light as well. With enough reflection and movement, people are bound to notice." She brought a hand to her mouth, focusing on the patrons once again.

The short senti did as instructed, gently pulling the yarn back and forth and making the mirror dance in the air. The movement itself only caught a few glances, but as the light reflected off the spinning mirror, it was a beacon for gamblers to pause and even turned heads at the bar.

Murmurs travelled across the wave of patrons, who started pointing out the mirror and questioning it. The volume began to rise even higher than usual, accusations being heard from every point of the floor. Customers stood up from their seats and confronted their opponents, yelling and painting the walls with vulgar language. Drinks were tossed at one another and glass shattered.

The two of them were so fixated on the turn of events that it was too late once Iris snapped to one of the many rioters who climbed onto a gambling table to grab the mirror, tugging it with full force. Marin's face smacked onto the banister, causing them to quickly release the yarn from their grip.

"Ouch... okay, that's our cue to leave. Let's get out of here!"

The uproar below them drowned Marin's words out but based on how they hopped up—with ease at that, despite carrying the suitcase—and made a dash for it, she followed suit.

Up here, she could stroll if she wanted to, but it would be a battle once they joined the open floor, vulnerable to the drunkards of the day and customers demanding their money back.

Marin was already at the bottom of the staircase as she began her descent, not bothering to check for guards as authorial demands echoed from across the room, forcing the patrons away from the chip clerk and challenging those trying to run out with armfuls of coins.

The senti was calling out to her, but panic set in as no words reached her ears in lieu of yelling, screaming, and more glass shattering.

"Dear God and Goddess above… bring mercy to my family for how much we will pay for these damages," Iris mumbled, her eyes scanning the crowd as she made the final steps and entered the formulated chaos.

Fortunately, she didn't need her ears to see Marin theatrically swinging their arms towards the main entrance, which had been busted open by the thieves of the day already.

Waves of people trying to run with their coins pushed her away from the main entrance. It was suffocating to be between so many people in such a small space that was the gambling house lobby, but she fought the waves with clawing fingers and using her less frivolous attire to squeeze through everyone while they were ensuring their clothing wouldn't get ruined in the mayhem.

It was hard to tell how far or close she was to the door, but she kept at it until she heard Marin's call.

"You can do it, Iris! I made it through!"

With a gasp, she clutched her deck to ensure it wouldn't fall and made a final effort to force her way through the crowd before the situation was under control. She wasn't going to let this endeavour go to waste.

The surrounding noise was muffled now, and she couldn't help but feel the adrenaline rushing through her, her heart beating fast and her legs pumping her to the imaginary finish line that was outside the Galacia Gambling House for the first time.

Emerging from the mountainous crowd, Iris finally took a full breath, with the door a mere meter away and Marin cheering her on. Anything that was happening behind her would be ignored and all she needed to do was get out.

As she crossed the threshold, she closed her eyes, unsure of what to expect once she got there. She heard a door slam behind her and someone—Marin—grabbed her hand and continued to run.

A gust of wind flew into her face and through her hair. She could hear rustling around her, but she couldn't tell what it was. Even as she ran, the sounds beneath her feet were unfamiliar, a scratchy quality to them compared to the dull carpet.

It wasn't until Marin forced her to stop by pulling on her arm that she stood perfectly still, not daring to even twitch.

She had done it—she left home despite her mother's wishes after all these years. She didn't dare open her eyes yet, there was already so much to take in. What was she going to do now?

"Iris?" Marin asked cautiously.

"Yes?" she replied.

"You can open your eyes now."

And that's what she did.

Chapter 6
six of pentacles

Iris Galacia had never known the outside world to be so beautiful.

It was like finally reaching the top of the ocean and breaking through the layers of tension stretched across the water. All of her senses were being bombarded at once—the touch of the breeze and tiled path below her, the smell of freshly cut grass and summer trees; the sound of laughter was dancing around them with chattering that didn't deafen her; the taste of smoke and alcohol lingered on her tongue, but it was subsiding by the second.

And what she could see… my, the sight of it all.

No words could describe what looked like a painted scene before her. Her view was framed by lush, green trees lining the stone tile path that led to a tall marble fountain which was gushing with crystal-clear water reflecting the bright blue sky.

She was used to the bedazzled dresses and ironed suits with pockets full of coins and smokes but, looking to the townspeople dotted around her, that style was replaced by cotton floral dresses and plain but comfortable-looking tunics with trousers.

"Please say something, we've been standing here for five minutes—okay, maybe not five."

She blinked and turned to the shorter senti, whose foot tapping gave their patience away. "I've never seen anything like this before."

Marin looked around. "It's nothing new to me, but I suppose it's different for you. We need to get moving, though. We need supplies."

Marin chose a direction and began walking. Iris followed. "Supplies? Like what?"

"Well, we're going to be travelling on a ship, and we'll need some survival items." The senti dug into their cloak pocket and pulled out a worn piece of paper. The wrinkles made it look like it had been dampened and then dried. "Changes of clothes, food, that cool new pocket watch a guy was selling... Did I already say a change of clothes?"

"Yes, you did— wait, why do we need a pocket watch?"

Marin shot her a cunning look. "Just a gift for myself."

"A gift? But is it necessary for the rescue?"

They held up a finger towards Iris. "Shhhh... you will understand in time. Hah, get it?" Chuckling, Marin continued onwards, folding the piece of paper gently once again and sliding it into their pocket.

Iris opened her mouth but shut it a moment after. With no words in response, and keeping track of Marin's heels to avoid being taken by the engulfing outside world, she had better things to focus on.

Soon, the peaceful tree-lined stone path turned to gravel roads. Wooden stalls donning fabric overhead covers were scattered across the area. Merchants yelled, and a clattering horse-drawn cart rushing past Iris would've clipped her cloak if Marin hadn't pulled her out of the way.

"Gotta be careful of those, you don't want to get run over by a horse." Marin winked at her before looking down.

"What is it?" She mirrored them; the gravely ground, Marin's boots, and her flats not answering any questions.

"Adding new shoes for you to the list. Those won't do for where we're going." Marin rubbed their chin before pulling her towards them again, another cart rattling by.

She thanked the senti before they continued onwards. While the gravel path was uneven enough to trip her steps, she couldn't help but look at each and every stall. Colourful vegetable bunches filled the wooden crates, and the air was permeated with the smell of freshly baked goods. A stall caught her attention when hanging jewels reflected the sunlight and sparkled in her direction. She had never seen so much jewellery in one place.

"I didn't know markets had… this much." Without thinking, Iris hovered over to the jewellery stand and looked over the rings. She rather liked her own golden band, but there were so many options to choose from.

"There's usually a lot more in markets like this, actually." Marin joined her, looking at the bracelets instead. "Caemi used to make up a large chunk of markets, even in Kyross."

She hadn't noticed anything missing with how busy the market was. "What happened to their stalls?"

"That depends on where the caemi were when the queen made her announcement. If they were working, guards would've pulled them away and left their stock to gather dust or rot. If they were packed up for the day, that's how they will remain until nobles sell off their stalls."

Iris nodded, bringing her thoughts away from the gloomy shift in conversation. Marin seemed to do the same, a flash of recognition appearing in their eyes as they spotted a building in the distance.

"A clothing shop! That's what we need."

She chased after the senti who was speeding towards a sea-green building with ivy hanging from the upstairs window. It looked more like a plant shop than a clothing one.

"I already have clothes, so I don't need any. Where do you keep yours?" Iris asked.

Marin turned around and placed a hand on Iris' shoulder, giving a solemn look, although she figured they were just being overly dramatic. "Trust me, I will not be wearing those clothes again after what they've been through."

"What does that mean?"

Their expression soon turned to a cheeky smile, and they made a sharp turn into the shop. Iris quickly spun on her feet to follow suit, suspecting she had to learn when Marin was just playing around.

"That doesn't explain anything."

Again, no answer, and the senti just ushered Iris into the store with a wave of their hand.

Iris pushed the door open and a small bell dinged, causing her to look around for the source of the sound. Marin only chuckled at her obliviousness. As she entered, an earthy smell met her nose. Shelves along the wall were decorated by potted plants of various sizes and greens. It was actually quite refreshing.

Soon after the bell had rung, a young woman joined Marin and her in the room from another, picking pieces of thread off her dress and adjusting the glasses on her face. She looked at Iris and Marin with a bright smile. "Welcome to The Dancing Dress, how can I help you?"

Marin walked up to the counter and leaned against it, propping an elbow on top. "Hello there, beautiful. Think you can help me pick out a few outfits?"

Iris had to admit Marin had a charming smile, although it didn't affect her very much. The shopkeeper's cheeks, however, blushed pink. It was cute.

"Of course, sir... ma'am? I-I apologise, I'm not very sure..." she stuttered but kept her composure as she walked around the counter and to a rack of clothes lined with leather and cotton fabric.

"Either is fine. The preference isn't significant." Marin reached for a pair of pants the woman was holding and felt it, especially checking the ends of the legs. "I prefer cuffs, thank you. As well as on the shirts. I'd also love to know your name."

"I can do that, sir. And name, my name is Bea."

"The name's Marin, and my friend here is Iris."

She didn't particularly appreciate the stranger introducing her by name, nor that they referred to her as a friend, but she decided to leave Marin to their shopping and look around. With a new environment came more exploring of the oddities and differences of what she was used to at home. There were a few things she could start with.

For one, the scent—rather than smoke, the clothing on the racks gave off an organic aroma. Whatever the material was, it seemed to attach to the fresh and natural smell of the surrounding plants. She couldn't find how else to describe it.

She peered around and found a bundle of herbs and what she assumed were slices of a citrus fruit hanging by the doorway as well as the front counter. Her only frame of reference for the fruit was the ones used in the bar for drinks. They were typically lemons or limes. They didn't give off a strong scent, but she could tell when she walked by them. What could they be for?

Iris noticed the shopkeeper was quick to move around the racks and fulfil Marin's request, tossing a piece of clothing into her hands, looking at it and either swinging it over her arm or putting it back to where it belonged. She could tell this young woman was well acquainted with the shop—perhaps she was even the owner.

As the other two were conversing and finding the clothes Marin needed, she decided to continue exploring past the smell and hanging fruits and herbs. The clothes looked fit for adventuring or casual wear, not so much as formal or what one would wear to visit the Galacia Gambling House.

She had a few dresses, the occasional cotton pants and blouse, but not much for outside of work. It wasn't like she ever needed clothes for that before this.

"Do I need adventuring clothes?" she asked aloud without realizing it and interrupted the conversation going on at the other side of the room.

Marin suddenly appeared beside her and placed a hand on her shoulder, a smile on their face. "That can be arranged. Your clothes aren't very suited for a journey like this one."

Iris took a moment to think about what they would do during this journey. If they were just travelling by boat and assumingly walking somewhere, would her clothes suffice?

"I can do without them as well. I don't want to take too much from this place."

"We still have that money in the suitcase which we can use for this, no need to worry about that." Marin bent down to place the luggage bag on the floor behind them before opening it to reveal the bag of coins.

"Wait, that's what the coins are for?" Iris' expression turned into a quizzical one.

"…yes? What did you think they were for? People used coins to pay you for services, did they not? Same thing for buying these clothes."

She sent a glare towards Marin. "I know how money works. I just didn't realise we'd have to…" Her voice trailed off as she walked over to a rack of clothes that appeared to be her size. With a lack of experience in shopping for anything, she couldn't have known the fortune she kept in her suitcase would be used for something like clothes. But Marin knew about this better than her, so all she could do was follow their lead.

The majority of the clothing in this section was easy to crumple in her hands and thin, which probably meant she needed multiple layers to stay warm. They also came in a variety of colours—did colours matter?

Iris ended up hovering from rack to rack, feeling the clothes between her hands and comparing the shapes and colours of different articles of clothing. It occurred to her that she didn't exactly know how to choose which clothes to buy, especially for a journey she had never been on before.

"Maybe I'll just settle with what I have." Iris came to a stop at the front counter where she returned to staring at the bundle of herbs with fruit. As long as Marin got what they needed, they could continue the journey.

"I can always help you take a look. We do have little ones come by and shop for themselves for the first time." The shopkeeper smiled, though quickly waved her hands in front of them. "Not to call you a child or anything, but I have experience with new shoppers."

She was reluctant to ask for help on something like this, it felt like she should've known this at her age. Though, the glowing expression from the shopkeeper convinced her to follow her through the store and pick out a variety of clothing.

Her theory on the thinner cotton clothing was correct. She watched Bea collect a bunch of items from one rack, explaining the thinking behind possible outfits and combinations that ensured things such as warmth, safety and general good care of the clothing.

"Do you have favourite colours?"

"Not particularly. It's nothing I think about." Iris couldn't recall the last time favourite colours had been mentioned, even in conversations with her clients. At most, she figured a distressed lover would mention their partner's favourite colour for some obscure reason, but that was the length of it. She didn't have a use for a favourite colour.

"Well… is there anything of yours you like the colours of? For example, my favourite colour is green, and it's reflective of my plant collection." That partially explained why she had herb bundles hanging around the shop. "I also tend to dress in green."

Iris' possessions consisted of her clothes, the items in her room, her reading table, and her tarot cards. She had her cards on hand, so perhaps that was the best way to discern her favourite colour.

She reached into her pocket, pulled out the velvet drawstring pouch her cards resided in, and gently slid them out into her hands. Without fail, every time she took out her cards and held them, a boost of energy emitted from them and joined with her own. It was a nice way to stay awake and alert during long workdays.

Bea peered over at what Iris was doing, a hint of recognition in her eyes. "Ah, tarot cards."

"Do you use them too?" Iris asked, a bit too quickly for her liking. Was she already going to meet another reader?

"Oh no, I don't." The shopkeeper shook her head with an apologetic smile. "It's just something I recognise. I haven't looked into cartomancy."

"Cartomancy?" A sinking feeling came with the realisation she didn't know what this word was.

Bea continued onto another rack, looking through the different articles of colourful clothing, holding up the ends of some to compare what she had over her arm. "Well, fortune-telling or divination using cards. Tarot cards are seen as a form of cartomancy or card divination. You're a witch, right?"

It didn't occur to her that her practice was regarded as something more than what she knew within the walls of her home. Bea spoke of tarot reading, or now as she knew it in a broader context, card divination, as if it were a common occurrence or normal to the outside world. Although she was unsure how to answer the latest question.

"I don't know enough to answer that." Aside from a vague childhood memory of perhaps a storybook on the topic and a few fleeting conversations. "Are you a witch?"

"Somewhat. Well, yes. I'm not used to telling others, since witchcraft is regarded as lower magic than caemi magic."

Magic—something she wasn't versed in at all in practice or knowledge. She had met her fair share of occultists and magicians during her service at the gambling house, though she had to admit most of them were caemi and therefore employed the use of caemi magic, as Bea referred to it as. Before this, she thought it was the only magic out there.

"What about those?" Iris pointed behind her, to the bundle of herbs and citrus by the doorway. "Are they related in any way?"

Bea gasped, excitement twinkling in her eyes as she wordlessly went behind her counter and lifted a step stool from behind it. Wrapping back around to where Iris was standing, the young lady stood atop the wooden step and held one of the potted plants, watching over them from the shelves.

"How about I show you?" Her voice was hushed, and her eyes were fixed on the plant in her hands. She placed it ever so gently on the countertop.

Iris stared at the plant, blinking. How a potted plant related to the bundle of herbs on the door, she didn't know, but she was open to being entertained by the giddy shopkeeper.

With the plant set down, Bea leaned onto the counter with her elbows propped up and her head resting in her palms. Bea's eyes hadn't left the plant since she grabbed it.

The plant looked like a plant normally would, and Bea was unmoving. "What now?"

"Shh…" Bea took a deep breath and continued watching the plant.

With nothing better to do while Marin was browsing the clothing racks, Iris mirrored the shopkeeper's actions and waited. With a deep breath in and out, she returned her gaze to the green plant once again. Shortly after, something that wasn't there before appeared in front of her eyes.

Resembling the twinkle in Bea's eyes from earlier, small glowing beings appearing as tiny orbs materialised around the plant and began zipping around. Their green nature occasionally blended into the natural decorations of the store.

"Hello there, little ones!" Bea giggled excitedly, the little orbs reflecting her energy by spinning about the shopkeeper. "Iris, say hello to the spirits of earth."

The spirits felt anything but out of place in the shop, mingling amongst the potted plants lining the wall and dancing around each occupant, Marin being a strong point of attention for the mischievous creatures. If anything, Iris was out of place, keeping her arms close to her sides as if touching the small beings would harm them.

"Hello… spirits of earth." Iris gave an awkward wave in the general direction of Marin, where most of the spirits were gathered now.

She watched as a shirt was being pulled out from Marin's pile on the counter and started floating in the air. The short senti chased after it, continuing to be swarmed by the spirits. "Get back here with that!"

Bea clapped her hands together, bringing Iris' attention back to her in a swift moment. "It seems like you aren't incredibly familiar with spirits."

The shopkeeper was correct in that assumption. Iris' mother and siblings never mentioned them, nor did she run into them in her own home. The most magic she came across were the caemi spending their time and coin in her family's establishment.

"Spirits haven't been a concern in my home." Since the appearance of the spirits, Iris started to feel tingling alongside her arms. It reminded her of the energy her hands gathered when shuffling her cards. "You mentioned spirits of earth, are these all of them?" The question was probably silly, but she was still curious to know.

Bea shook her head with a laugh. "A concern? I wouldn't call them that. And no, they aren't. But they work like a force together to represent the element of earth. It would be wrong to only refer to the spirits as their own individuals when their life force does so much collectively."

"If they are so powerful, what are they doing here, then?" She hoped to not sound so blunt to the lady who was only trying to inform her, but the question flew from her mouth before she could stop it.

Bea tapped her chin to think. "Well, the elements and the spirits behind them are around us all the time, even if you can't see them."

Perhaps she was wrong about spirits not being in her own home then. "I see, do you have other spirits here?"

"Likely so, but maybe not in the same volume. Let me go back to your original question." Bea walked over to the herb bundle by the counter. "While the spirits are everywhere, you can do things to build a connection to them or attract them. For caemi, this is much easier, as they naturally emit magic, even if not the same as the spirits themselves. Magic attracts magic."

"So these bundles, are they meant to attract the earth spirits?" Iris couldn't help but reach out and hold the bundle in her hands, feeling the fragility of the dried greens. She gently lowered them as to not crush the herbs.

"Multi-purpose, but yes. The herbs will attract earth spirits who will help my plants thrive. In return, I cultivate a beautiful environment for them to rest. Now when it comes to the herbs, I've bundled some which are known for having protective spirits that watch over them. For example, rosemary makes most of this bundle. Her spirit is known for bringing protection to wearers, carriers, or those who keep the bundles in their homes."

Iris soaked in the information, a rising curiosity and joy in her chest as more of the world opened up to her now. She almost felt a rush to ask more questions. Or was it the spirits affecting her mood? If the plants made her feel refreshed and energised, what could the spirits do?

"That's incredible." She let some of her excitement leak into her tone. "Perhaps I will run into more spirits along my journey."

Bea opened her mouth to say something but glanced around and shuffled closer. Her cheerful expression from just a moment ago was now replaced with a sad undertone. "Unfortunately, you may have trouble with that. I mentioned magic attracts magic— the caemi trading their power with the spirits so they could maintain presence. Now… you know. I'm putting in the extra work with my plants to help spirits stay around."

She did know. With the caemi being deported, it seemed this was one amongst other things that were affected in Kyross. How would the lack of spirits influence the land?

"Things are really changing with the caemi being moved," Iris reflected, and Bea shook her head sadly, taking a step back.

"I don't blame the queen. Her guards and men have been spreading the news of the caemi violence—organised crime and raids, threatening with magic and their enhanced physical ability.

Those cat and fox caemi can be incredibly sneaky with how they conceal weapons, and wolves are known to resort to their strength."

She watched as Bea looked up at the spirits returning to their plant habitats, the room darkening as the spirits made themselves invisible.

"Anyway…" Bea cleared her throat and straightened herself, reminding Iris of her own process to remain professional in front of customers. "I apologise for going off on a tangent. Have you figured out your favourite colour so we can continue?"

She found the change of conversation abrupt, but she understood if it was a sensitive topic for the shopkeeper. With the cards in hand, she flipped through them until she reached *The High Priestess*. This was one of her favourite cards and, like the woman in the image wearing a blue cloak, she too wore one during her readings.

"Blue seems like a good place to start," Iris said.

Only a few minutes passed, and the counter was full of clothing for Marin and some new clothing for Iris, which was completely different from the wardrobe she was used to.

Her mother's shopping resulted in clothes that were mainly for show, so that she could appear in the way a Galacia should. This meant clothing that imitated expensive materials and manufactured jewels lining the hems. Her wardrobe consisted of dresses that reached her feet and cardigans that were too delicate for her liking. It was mostly uncomfortable, especially on days when the gambling house was warmer, but she'd learnt to deal with it.

Before her were pants, tops and jackets that appeared to be scratchy and cheap but, upon feeling the material itself, lend themselves well for their prices. A small bubble of excitement rose inside of her at the thought of swapping a floor length dress that was terrible to run in for a pair of pants which she had longed to wear but refrained from in her time at home.

Everything was neatly folded, and Marin offered Iris' old clothes as part of payment in exchange for having space to store their new wardrobe.

"Wait, but those are the clothes my mother bought me." Iris crossed her arms, walking over to where Marin was emptying her suitcase onto the floor.

"You have new clothes now. How else are we going to transport them?" Marin asked in all seriousness.

She found it a little unusual when Marin acted like this. Most of the time, they were the chirpy, outgoing type that enjoyed making a joke of things. "I don't suppose we can find another suitcase I can carry?"

"The lighter we travel, the faster we can get to Excava. I didn't pack every single one of your dresses in here, so you still have some back home. But for now, we need to make room for these clothes."

Iris nodded silently, unable to argue against the logic presented before her. Instead, she helped pass the folded clothes to Marin to pack. She was also wondering where Bea had gone. After taking the coin part of the payment, she headed back through the door she had appeared from earlier but hadn't returned just yet.

"Now that we have clothes, we can get something to eat before the trip. Then we need to get a ship ride to Excava. Hopefully, that shouldn't be too hard, since we're in the literal trading capital."

"Are we just taking any ship, or do you have connections with someone who owns one?" Iris inquired. With figuring out Marin's type, she found it likely they would make friends with people in different occupations. She had also come across these people in her business, but they usually had plenty of money to establish their connections rather than charm, which Marin seemed to use instead.

"Oh, please, why would you assume that?" They were back to their wide, cheeky smile as they clipped the suitcase shut and hoisted it onto their back. "I know two someones. But whether they're scheduled to be in Vestirr is another story."

They tossed a small pile of clothing that was left out towards her, which she almost dropped in her attempt to catch each item. They gestured towards one of the walls with a tall booth, a curtain covering its front side. "Take these clothes and change out of your dress. You can keep the cloak though, it does look nice."

"I suppose this means my dress isn't suitable for sea travel or something along those lines?" Iris raised an eyebrow, making her way to the dressing booth. Her question was more to humour the short senti, as she was already sighing in relief to be wearing more 'outside worthy' attire.

"More or less. It's harder to run in a dress than it is to run in pants designed for it." Marin chuckled with a roll of their shoulders to adjust themself. "You get changed. I'll sort out these old clothes, which will probably help Bea's business out as well."

Soon, Iris returned newly dressed and took her time to feel out the new pants, tunic and boots she wore, her usual cloak worn over the outfit. Bea showed up at the front counter with a couple of books.

"Looking nicely dressed, Lady Iris." Bea smiled with a nod. She also looked Iris up and down before looking away quickly.

"Oh, she's not a *Lady*," Marin mentioned. "We aren't nobles."

Indeed, they weren't. Iris considered herself and her family to just be middle class, as they were a working family. They didn't have the luxury as the nobles and higher class did, and her mother often reminded her and her siblings to be mindful of their spending and even to give up most profits to her to account for business expenses.

"Really? Apologies then. With how much you were willing to pay and donate to me, it was an honour worth calling you noble."

Iris took a look at the pouch of money in Marin's hand, now emptier, but still carrying quite a bit of gold, which she assumed would be enough to bring the two of them to Excava. Them being nobles was an honest assumption from the shopkeeper but, at the same time, this money wasn't technically hers.

"I wanted to give you a gift in any case." Bea held up the books. "I noticed you were interested in witchcraft and cartomancy. These books could keep you company on the way. I've read them a few times over already."

Bea handed the books to Iris, and she couldn't help but shift her gaze from them to the shopkeeper. Were these really for her? She couldn't hide her curiosity and, admittedly, she was excited to read the books. She reached to grab them, her hands overlapping Bea's before she pulled away. Even just holding the books and looking at the covers filled her with delight.

"I can't express my appreciation. I shall return these when I get back from the journey." She held the books close to her. She could read these on the way to Excava.

There was a moment of quiet appreciation amongst the three strangers, but it was soon broken as Marin firmly placed their hand on the counter. "It was wonderful meeting you and purchasing from you, Bea, but we best be off now. A few more things to gather, and we'll be on our way."

"Of course. Thank you for shopping at The Dancing Dress. May Ter and Mian watch over you on your trip."

Chapter 7
seven of cups

The smell of freshly ground coffee beans drifted through the air as Iris sat snugly at a table, waiting for Marin to return with food. Looking around this time introduced yet another perspective now that she was seated compared to the constant movement of the day. She was in her own world, while the others around her were serving customers their drinks and said customers conversed.

Iris had her own plans, staring at the books in front of her.

One of the books covered witchcraft and the natural magic that came with it. The other, based on a quick flip through, was a compilation of information about divination, including tarot.

Information she never had the chance to read back home was at her fingertips, and there was no doubt she wanted to consume it all. If she wanted to read at home, she had to read what her mother assigned her. It was interesting, but not this. It wasn't what she loved.

She ran her hand along the book and slowly made her way to the edge of the cover, lifting it ever so slightly. Should she wait to read it? But then, what would she be waiting for? Her own hesitation was being dismantled by the logic of the situation, and so she went for it, opening the book to the first page.

At first, the words came to her as a blur, sentences appearing as black shapes on white paper, slipping away as she flipped the page. Having not practiced reading for a long time to focus on her work, she was finding it difficult to process what was written.

She pursed her lips, flipping a few pages ahead in hopes of finding something that would be easier to read. The following pages were similar to what Bea was explaining with more depth, including natural landmarks housing spirits of larger power, which in turn powered the natural environment's ability to thrive.

Iris was taken out of her thoughts when a few plates were placed on the table in front of her.

"Hope you're hungry, I got a bunch of food. Actually, even if you aren't, I can surely finish this." Marin laughed as they took a seat and rubbed their hands together in anticipation, eyeing the food. They went to grab a fork when they paused, glancing at Iris. "How's the book going?"

She gripped the book shut and placed it flat on the table, bringing her focus to the senti in front of her. "I can't apply a lot of it to my knowledge since I haven't been outside to see nature, for example. It's still very interesting to learn." She paused. "Why are we taking so long to get food? I thought we had to make the most of our time."

"I mean, we need food for a journey like this, otherwise we'll fall ill. You know it's important, right?" For some reason, the cheeky smile on Marin's face made it hard to take them seriously in this instance. One moment they were determined to get Iris moving, the next they were relaxing in a cafe in a quaint-looking street surrounded by laughter and music. She watched as Marin stared at the food, but from their eyes, she could tell they were thinking of something else.

"What are you thinking?" Iris asked, adjusting everything on the table to fit.

Marin looked up and blinked. "I'm curious about your life. I mean, you've told me some things already. I know you've stayed in that gambling house your whole life, and that it's smoky, and that you work there. Tell me more."

She raised her eyebrows. "Why do you want to know about this? What will you do with this information?"

Marin laughed, sticking a fork in a small cake and picking a piece to eat. "You're acting like I'm trying to take something from you. I'm asking you these things to get to know you."

"Get to know me?" Iris grabbed her own fork and mirrored Marin's action, tasting the cake. It was soft and sweet, with fresh fruit between sponge and cream.

"Yep. We're going to be travelling together for a while so why stay strangers? Let's at least get to know each other." They gave Iris a wide smile with a thumbs up.

There wasn't much she could say to disagree with Marin. She usually didn't share anything about herself with people, especially not her clients. Though, as Marin said, they were travelling together, and they were not a client.

"Well, I'm a tarot reader…" She had to take time to gather her thoughts. "It's my job as well, and for that, I am lucky. I get to spend my days with my cards and reading for people." Given, they were people she hardly remembered as they came and left, but she still liked the act of tarot reading.

"It sounds a little boring, to just sit all day and do nothing." Marin began to laugh, but Iris frowned.

"Tarot isn't nothing, it's like an art. I don't appreciate you treating it as such." For the sake of her connection with the cards, she found it important to protect their name.

Marin waved their hands in a flurry. "No, no. I'm not trying to ridicule you or anything. I just prefer spending my time moving and doing things more actively. It's amazing to find something that gets you excited. That's what passion is about."

"Passion?"

"Well, it's what you put your heart and soul into. Not the same soul as the magical auras of caemi…" Iris wasn't familiar with that either, but she let Marin continue. "…but it means you have a different drive towards this activity or topic you enjoy than other things in life."

"So, my tarot?" Iris mused, glancing down at her cloak pocket where she could see a very card-looking lump protruding. It was reassuring that her deck remained by her side.

"Exactly." Marin leaned forward, but at the same time stabbed their fork into a piece of potato and ate it. They did seem pretty hungry, so she couldn't blame them. When was the last time they ate if they arrived at the gambling house earlier this morning? "I have a passion for travelling and finding new things to learn and do. It's a much broader passion than tarot, but I love it nonetheless and seek to embrace it every day. This journey may look like an obstacle, but I got to meet you. That's a plus."

Iris raised her eyebrows. They had only known each other for a day, so she couldn't make any assumptions about how she felt about this person. For now, Marin was a guide and someone to stick by during this journey if she wanted to impress her mother.

"You seemed to like that young lady very much." Iris turned the subject around, not wanting to think about her impulsive choice too much. She played with the spine of the book, noticing how the hardcover edges were worn from use. Signs of love and usefulness.

"Bea from the shop? You're referring to her like you're an old lady. I bet you two are the same age." Marin crossed their arms and leaned back in their chair.

"Yes, Bea. You were flirting with her." She recalled all the love readings that involved young men and women asking about their relationship, and how a few partners seemed like they had eyes for others due to 'flirting'. She hadn't experienced it herself, but Marin made it obvious. "Do you wish to court her?"

"Old lady talk." They shook their head and pursed their lips together, then took a moment to lean forward again, their crossed arms resting on the tablecloth. "Flirting, yes. Courting, no. I'm asexual, and somewhere on the aro spectrum. I'm not very interested in that kind of thing."

She raised an eyebrow. How could someone flirt without wanting to be in a relationship with a person? "I don't understand. Why do you flirt then?"

A smile returned to Marin's lips, lighting up their eyes like stars. "I am incredibly charming, so why not use it? It gets me out of sticky situations, and shall I use the 'I got to meet you' card again? Because that's the sort of thing this talk can do."

This time, her shoulders lifted to the compliment. They seemed rather insistent that meeting her was a positive thing.

"So flirting can just be for a little fun, it doesn't mean I want to pursue a relationship, or anything intimate. It's different for everyone, but that's me, and isn't that most important?" they added, with a wink to seal the deal.

"Anyway," Marin continued, reaching for a pastry and leaving crumbs as it travelled to their mouth. "You should read the book. Who knows, maybe witchcraft will become a passion of yours. You know, my friend is into witchcraft, too. You'll get along well."

"Ah, so she's also a witch…" Iris said to no one in particular, but pulled the book closer once again, her hand hovering by the edge of the cover. "I am quite looking forward to reading more." A small smile peeked through her lips.

"Make sure to dig in too!" Marin said with a half full mouth, pointing their fork at her. "Very important."

⛤

By the time they had finished their lunch and paid for it, Iris was up to chapter three of the book about the tools of witchcraft—the mention of tarot cards made her want to skip ahead just to read about them. Seeing tarot outside of her home, and what she knew, was like seeing someone familiar in a new place, or as if she were lost but found something to help her find her way.

"Hey, Iris." Marin poked her arm, which caused her to flinch, but she kept a tight grip on the book. She knew they were leading them to the docks to find a ship, except, once again, she found herself following footsteps in an effort to navigate her way. With the book being her main point of focus, she just had to make sure the floating suitcase was in her peripheral vision as they went.

"Yes?" She lowered the book and before Marin answered, she noticed they were approaching the docks. White birds were cawing on wooden poles, and the air was salty.

"I think you should put the book down now. If you keep your face in it, you might accidentally walk off the dock and into the ocean. Wouldn't want that, would we?" They chuckled, which caused Iris to frown, but at the same time, they lowered the suitcase and reached out to grab the book to safely store it away.

"You're the one who encouraged me to read it. Why are you laughing?" She shook the sores off her hands, realising it wasn't the best to hold up a large book and walk with it at the same time. Perhaps she would have a comfortable spot on the ship to read.

"Don't worry, I just thought the image of you walking into the ocean was funny. But it's better to be safe and you can keep reading when we are on the ship. Now then…" Marin's voice trailed off as they glanced around, likely searching for any of their connections being docked nearby.

They walked along the stone footpath, which was parallel to the gentle ocean flowing beside them and into the distance. The ocean was yet another thing she hadn't seen before except in a few paintings, so she was staring at it while Marin looked at the boats and captains resting around the area.

Crew members were also scattered about, hoisting new cargo and supplies onto the various ships. They seemed to be in a rush to get the job done while captains conversed with each other.

"Goddess, save me now… I don't think my guys are here."

"Your guys?" Iris tilted her head, looking away from the scenery and being met with a frantic Marin running their hand through their hair.

"You know, my connections. My guys. I don't know their schedule or if they'd be here at all." They started pacing and waving their arms around. "What are we going—"

The rest of Marin's question was drowned out by the shouts and shrieks of the people nearby, shifting the gears of both of their minds to turn to the source. A crowd was gathered, but it wasn't until two guards being followed by a crying lady came into view and split the onlookers apart that a crumpled caemi on the ground was revealed.

With a gasp, Marin rushed over to the dispersing crowd, and Iris had no choice but to follow behind, already drawing out of breath once they stumbled to a stop. She hoped their trip to Excava Kingdom wouldn't involve much running at all.

Many of the townspeople around them murmured and mumbled, some about the caemi, and some wondering what was happening. It didn't take long to realise what was going on when the guards drew their weapons and stood above the shaking caemi.

"Stand up," one guard demanded, planting the end of her spear into the grout of the stone tiles. "That is an order."

Iris felt the crowd shiver at the demand, having to watch the helpless caemi in the centre of the circle yet not being able to take their eyes away. The caemi had long golden ears on top of their hair resembling rabbit's ears that would normally be standing tall if not for the many eyes on them and the guards standing at attention.

The caemi nodded quickly, the tears in their eyes flying out and disappearing under the midday sun as they stood up and revealed their pants torn at the ends and a shirt of holes. They didn't dare move from where they stood.

"Do you understand what you have done?" the guard continued, her eyes trained strictly on the trembling rabbit caemi.

"I was simply trying to get my belongings back from—"

Before the caemi could answer, the other guard used the pole of their spear to smack the caemi in the side, causing Iris to grimace and grab onto her hip. Many of the onlookers walked away as it happened, though many more remained to stare at the commotion.

"I said, do you understand what you have done?" she repeated, ice lacing her words.

Iris frowned, unsure of what had happened but feeling as though the caemi didn't deserve such harsh punishment. Surely, they only wanted their clothes back, judging by the state of what they were currently wearing.

Marin tugged on her sleeve and she turned to them, now seeing a more serious expression than any other she had seen on their face before. With eyebrows furrowed and a stern squint, they limbered up their arms.

"I'm going to stop them," Marin hissed in a low voice.

"Wait—"

She couldn't get another word in as the short senti burst past the remaining onlookers and dove between arms, emerging into the clearing and inserting themself between the guards and the caemi.

Iris stood in disbelief as she watched the guard smack their polearm into Marin's side instead and, while the smack was audible, Marin remained unmoving, staring up at the armoured city guard whose eyes were threatening to pierce them.

"You dare get between a guard and her task?" she asked, just as unmoving as the other. "Move away before you receive equal punishment as this criminal."

Marin sneered, which took Iris by surprise. Their typical upbeat and charming self was now replaced by ambition to stand against this guard. Would they really go so far when they didn't know the whole picture?

"I will not stand by to watch you harass another." Marin held their arms out as if to provide a protective shield for the caemi who was ever confused at the sudden act of heroism from the crowd. "If you must escort them, escort with patience and regard for their rights."

"Justice doesn't have time for patience and regard when caemi are to be taken into questioning on sight. This is your last warning to move, little senti."

"Your kind has no respect."

With eyes still staring at each other, each second passing by more threatening than the previous, Iris watched as Marin reached into their pocket. Surely there was no weapon concealed in such a small pocket and, even then, Marin wouldn't be reckless enough to physically attack a guard, would they?

In one swift movement, Marin lifted their hand from their pocket in the form of a fist and it flew towards the guard's face. The guard smirked, predicting the move and shifting their own hand to block the incoming punch.

Iris braced, expecting for the guard's larger armoured hand to injure Marin's on impact but was surprised to see that, instead of following through with the swing, they opened their hand to reveal a handful of sand that flew into the eyes of the guard.

Chaos ensued as the guard clamoured about, her composed self now panicking, clanging of metal sounding through the air, and her perfectly standing spear falling to the ground with a pathetic clatter. Marin laughed heartily, evidently proud of their little stunt, but the fun was outlived when the guard's companion readied their spear and pointed it to Marin.

"You will pay for your insolence!" The guard went to charge Marin, but they were quick on their feet, now bounding towards Iris, the spear right on their back.

"Iris!" they called as they circled around the berserk guard, who tripped on her own spear and fell to the ground. "Get the caemi somewhere safe, I'll meet you there after I lose this rotten guard!"

Marin made a turn, out of the crowded circle, and towards the port-side marketplace. The guard followed behind with a sharp turn, forcing Iris to take a step back and stare in disbelief.

She regained her composure and scurried towards the rabbit caemi, who was sitting in shock. It was only natural with how much was happening so quickly.

With no idea how to navigate Vestirr outside her family home, she opted to help the caemi up and thought to drag them in the direction of Marin's chase, hoping to come across the strange senti once they got out of the guard's view.

If she wanted to continue this journey with Marin, she would need to do what they said and learn to navigate on the spot. "Come, we need to get somewhere safe." She looked up at the caemi's ears, knowing they were a direct signal for guards to confront them.

If there was one thing she could assume to help, it was covering the ears up, and while she didn't have the suitcase of clothing as an option, she did have her cloak.

She swung it around and off, wrapping the caemi to cover most of their head and clothing, hiding the fact they were a caemi under pursuit. With that done, she walked as fast as she could through the crowd, who didn't seem to have any objections to her taking the caemi other than the woman from before crying after them. It was before long that they had walked out of earshot and out of attention's way.

"Why are you helping me?" the caemi asked meekly, following Iris closely as she frantically took in her surroundings at five times the speed she usually liked.

What surrounded them were stalls set up along the port, mostly selling what she'd expect, including fish, bait, and other produce coming from the sea. With the stalls came merchants, and then came customers. The smell of fish made Iris recoil and want to pinch her nose, but she had to keep her arms free to push past the moving crowds.

"I don't know, but my companion seemed to put on quite a show to help you," Iris replied without looking at them, now trying to peer over the crowd. She managed to spot an alleyway that was blocked by a few cardboard boxes while the two stall keepers besides the alley were occupied with customers and showing off their stock.

She waved the caemi to follow her and snuck between the stalls, avoiding the attention of the people around them as merchants called others to their sales and deals for the day. It was the perfect cover for the sound of cardboard boxes scratching against the concrete to make an opening for her and the caemi to fit through.

"Who are they?" The caemi observed the alleyway they had entered. It smelt of raw fish and wet cardboard, causing their nose to wrinkle.

Iris didn't appreciate having to stand in this gap between buildings, water dripping from the gutters above and puddles forming below them. She hoped Marin had a good reason for leaving her to deal with the consequences of their actions.

"Their name is Marin, we only met today." Iris shook her head, feeling a looming disappointment at having to say those words. A businesswoman of the Galacia Gambling House following a stranger's shenanigans—but she had to, if she wanted to prove her worth.

"I am forever grateful for Marin, then. It's nice to meet you both." The caemi smiled at Iris, though she didn't return it. There were only so many strangers she wanted to welcome into her life, and one was already a lot. "Tell them I—"

From the sky, something fell. That something being very Marin-shaped.

With a solid thud, Marin landed in front of them in a low crouch, their feet somehow flat on the ground instead of the entirety of their being.

"Oh good, you guys made it safely." Marin stood up, dusting themself off and them holding a hand to the caemi. "My name is Marin."

"Marin, what in Ter's name was that? Did you just jump from the rooftops?" Iris didn't know how much more Marin could make her gasp in disbelief as she stared up at the roof. That was at least two stories high.

"Don't be so worried, Iris. It's not that high, and I managed to get the guard off my tail with that trick." They grinned with a thumbs up.

It was like they had done this many times before, but Iris didn't want to give herself the headache of trying to work out the many reasons why they would have. "This better be the last time I have to do something like this…" The quick decisions she had to make prevented her from properly taking in her surroundings.

"Thank you." The rabbit caemi took Marin's hand and shook it vigorously. "You truly didn't have to do that, it was my mistake for revealing myself in public."

The senti gently patted the other's hand with a small smile. "Any caemi in trouble is a caemi I save. They had no business hitting you and shouting at you. What did you do, anyway?"

"You know the girl who was crying for the guards? She's an old friend of mine, and I used to stay over at her house sometimes. She has the only belongings I have left as my other clothes were taken by guards when they were investigating houses for caemi."

"Why would someone who shares history with you call the guards on you too?" Iris wondered, and the caemi responded with a bitter chuckle.

"Funny things happen when the queen spreads lies about your race. She said we are all violent, but all I wanted is my clothes back. I would've left solemnly, but not without my things. And not without saying goodbye. It seems she didn't share the same sentiment."

Marin opened their arms to embrace the caemi, and they took the offer, holding onto the short senti and sniffling. "It's probably best I make my way to Syriphia instead. I will at least be in a more accepting environment while I find new clothes."

A small pang hit Iris' chest as she watched the two let go and step away from each other. There wasn't much she could do to help as they hardly had clothes to spare, and there wasn't much they could do from now, knowing they had to be on their way soon.

"Listen, stay safe." Marin spun the suitcase around to their front and opened it, pulling out one of their tunics. "And take this, it will help during the cooler nights of travel."

"I don't know how to repay you, Marin, and…" They glanced at Iris, clipping off the borrowed cloak at the same time and handing it to her.

She pursed her lips as she took it. "Sybil, you can call me Sybil."

"Marin and Sybil, I hope your days from now are blessed by the patrons above. Is there anything I can do to help you before we split ways?"

Iris left the thinking to Marin and, as expected, they perked up with an idea. "Can you recommend us a ship to travel on to Excava? We really have to be on our way now, since I got a bit distracted."

Distracted was an understatement, but it would help if they had guidance from a caemi who was also going to be travelling across the sea.

The caemi beckoned them to the entrance of the alleyway and scanned the docks, their eyes setting upon a ship with a crew conversing in front of it. One of them was sitting on an upside-down crate with a peculiarly shaped hat.

"Well, all you have to know is that ship there—"

As soon as the ship was pointed out, Marin roughly moved the cardboard boxes aside to make their way there, the rush to get to Excava returning to their eyes and movements.

"Quick, Iris! Before they leave without us!" They turned back to Iris to wave their arms before taking off again.

Iris smacked her forehead. The hyper-energetic senti had revealed her name despite her efforts to remain anonymous to the stranger.

"Hey!" Marin waved their arms as they ran in the direction of the idle group. A few of them turned their heads, excluding the captain.

The young senti stood among the travellers who were much taller than them. It was slightly entertaining to Iris, though she kept a straight face as she approached from behind. The looks from the travellers weren't entirely friendly, but at least they weren't telling them to leave.

"What is it, lass?" one of the travellers said. She had her arms crossed, and a bandana was covering one of her eyes. It went well with her stylish outfit.

Marin wore a beaming smile. "I was hoping your captain and crew could help my friend and I across the seas." They faced the captain and held their hand out to shake. "Good day, captain."

The captain turned her head towards Marin and silently shook their hand, then turned towards the bandana traveller. Her fingers danced around her face and touched different points.

The bandana crewmate nodded and moved her hands in response, silence between them. Marin didn't seem phased watching the two and waited for them to finish.

"I didn't realise. Could you tell her I'm sorry?" Marin asked with an apologetic look.

"Of course." The crewmate signed to the captain. "I suppose we shouldn't expect you to know sign language."

"Sign language?" Iris asked in a quiet voice. She hadn't come across anyone who used sign language, nor did she know what it meant when someone did. "What is that?"

Another crew mate stepped forward, a taller man who was carrying a box of what looked like fruits. "Our captain can't hear. Her ears don't work. Doesn't make her any less a captain, though."

The group around them let out a cheer, and she noticed the captain wore a smug look. She must've sensed the group's energy despite not hearing.

It made sense she didn't come across any sign language users in her time at work, since it was difficult to give someone a tarot reading if they couldn't hear.

Iris decided to remain quiet as Marin continued, "Ah well, as I was saying dear… would you ask your captain kindly if we could catch a ride to the Excava Kingdom?"

The bandana lady signed to the captain, and the captain signed back. Iris couldn't understand it, but from the frown on the captain's face, this didn't seem like it would go in their favour.

"You do realise there is a lot of traffic to Excava at the moment due to the queen's orders? More crew means more danger," the bandana lady translated.

"What if we pay?" Iris offered, looking at Marin, who nodded and took the pouch of coins from their cloak.

The group gathered around to listen to the jingling coins as Marin played with the bag, except for the captain, of course, who sat there watching. "We can offer gold in exchange for a trip to the kingdom. How's that?"

The crew looked at each other in thought before the captain signed once again.

"She says we don't just take the gold. We want something valuable."

What items of value would they be after? Sentimental or monetary? Other than her tarot cards, Iris didn't have anything else to offer, and it wasn't like she was giving those up anytime soon.

Marin dug into their pocket, pulling out a golden pocket watch. When did they have time to get that? "How about this?"

The captain held her hand out with a beckoning motion, then flattened it. At first, Marin stared at her before placing the watch gently in her palm. She took a moment to examine it and also handed it over to the bandana crewmate, who held it up to her ear. They exchanged a few more signs before pocketing the watch.

"This will do. Pegs will get your suitcase on the ship and we'll take the payment upfront, thank you very much." A shorter person appeared from behind the bandana lady and they did indeed have pegs clipped along their jacket. Iris assumed that was where the name came from. Marin handed over the bag and watched Pegs bring it up to the ship in silence, though the clamouring of the others filled that gap.

"We'll be heading off soon." Bandana lady grabbed the coins as Marin held them out to her. "Hop on, and I'll introduce you to the lot."

"It seems we have a way to Excava now." Iris was honestly surprised at the result, not expecting their first impressions to bode so well. She supposed they were a friendly bunch and were willing to go ahead with payment. "Did you have to give up your watch, though?"

Marin shrugged as they took the lead on walking up the ramp and onto the ship, now fixing up their hair after all the ruffling. "I'll find another in no time. It's not like I was going to give away your tarot cards or books, right?"

She couldn't find a way to disagree. Marin didn't have the watch for long after all, no matter where they had found it. Her possessions were too scarce and precious to give up. Incredibly hard to replace.

As she stepped on the ship, she could feel herself slightly leaning left to right, causing her to whip her arms up to balance herself. She took a moment to look around the ship deck, which had a hole in the floor alongside a ladder, perhaps to enter the ship's interior.

Above her head, there was a bird's nest, which she assumed was good for looking out across the sea. Other than that, stacks of barrels were tied onto the deck and some wooden cargo boxes were down at the end, emitting some unusual smells.

The bandana lady was now sitting on half a barrel where the closed end of it was facing to the sky as a makeshift chair. "So, I'm Risala. I identify as 'she'. We call the captain Josey, but she don't care what we call them by. The tall guy over there?" She pointed at the man who was carrying fruits before. "That's Paddy. You can call him if you ever need to reach a shelf, but never to duck under a cabinet."

"Don't remind me, Ris." He glared at her, to which Risala only grinned.

"Finally, Pegs doesn't go by any he, her, they, whatever. Just Pegs. But they don't mind if you needa use one."

It took a moment for Iris to work through each introduction, a list of strangers now being fired at her mind. If they were going to be spending a few days together, it was good practice to know how the crew members liked being addressed.

Marin didn't show any signs of hesitation, smiling at Risala. Considering they liked to travel and get around, they were probably used to meeting so many people at once.

"Marin, I use they and he." He smiled with a nod of approval.

Iris noted Marin didn't only use the non-gendered pronoun, but the masculine one as well.

"And the lass?" Risala gestured her chin towards Iris.

Iris didn't expect to be put on the spot, and despite knowing the answer, she took her time. She had been referring to herself with feminine terms, and she didn't have any issues with it. She was yet to understand the usage of the other pronouns, such as how Marin used 'they' and 'he', though it didn't change how she saw Marin. Though on another thought, did she have to share her name? Typically, she wouldn't to a customer, or a stranger for that matter.

"You can call me Sybil, and 'she' is fine."

Marin raised an eyebrow at her, but left the introduction to her as to converse with Paddy.

"Sybil it is, then. It's nice to meet you, Sybil." Risala held her hand out to shake, and Iris took it with a firm grip. "Huh, a strong hand with this one. Welcome aboard."

Chapter 8
eight of swords

Sea salt on every surface and invading her nostrils was something Iris had to get used to, but the alcohol? Not so much. Having worked near a bar for most of her life, it was easier to tolerate and, after a short while, she didn't notice it anymore.

Travelling on the open sea consisted of watching the crew pop bottles open and drink while the sun burned brightly above. Crashing waves against the ship made for a peaceful atmosphere if it weren't for needing to constantly balance while on the top deck. The crew didn't have much issue with this, though.

After declining drinks, for she wanted to use her free time reading, and having enough of staring at how much wood there was on the top deck, she made her way inside the ship to explore.

What fascinated her most about the hallways and rooms were transparent prisms fastened to the ceiling with their points hanging down. She figured out this was their way of lighting up rooms and halls below deck without needing to keep too many lanterns or lights on the ship; the sun shone through the prism, which then scattered light all over.

The wooden planks beneath her made strange sounds, almost like a mix of creaking, groaning, and murmuring. At one point, she made it out to be a voice of sorts, like someone was speaking to her from underneath, but testing the planks a few times with her steps also resulted in random noises that could pass as speaking. It was like the ship itself was as cheeky as the spirits she met with Bea.

She admired a range of doors that lined a hallway, taking note of their weathering blue paint, which had a certain novelty to them. Each door also had a different handle, as if they were replaced as they got damaged one by one.

A few doors down from where she was standing, Marin's head popped out.

"Iris! Come look at our room!"

Before she could respond, Marin was already back inside the room. There was a racket, and then a thump.

Rounding the corner and entering, she saw Marin sprawled out on one of the two beds, his clothes everywhere, while hers were still sitting neatly in the suitcase. The room itself was lit by a single lamp with a small flame and included a window between their beds. A dresser with a missing drawer was against the left wall, a small desk sitting beside it. But there was nothing on it. She assumed the crew didn't keep much on desks because of the moving ship.

"Pretty cosy, huh? I think I'm going to like it here."

"Why have you thrown your clothes everywhere? You should take care of them."

She walked up to the other senti, picking up a few of the clothing items to check them. Fortunately, they were undamaged. She then dropped them, it wasn't her mess to clean.

"I didn't realise you were my mother now, Iris." Marin laughed as their head dangled off the edge of the bed. "Kidding. I was planning to pack them into the dresser so we'd keep our clothes separate during the trip. I just got distracted."

She nodded in understanding as she sat on what would be her bed for the next few days. The bed felt tougher and smelled different from her own bed.

As she watched Marin mess around, the reason they were on this ship together came to mind. They were on their way to Excava Kingdom to save Marin's friend and so she could meet her. The intentions were all well and good, but did Marin have a plan for getting his friend back?

"What are we going to do once we arrive in Excava?"

Marin didn't spend much time thinking, likely knowing this question was coming. "We'd have to travel to the castle grounds, as that is where they keep their… confinements. Underground. That is where they are keeping her right now until she's sent out on a ship to Syriphia."

They swung themself around to be sitting up once again, crossing their legs on the bed and resting their elbows on their knees, chin in hand. "We'll make our way into the castle—"

"Wait, we're breaking into the queen's castle?" It sounded absurd, even just coming out of her mouth. Part of her thought Marin was joking, but perhaps that was just her trying to justify them saying it. She knew deep down they were not lying because of their tone.

"No, no, of course not. It's not that bad if you think about it. We're trying to rescue my innocent friend from the grip of the Excavas and their guards so I can personally ensure she gets to Syriphia safely. See how that's better than *breaking into the castle?*" They held their hands up and wiggled his fingers as they emphasised the last part.

"I see…" She didn't really, but she was interested in knowing more. "What about the other caemi that were captured? Are they innocent, too?"

Marin took a moment of pause to think, drawing in a sharp breath. "Gods above, each day more caemi get captured and I wish to save them all, but…"

"But?" Iris leaned in curiously. As she didn't have as much experience around caemi as Marin did, she wasn't familiar with the drive connected to caemi justice, though she found herself wanting to reflect Marin's vigour, knowing there was more to caemi than the queen's messages, and that they deserved proper treatment.

"There are probably hundreds in Excava alone that were taken to isolated prisons before they're shipped like cargo to Syriphia. I mean, what do you expect in the capital of Kyross? Caemi entertainers, sellers, even just citizens. It was a privilege to live in the capital and now… they are making caemi pay a price they don't owe."

She remained silent as Marin turned to look away. She could see the distance in their eyes and a frown growing on their lips. It seemed they did believe the caemi were innocent.

"What about the assassination?" She thought back to her conversation with her older brother, which also made her wonder if she'd run across him but, for now, she didn't worry about it. The caemi were being deported by the command of the queen after her near-death experience, so was her call reasonable?

"What about it?" Marin snapped at her. It honestly took her aback, and she held her breath for a moment. It made her feel… uneasy, despite knowing what Marin was like—a jokester and passionate young senti. The surrounding sounds seemed to drown away.

"I mean…" she began slowly, looking back at Marin who continued to stare at her, wondering why things seemed so muffled at this moment. "Did they find the caemi behind it? Would they be part of the captured crowds?"

The young senti sighed, and shook their head, sounds rushing back as they did. "It's nothing we're going to hear about, but I have a feeling the queen has got it all wrong."

There was still something off about what Marin was saying, like they knew something she didn't. But at the same time, they were focused on rescuing their friend and just wanted her to be safe.

"Anyway," they continued, clapping their hands. In a fleeting moment, their expression returned to their gentle smile with shining eyes and they laid on the bed once again. "When we get there, I can explain better. I can probably show you a few things to get an idea. It won't be dangerous, don't worry. Though your expertise may be useful."

She assumed her expertise meant tarot, but couldn't see where that could fit in. Before she could ask further questions, Marin had already gotten up, thrown their clothes into the dresser as they walked by, and exited the room without another word, leaving Iris to spend time reading alone.

It was the next day when Iris had changed into fresh clothes and headed up to the top deck of the ship with Marin to join everyone for a meal. She found it difficult to spend too much time around the others, even after so long in a gambling house. Perhaps it was because there were fewer people that she became uneasy. Fewer people meant more focus on each of them, meaning more interaction.

During her time at the table, she noticed the meals were different on board. There was much more fish in their diet and even soup, though she supposed it made sense since they were on a ship.

She also took the time to take some of Marin's advice about learning more about each other if they were going to travel together. With that, she curiously asked Risala about her bandana, which earned a gasp from Marin.

"You don't just *ask* someone why they have a bandana over their eye, Iris!" They facepalmed and shook their head.

"It's quite alright, lad. I'm more than happy to answer." Risala gave them a crooked smile. "This eye can't see very well, and the light of day can hurt it, so I cover it. It means I'm half blind, but with Josey around, it's not so bad."

Iris nodded, looking between the two as Risala signed what she had just said to the captain. "I see. Is it a case where you help her hear, but she helps you see?"

"That's a way to put it! What better of a best friend than one who helps you hear and see?" Risala heartily laughed, then translated it for Josey, who laughed alongside her.

The laughter set a positive mood, and Iris started to see why learning about others could be a fun activity to pass the time. It did make for good conversation, and answered questions she had about other people she had to spend time with.

And even with the conversations and bustling of mealtime with a ship crew and Marin around, it was a quiet day compared to the previous one. The sound of the ocean replaced gambling patrons or loud dancing music. Sea salt and laughter in the air replaced the smoke of cigarettes and cries of people losing their money.

Today, she wasn't surprised by a senti breaking into her room or concocting a plan to distract guards to sneak out. She also wasn't out buying clothes or witnessing arrests.

The feeling of waking up in another place had startled her and made her assume she was still dreaming, especially since the murmur of gambling from downstairs was replaced by murmurs from under the floorboards. It was only when Marin shook her bed that she recognised them and remembered where she was.

What caught her the most off guard was not needing to set up her business and shift for the day to serve customers.

It didn't prevent her from thinking about the moments she would've been getting ready, setting up her booth, grounding herself, shuffling her cards, and then preparing for customers. She also wondered what the time was, and if she would've been working right now. It was a quiet day, but with a busy mind.

Marin was acting their usual self. At least, as usual as she has come to know them as so far. They had friendly conversations with the others and did play fights with wooden branches. Iris was completely content listening, and it was relieving to not be confronted with questions or a need to contribute to the conversation like in her family meetings. It seemed Pegs shared the same sentiment, as Pegs had joined her later in the meal, while Marin was challenging Paddy to an arm wrestle.

During her time idly looking around for anything else to take note of, she caught a glimpse of another ship member. It was only a shadow, but a large one at that. She was curious why they hadn't been introduced yet.

Though, her mind became distracted by a flash of colour coming from the corner of her eye. This time, she knew it wasn't a shadow because of its blue and green nature.

By the time she turned her head, there was nothing there except for another splash appearing on the other side of her peripheral. Rather than anywhere on the boat, it disappeared into the distance.

Marin walked up to her and placed a hand on her shoulder, causing her to jump. "Iris, are you okay?" They stared at her with a look of concern.

"What? Of course I am." She took a deep breath, looking away from the senti to avoid any more questions. She couldn't be letting herself act so recklessly in front of these strangers.

"Okay…" Marin shrugged, shifting their expression to a smile. "Paddy wants to show us something, wanna see?" She didn't have much of a choice as Marin grabbed her arms and pulled her away from the upside-down crate she was sitting on.

As they made their way to the edge of the deck, the waves washing up against the edge of the wooden ship caught her off guard. Stumbling, she quickly grasped the railing and held steady. The vast ocean was a view she was unfamiliar with, the blues and greens reflecting the sky, making a beautiful mural of colours on the water.

"Hm, I've never seen the ocean before," Iris mused to herself, then brought her attention back to Marin and Paddy, who were both leaning their backs on the rails.

"It's quite the magnificent sight. Despite travelling the seas almost every day, I still love watching it." Paddy smiled proudly, as if he had raised the waters as his own child. "There's a reason it's so beautiful, too."

"And what's that?" Iris continued, staring at the water.

"Spirits!" Paddy announced triumphantly. "I adore their work in the ocean. They're well known for their earth-work, but the water-work should be just as appreciated."

Iris recalled her conversation with Bea and her experience with the orbs of light. "Ah, I saw spirits of earth just yesterday. They were little balls of light."

"That's a common misconception about a spirit's appearance. They don't actually look like little orbs of light." The tall crew member spun to look at the ocean and continued to ramble. "Spirits are not like senti and caemi, they don't have a proper physical form. They more commonly appear as small lights as that's a form mortals can perceive. Their real forms, well I've never seen them before, but I've looked into it, and apparently, we can't perceive them unless we were spirits ourselves."

Just as he had finished this sentence, drops of water rose from the ocean, circling and performing until they formed an arch back into the water, disappearing into ripples. Iris gasped, watching, now realising the colours she had been seeing were the spirits.

"They're dancing," Iris whispered in childlike wonder, any thought of staying professional being sent overboard as she watched the sparkling water droplets create small images within their liquid and then fall into the ocean like they were hiding away. She had never seen anything like this before—any sentience outside of the blurred faces she saw every day.

Marin undid their vest and hung it over a barrel, the bright sun now shining overhead. "I've seen my fair share of spirits, though I've felt just as many. Can you find them in actual objects?"

Paddy smiled excitedly. "Yes! It also helps them get energy from natural forms. A tree, for example. A spirit can become part of a tree and be regarded as a tree spirit. As the tree grows, the spirit grows. The spirit helps the tree live longer than it should, or even influences senti and caemi to help the plant."

The spirits continued to jump up, now forming shapes of fish with flowing tails and seashells as if they were imitating what they saw on their worldwide journeys. At one point, she watched a few droplets gather together, making a blob and then slowly sculpting it into a reflection of Iris herself. She couldn't find the words to say to the spirits as they copied her action of moving her hand up to her mouth and then waving it around.

"That explains more about the potted plants." Iris hummed to herself, the spirits of water coming closer to her and almost beckoning her to hold her hand out. "How do you know so much about spirits?"

The tall man turned to Iris to answer, noticing her holding her hand out and a water spirit coming towards it. He quickly moved past Marin to grab a hold of her hand and force it upwards and back in the perimeter of the ship, the spirit falling back into the water.

Iris blinked, shaking her hand out of the grip of Paddy's and stepping back. "What are you doing?"

"Don't put your hand out to the spirit." Paddy shook his head, his face wearing caution. "Have you heard of siren stories? Spirits of water can be like that—luring you into their beauty and taking you away. We don't want that now, do we?"

She let out a small 'oh', feeling her cheeks flush with embarrassment. Her awe and inattention almost caused something horrible to happen, and she humiliated herself in front of Marin and the crew.

"To answer your question, it's a small research project of mine. Witchcraft isn't so much my thing, but spirits are fascinating, especially alongside the existence of caemi. Ocean spirits have helped us, sea travellers, for the longest time with navigation, calming the waves and even with food. A little unfortunate that with less caemi around, the ocean spirits are less likely to hang around Kyross waters."

"I'm sure you can work around it," Marin offered, patting Paddy on the back.

"Of course, we always do." He exchanged a knowing look with Risala.

After taking a final look at the spirits and sending the ocean a piercing glance, she farewelled the crew and Marin and left them to their games while she returned to her sleeping quarters to think.

Reflection. During quiet moments on shift, she allowed her mind to search for anything she could work on. Though, being at home or work all the time didn't give a lot to work with apart from family and her business.

Now, it would be a little different.

First, she was still reflecting on the previous day. She didn't give herself time to process it before falling asleep last night, as soon as her head hit her pillow.

Her mother never specifically emphasised dangers regarding travelling and the people of the outside world, but she couldn't help but think something was wrong. So far, everything had been so quickly moving that she barely had the time to take in the events and her surroundings before they had to keep going. There were splashes of different scenery, sniffs of new smells, and sounds she had never heard before. It was only now that she was in one place for longer than an hour.

Was Marin being honest with her? Was she right to earn money this way? Would her mother be happy with the pay she would get from this trip? Should she have told her family before leaving? Should she have stayed where she was familiar, even if so far she was safe with Marin, learnt new things, and eaten a variety of food?

Questions. There were so many questions swirling in her mind, and she couldn't make them stop.

It was quiet, with only water splashing against the wooden side of the ship, which creaked with each rock, back and forth. But her mind was so loud. She usually had to be at her table to calm down at moments like this, but now she just had this bed, this room, and her cards.

So her cards were what she took out. The touch of each one rippled calm and serenity throughout her body within an instant—it was her sure-fire method if she needed to ground urgently.

Her quick breathing slowed to deep, mindful breaths, and her mind was sorting through each thought by either reasoning from Marin or telling herself to not think about it now.

The questions and problems were only small, and she shouldn't have made them so big. This was something she often reminded herself of during her line of work, as customers would approach her with bigger problems or issues that appeared much more emotionally taxing. It reminded her of the drunken lady. The lady's problems were bigger than Iris' ones. Did they even count as problems?

To distract herself from developing a loud mind again, she began shuffling her deck to move into a rhythm. The cards glided up and down, past and through each other, a song coming from the sound of thick paper sliding against thick paper.

A walk would help take her mind off things, too. The beating of water against her window was starting to irritate her. It was strange. She was used to shuffling in a house full of people, but couldn't make herself do it in a quiet room.

She made her way to the hallway, tarot deck in hand, and began walking down. It was on the way back to the indoor dining room, though she recalled the kitchen was another place she had to visit. Perhaps she would take a look before she pulled some cards for herself.

She closed her eyes as the cards went from one hand to the other, and now she could sense that familiar feeling of energy coming from her hands and surrounding the cards. They danced around her fingers and laid on her palms, tickling at her wrists. She liked this feeling, like a connection building between her precious tarot cards and her. She assumed it would make her readings more accurate and easier to read. Of course, the cards were always right.

Just as she was getting into the rhythm of her shuffling, a card flew out of the deck and landed somewhere in front of her. As she opened her eyes to search for the card, there was a stomp, and sure enough, it came from someone who was standing with her in the hallway.

It was the shadow from before. Well, the person whose shadow she'd seen a while ago. A large man before her with a beard wrapped in some sort of cover, holding a large knife. It was hard to make out the rest of the figure because of the low lighting in the hallway. She would've jumped in surprise at the sight if the cards in her hand weren't more important to keep a steady hold of.

The two of them didn't say a word as Iris looked down, now realising what the stomp was. The man was standing on top of the card that had flown out, the top of it only peeking out from underneath his large boot. Seeing her precious card being held in such a rude way made her blood boil.

"Get your foot off my card." Iris maintained her composure. It wasn't correct to lash out at a customer… well, person. This wasn't the first time someone had abused her cards like this. "I don't know if you'd like being stepped on, but my cards surely don't."

She looked up to keep eye contact with the man, though he was rather tall, which made it difficult to maintain authority in this situation. She didn't let herself be swayed, though.

Her hand reached into her pocket to pull out her tarot pouch. She slid the rest of the deck inside for safekeeping before she crossed her arms and waited for the man to respond. A part of her couldn't help but look between the man and the knife he was holding. Was that blood on it?

"Hm." He simply grunted and shuffled his foot, but not really moving it off the card just yet.

Iris blinked. Was he out of his mind? It was a simple demand, and he wasn't able to follow through or reply in any way. She opened her mouth to challenge him once more when he lifted his foot as far up as he could, attempting to balance on his one foot that remained steady on the ground. It appeared as if he was trying to look for what he was stepping on, but couldn't since the card was tiny compared to him.

Amidst the struggle, Iris crouched down to grab the card, dusted it off, and checked it for any scratches. The Three of Cups. Fortunately, there wasn't any visible damage. After Iris slid the card back into the rest of the deck, the man let out a sigh of relief and lowered his leg.

"I appreciate it," Iris began cautiously, not sensing any further response from the man, but wary of the knife in hand. "These cards are very important to me."

The man grunted again, staring at Iris. Curiously, he turned away and beckoned with his empty hand for Iris to follow him further down the hallway in the direction she was already heading. It felt like a bad idea to follow a large, buff man who didn't say much and was also holding a huge knife stained with what looked like blood, but it also felt like she didn't have much of a choice.

Chapter 9
nine of Wands

She was led into a room similarly sized to the one Marin and she was staying in, with a bed sitting in the corner and a dresser alongside it, which was also being used as a bedside table. A hanging ceiling lamp was swaying back and forth with the motions of the boat, but it still provided cool lighting to the room—a welcome tone after being exposed to warm light so much.

A table and a couple of chairs were placed next to the wall opposite the bed, a cup on the table and a few visible circles stained into it. She also noticed a few books stacked in a corner, but the cobwebs gathered around them reminded her of the books that sat in her room to age away after she lost interest in them or didn't need them anymore.

"Sit," he said. It didn't sound like a demand, but she still did as she was told and took a seat at the table as he settled across from her.

She watched as he took off his beard cover, and also his face of surprise when he brought his hand up and realised he was carrying a knife. He quickly got up again and walked over to his bedside table—dresser—and placed it down. She didn't want to admit she felt safer now that it was on the other side of the room.

He sat down once again, dusting off his front, which, now that it was brighter, she could see was an apron. Putting the knife, apron, and beard cover together... this man had to be the ship's chef.

"The cards," he began in a low voice, though was leaning towards Iris to peer at the pouch she was still holding by the drawstrings in her hand. "What do they do?"

It took her by surprise that this large man who could carry around a heavy knife without realising and didn't say much was curious about her tarot cards. Typically, when people came by on shift and didn't know what she was doing, they were a bit obnoxious about it. There wasn't much she could do, since they had the money to speak to her in that way, and she needed to be paid said money for her work.

To see this man with a curious expression and an innocent interest was refreshing. From the way she felt sitting in this room, and having taken a good look at the man, she could tell he had good intentions and only seemed intimidating at first.

She held the pouch in her hands, slid the deck out, placed it gently on the table, and fanned the cards out in a line face down. "These are my tarot cards. They are a tool that helps me give advice or guidance. I have the answers to those who have questions."

With a flick of a switch, Iris was now Sybil, a mystique air surrounding her as her hands hovered over the cards. Sitting at this table, it was like sitting at her booth back home—it was almost enough to make her smile. Tingling rushed up her arms as she could feel the energy of the cards.

"Tarot," he repeated, getting a feel for the word. While Iris preferred to pronounce it with a soft 't', sounding like 'taro', he said the word with a hard 't'. It didn't make too much of a difference to her, since he was just learning.

His hand hovered towards the cards that were laid before him. He hesitated to touch them, as though he understood she didn't give much of a go-ahead. "Sorry."

"You can get a feel of them later," she replied, folding her hands on the table. It wasn't the same as her clothed table, but it was close enough.

"No, sorry for before. Didn't see card."

Ah, so he was apologising for stepping on the card. She supposed she was rather upset about it, even though she didn't mean to show it. It was more often than not that people wanted to mess with the cards just because they could. That energy was sent right back in the reading, though, with the cards not holding back on revealing secrets she wasn't supposed to know.

"It's quite alright." She offered a gentle smile, not just out of formality, but because she felt it was the least she could do for his politeness. He returned the smile with a lopsided one.

They sat in comfortable silence for a moment. Iris was used to waiting for the customer to proceed with the conversation and didn't prompt unless needed. For now, she explored the feeling of serving someone, even though she wasn't at home. Would she have to ask for payment? It only took a second before she knew the answer. No. Why would she if her mother wouldn't know? She would be paid at the end of the trip.

"Can I ask a question?" He looked down at the cards, staring at them like he was trying to work out what was on the other side. "To the cards."

"Of course you may. What question do you have?" She prepared to shuffle, picking up the fanned cards and taking a few deep breaths before the chef shook his head.

"You show me first. Ask a question to the cards. I want to see."

It was incredibly rare that she would be asked to read for herself as a demonstration to a client. Every time, she would say no due to it being unprofessional and a waste of the client's time. While she could've charged more in those instances, she found it meaningless to read for herself in front of those people. Why would they care?

This time, she didn't hold such restraints. The chef wasn't one of those stuck-up clients who just threw money at her to tell them good fortunes. While she didn't know what he wanted to ask, he was patient enough with her that it felt wrong to assume otherwise. Perhaps it wouldn't do harm to demonstrate.

"I'll do a simple future reading. I can use the cards to see an event that could be coming up for me." With everything happening in these past few days, it was unpredictable what the cards would say. It was easy to assume when she was at the gambling house—the cards would read about her business or family. What would they say here?

She let out a deep breath and straightened the edges of the cards. Following a quick overhand shuffle, she cut the deck and laid out three cards, face down, between her and the chef.

Before flipping the cards over, she looked up at the chef, who was intensely following the process, his eyes fixed on the cards and humouring her. Watching his gaze was like looking in a mirror, where she saw her younger self, ever curious about the world of tarot and the power they held.

After a moment, she flipped the three cards right side up.

Five of Wands, Three of Swords, Six of Swords.

The result of the cards caused her to grimace. While the Six of Swords indicated moving on from the situation into more peaceful waters, in conjunction with the Five of Wands and Three of Swords, there was going to be trouble and something she would have to go through or leave behind first in order to proceed.

Despite the generally negative message from the cards, the chef was thrilled to see them, like a surprise he had been waiting for had finally been revealed.

"What do the pictures mean?" He leaned in closer to get a better look at the cards.

She ran her fingers over each card, mulling over the imagery and symbols. The Five of Wands pictured a few young people fighting with staffs. It felt like a fight or disagreement would be coming up between multiple people. She couldn't help but think there would be trouble amongst the ship's crew. But why?

"This first card is the Five of Wands. These are the wands, and there are five. That's where the name comes from." She pointed to each wand on the card. "This is a card of disagreement. Since this card is part of the minor arcana, it shouldn't be too large of a situation, but it seems to involve multiple people."

The chef let out an 'oooh' before nodding.

The Three of Swords had more simple imagery. Three swords were stabbed through a heart and rain was pictured. On the positive side, expression of emotion was encouraged to move on from a situation. Negative feelings were part of life and had to be worked through in order to get somewhere. She found this card commonly popping up in love readings that concluded in telling the client to work on moving on from their lost love, or perhaps a breakup was in order.

"This is the Three of Swords, and you can see why. Since this card follows the Five of Wands, I assume this means emotional release and hurt feelings will come from this disagreement." She pointed between the first two cards. "Something will happen here, where someone…"

For some reason, Marin came to mind. There wasn't an indication in the reading as to what the disagreement would be related to, but usually, if someone or something popped into mind during a reading, it was a clue to working out the story.

"My travelling companion, Marin. It seems they will fight for something with others, which will cause them to be emotionally distressed."

"You know just from the pictures?" The chef held his hand out to take the card, but didn't wait for permission. Iris felt it was okay to hand him the two cards she had read.

"With practise and experience, I can recognise the symbolism and patterns involved. Messages come to mind occasionally, in the form of images and metaphors, that help me read for others. It's amazing, not only for my family business, but for how I feel drawn to tarot."

It was true: this was one of the few things she was interested in. Initially, her mother hadn't questioned it, and she likely had one of her brothers to thank for that.

It had taken a while for her small hands to shuffle the cards, but it just felt right. Her first reading had been for her brothers, and the message couldn't have been clearer: their parents would find her brothers' stash of bottle caps they had stolen from the bar. At first, they hadn't believed her, but sure enough, that night called for a vocal lecture about stealing from the bar.

It was nice to think about the days she and her brothers played around with the cards, but one day they had just stopped and left her to do readings on her own. When she'd tried to ask them about it, she was only met with responses along the lines of, *"We need to focus on the business now, Iris. And unless you find a way to contribute, the boss won't be happy."*

She hadn't realised the boss was her mother until she had her first meeting. She'd received a warning that day, too.

"You okay?" the chef's deep voice snapped her out of the memory, bringing her back into the room they were sitting in and reminding her she was not at home right now.

She cleared her throat and nodded, straightening up and regaining her composure. "I was just... sorting through some thoughts. Let's take a look at this one..."

She touched the last card, which pictured a woman with a small child travelling on a boat, a man rowing it along. Their journey surrounded them in turbulent waters, but the imagery of calm waters ahead was an optimistic sign that things were going to get better.

"This one is a bit on the nose with the ship on the card. This situation won't necessarily end on an incredibly positive note, but it will be looking up for those involved. It will require a journey of moving on and only taking what's needed going forward."

She hoped this meant Marin would be okay again. Even if she had conflicted feelings about interacting with Marin, she knew they had good intentions for Kalaya and wanted Iris to be safe and happy as well. The least she could do was have well wishes for him.

"So the cards, they are a story." He laid down the two cards besides the third once again. "A fight, hurt, and then forward. Like being okay again after realising something."

"That's exactly it." Iris smiled. It made her happy he was paying enough attention to recite what the cards were saying back to her, even in simple terms.

"I want to know if things are okay back at home," he said quickly. "That is my question."

He looked away, diverting his eyes. It seemed he was hesitant to reveal what he wanted to know. Perhaps she could find out more about him through this reading.

"I'm curious, is this something you often think about?"

"…yes. Of course."

"You don't talk about it to the others at all? It seems like something you hide based on how you're acting."

He looked back at her with raised eyebrows, lifting a finger to say something back, but then stopping. He took a few moments to think about it. "I keep to myself. Stay out of the way."

For some reason, this made her a little sad. Most of the time, the people she read for would tell her stories that were meant to be sad, but she didn't feel much of it, mainly responding in a way to appeal to them. It was part of her job.

Perhaps it was because she felt a similar way sometimes at home. She kept away from her sibling's business so she wouldn't get in their way.

"Well," she began, "I can do a reading about what's happening at home for you."

She slipped her cards back into the deck, silently thanking them for the reading. Then came the shuffling, the cards shifting into place for the perfect draw, and her mumbles surrounding them in the question they needed to answer.

With a final three beats, she stopped and pulled three cards to read for the chef.

The Empress, Two of Cups, Six of Cups.

Just looking at the cards, she could feel a smile and a bubbly feeling in her chest. This one was much better than the previous reading, and she was glad something like this popped up for the chef.

"This is wonderful," she started, running her fingers over the cards and noticing something. "You have a wife and two children?"

The chef gasped, smacking his hand on the table a few times, causing it to shake slightly, and nodding. "How did you know? My wife is back home with my little boy and girl."

This made Iris chuckle. "Well, the first card pictures a strong woman. Hmm… she grows her own food? Perhaps even sells it to friends? She is very good at managing what she's in charge of."

He sniffed. "I'm very proud of her. Even though I am earning money for her, she can get through anything. Even hunger. How is that?"

It appeared he was truly in love with his partner. It was a refreshing change from the constant heartbreak and crying in typical love readings.

"I can see there is a good balance between the two of you." She pointed at the middle card depicting a woman and man with cups, a caduceus between them with a lion head adorning angel wings. "Your relationship is strong and healthy, built upon supporting each other, yet you can maintain yourself. This is a good sign that, despite being away from each other, you two are always going to be there for each other."

At this point, tears welled up in the chef's eyes and she could feel a sniffle coming up herself. She didn't let the feeling get the better of her, though, as she continued, "Your son is growing up to be a good young man who helps his little sister out. They are in touch with their child selves and are exploring the world from their eyes instead of worrying too much about the ongoings of the adult world. Particularly with you. They know you are working hard, but don't pressure themselves to support the family."

"He's always been a smart one." The chef took out a handkerchief to wipe his eyes. He looked at the Six of Cups. "And my daughter... that's her in the card?"

"In regard to this reading, yes. They are meant to represent your children."

"And this one is my wife and I?" He pointed to the Two of Cups.

"Indeed."

Iris gave him a few moments to pick up the cards and hold them in his hands, staring at the pictures. It made her think he was trying to stare so deeply into them so he could picture his actual family members in the cards.

Abruptly, he placed the cards back down on the table and got up, rushing over to Iris. She shut her eyes as the large man barrelled toward her and opened her eyes to find her feet off the floor and her body in the embrace of the man.

She was much smaller than him and was almost squished between his arms and chest. Now, she didn't like being touched by others. She knew that much based on how much she pulled her hand away from the young women clasping hers or adjusted how she was sitting because of men letting their fingers wander along her arms during readings. Sometimes, random people would pull on her cloak, like it was a show in itself. Even Marin poking at her would cause her to flinch.

Though this time it was actually very warm more than anything. And a bit soft. Her tensed body relaxed as she let out a deep breath and let the emotional man keep his arms wrapped around her.

"Thank you so much. Letters are hard to get when on ship. I miss my family."

"Will you... be seeing them again soon?" she inquired, her voice a bit muffled.

"Soon. A few weeks. There are some trips to make. I will have enough to see my family for a while."

Iris remained silent. She didn't actually know what to say now. She didn't have her own wife or children she would be returning to. She supposed she had her family and business.

"When I get back home, I will be back with family, too. Though, the business is more important."

"To them or you?" he asked, letting go of Iris and allowing her to dust herself off.

She opened her mouth to answer, only to be interrupted by a cry and rapid knocking coming from outside the room.

"Iris! Are you in there? You need to come with me quickly. It's horrible!" The desperate cry and knocking became banging on the door.

"Who's Iris?" the chef asked, going towards the door to see what was happening.

She was frozen where she stood. "I'm Iris."

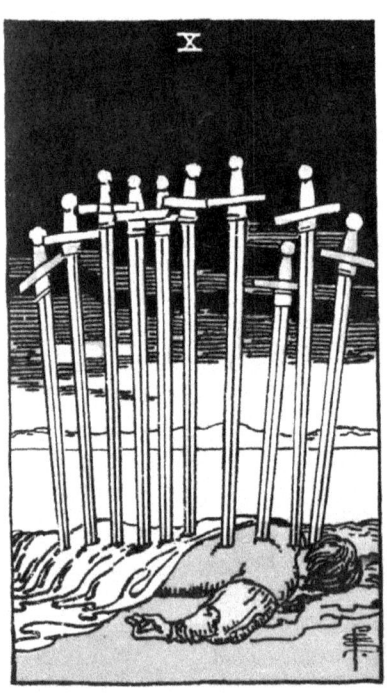

Chapter 10
ten of swords

Iris had to run to keep up with Marin's quick steps, their navigation through the ship proving flawless as they rushed to who knows where. They passed their sleeping quarters and walked into a large, empty room. She didn't think much of it when she first saw it—a few massive boxes in the corner, and that was it—but it seemed Marin had found there was more to the room.

The large crates were pushed away from the corner and toppled over, revealing a trapdoor hidden under them. The short senti lifted the trapdoor, which presented a ladder leading into darkness—another level of the ship Iris had no idea about.

"Marin, are you going to tell me what's happening? What's so horrible? And why are we here?" The questions flew out of her mouth as fast as she thought of them, her articulation tossed away for concentration as she made her way down the creaking wooden ladder after Marin.

"It'll be easier to explain once we're there," they replied in a low voice, causing Iris to shut her mouth. What was so bad for Marin to act like this now?

They made their way through another hallway, the lack of crystal prisms in the celling making their surroundings dark. Iris instinctively reached out to ensure she wouldn't walk into anything and found her hands caught in Marin's so they could lead the way.

Despite this situation being suboptimal, she had to follow along if she wanted to get out of there as soon as she could.

"Just over here," Marin said. She didn't know where *over here* was, or how close they were, or how Marin could tell, but remained quiet.

"Who's there?"

Iris jumped at the new voice appearing in the darkness. It was a hoarse voice, unlike anyone else's on the ship, which meant it was someone she hadn't met yet. Who else would be down here in the dark?

"Don't worry, it's just me. I've come back with my friend this time," Marin responded to the disembodied voice.

"How did you find someone down here?" Iris asked, coming to a stop as Marin let go of her hand and shuffled around. "Aside from that, why were you down here if they've clearly covered the entrance?"

"I think there are more pressing matters right now. Listen, there is a caemi down here with us."

"A caemi?" She didn't mean to sound so surprised, but considering everything that was going on, a lone caemi on a ship of senti was the last thing she expected. Were they the reason for the strange plank sounds and the murmuring early in the morning?

"Yes. I may have accidentally run into the boxes covering this trap door and I found this section of the ship. They were sitting in the darkness and tied up, so I untied them, but now I don't know what to do."

"And so you decided bringing me down here was a good idea?" Iris was sceptical that she could be of any help, but she was also worried about the caemi. How long had they been here and were they ever fed and hydrated? "Did you at least bring something for them to consume?"

"Of course I did! What do you make of me, Sybil Iris?" They tutted in the darkness, but she could tell by the quiver in their voice that their jokes were attempting to make light of a tough situation.

She heard Marin unclip a small bag and take a few things out. Fortunately, the first of those things was a small oil lamp and a few matches, which she came to see once the senti illuminated the area.

The caemi was one she recognised as a wolf caemi, as their ears that were rounder than a cat's ears and shorter than a rabbit's or foxes. They also had dust covering their face, likely because the floor they were on was not maintained. There were cobwebs and old wooden crates scattered around.

The short senti crouched down and took a seat beside the ragged caemi, then pulled out some bread and a canteen of water from their bag and handed it to them. Iris hardly blinked before the loaf was left to crumbs and the canteen emptied.

"Thank you." The caemi's voice was still hoarse despite drinking the water. "My name is Appius, may I know yours?"

"I'm Marin, and she's Iris." Without wasting a second, he turned to Iris with a stern look. "They don't know why they're down here or what the pirates want with them. Since they put them down here, they haven't visited since."

Her eyes widened. "Will this happen to us as well? We haven't known the crew long." How ironic, considering Marin was still hardly someone she knew, and she was trusting them with leading her away from home.

"I'm sure we can handle it if they try to capture us. With my skills and your smarts, they won't catch us." They gave Iris a determined grin. "Now, if we want to help this caemi out of here, it'll be impossible while we travel. We will have to wait until we get to Excava and, even then, being in Excava with a caemi would be trouble."

The only suggestion Iris had was feeding and hydrating the caemi for the rest of the trip by bringing down food and water each day. Her other idea was to keep the caemi in their sleeping quarters, but if the crew were to check this area or their room, they would be found out. Marin was right, they would have to wait.

Just as Iris opened her mouth to share her thoughts, Marin perked up with widened eyes and quickly put out the lamp, using their free hand to cover Iris' mouth to muffle her words.

"Shush, someone's up there…" Marin mumbled under their breath. While she couldn't see Marin anymore in the darkness, she could feel them looking up and around, as if to track the noise above the ceiling.

"Oi!"

Iris shivered at the echoing, booming voice. Based on the direction and tone of the voice, Risala was above the hole they had come down.

"It looks like a rat has gotten into the under-boards of the ship. Show yourself now before I come down there and get you myself!"

A prickling feeling climbed Iris' spine as she froze. It was a horrible idea to come down here without knowing what she was getting into. With Risala at the only place up and down from here, they would have to face her.

"I'm so sorry, guys." The caemi sniffled. "If you hadn't found me, you wouldn't be down here right now."

"No, no—don't cry. Finding you and getting caught is better than not finding you at all." Marin shuffled away, presumedly to comfort the caemi.

"Do you really want me to come down there and get you?" Risala's loud shouts had now shifted to a poisoned sing-song.

"Listen—" Marin started. Iris couldn't see them, but she looked in the general direction of their hushed voice. "I'm going to go up there. I'll pretend I'm the only one who came down. I want you to hide, Iris."

"Wait, no." She didn't know why she responded so quickly—since when was she worried about what Marin was doing? "What are they going to do with you?"

They chuckled solemnly. "No idea. But no matter what, I will make sure they don't cover the exit. Count to thirty before coming up after me. We don't want them seeing you here."

"But what should I do once I get up there?" In a panicked moment, Iris reached out and grasped Marin's arm. "I've never done anything like this before."

Marin patted her arm, getting up and ready to give himself in. "Use what you're best at, I'm sure you can do something with it. I'll see you soon."

Her grasp on the senti slipped as they walked towards the exit and Risala, ready to take whatever the crew was going to throw at them for uncovering their secret.

Twenty-eight, twenty-nine, thirty.

Iris sat in silence after mumbling her count to thirty, as Marin suggested. She had heard Risala ridicule the senti and then seemingly tie them up with strong vulgar protests from Marin. After a few moments, they had left the room above, fortunately without moving any of the boxes back on top. They were likely too distracted by Marin.

"We need to save them," Appius quietly suggested.

"I know."

If she wanted any chance at helping Marin and this caemi, she would need to think fast and use what she had to her advantage.

What did Marin mean by using what she was best at? Her mind raced through the last few weeks—her time was taken up by tarot reading and performances for the people receiving them. Tarot cards were a tool known for predicting the future, even morbid ones, with assumptions about certain cards in a negative light when, really, they could be interpreted in different ways.

What else did she have? There was the chef, and there was the caemi. She assumed the rest of the crew would be above deck with Risala and Josey. If she planned to use her cards, the chef would be able to help back up her claims, considering she had given an accurate reading to him just earlier.

"What can you do?" She fumbled around for the lamp and lit it once again with a match Marin had left them.

"I don't understand…?"

"Okay, what can your caemi magic do? Do you have *any* idea why the sea travellers would capture you specifically?"

"I believe they chose me randomly—wait, the sea." There was a hint of recognition in their voice, which gave Iris hope. "I have an affinity with sea spirits and I usually spent my time at the docks, you know, before the queen did that whole thing, so I could help sailors and travellers with blessings. I can speak to the spirits and request them to do things in exchange for offerings and spreading the word about them."

Her mind returned to the siren-like nature of the spirits of water, which made Appius' skill much more admirable. It was also an opportunity to use it in the plan that was beginning to cook in her mind.

If she selected the right cards, she could play the messengers of the spirits, her words coming to life with the assistance of Appius, and her claims being supported by the chef himself.

If Marin caught on, he would be able to play along and they would have a show to blow the travellers away and gain their trust.

It was a matter of creating a common enemy instead of antagonising each other.

"Come with me, I'll explain on the way." She couldn't help but think she picked that up from Marin. "I'm going to save Marin, and I need your help."

Chapter 11
the magician

Iris hurried up the main ladder, strong wind and the smell of salt rushing into her face. She surfaced on the top deck, which revealed a struggling Marin in the grasp of Risala and Paddy. They stretched Marin's hand up in the air and picked them up, their feet dangling.

Rope was tied around their mouth to prevent them from screaming, but the thrashing around continued. Angry expressions were painted on the faces of the crew, with even Pegs standing in the background, fixing a plank to the edge of the ship.

Considering Captain Josey was ready with a sword in hand, the tip hovering by Marin's stomach, Iris had to work fast.

"Try to escape again, and Josey here will be sticking her sword right into your heart. You hear me, you little rat?"

Muffled screams came from Marin and only led to more struggling and swinging around. Iris approached them swiftly, though not too aggressively, as to not anger them more. In her position, she couldn't help but be reminded of the Five of Wands.

"What's going on here?" As far as the crew knew, she had no idea what was going on.

Risala and Paddy turned to face her. The captain remained watching Marin—not that they would be able to hear her, anyway.

"Your little friend here," Risala hissed sharply at Marin as she squeezed their wrist, earning a whine from them, "decided it was okay to poke their nose into our business and try to mess with us. Didn't you?"

In contrast to the friendly demeanour the crew showed them when they'd first met, they were beginning to scare her—but she couldn't let her fear get in the way of her plan. She needed Marin to be safe, no matter how many lies it would take.

"There's something much deeper at play." Iris bared caution to the side of the ship, as if something was going to appear at any moment. Her tone was surrounded by mystery and her face was forlorn. "I come with a message."

"We don't have time for your message after what they tried to do. We let you two get on our ship for a ride, only to be stabbed in the back by this child playing hero." Paddy drew a small dagger from his belt and held it up to Marin's neck. More struggling ensued to avoid getting cut.

"You must listen to me." She kept her voice level and serious. As they squinted at Iris, the sunlight casting a long shadow of herself towards them, she pulled out her tarot cards.

"Why should we? Maybe we should tie you up as well, Sybil." Risala let go of Marin's wrist, causing them to thump onto the ship floor and crumple. They weren't thrashing anymore, only being held still by Paddy now. "What are you holding? You aren't going to try to fight us, are you?" She laughed alongside Paddy.

"I bring a message from the spirits of water." She held her hands up defensively, also displaying the cards. "My name isn't Sybil, but it is signifying of my occupation. I can divine the future, and the spirits have sent a message to share."

The mention of spirits caught Paddy's attention. "Why would they send you a message?"

"It's what I do. I get messages, and I happened to get an urgent one. Considering we're in the middle of the sea—" The ship began to rock, and the waves became rough against the sides. "It isn't out of the question these spirits to have something to say."

"Speak your message, Sybil." Risala jutted her chin out at her. "Make it quick."

She held up the Two of Pentacles.

"They feel an imbalance." She displayed the card with a man juggling two pentacles, rough waters in the background. Her choice of cards was methodical. "See how the waters are unruly in the background, and how the man is struggling to hold his goods? A strong indication that danger out of your control may be coming your way."

As she interpreted the card, the ship leaned from one side to the other roughly, the imbalance she felt in still waters being put to shame. She selected the next card.

"The Tower," she announced, the card depicting lightning striking a tower and destroying it, with two figures falling out of it. This was one of the cards people feared, yet it didn't always mean bad things. She knew her deck found amusement in scaring clients using cards of this nature. "A horrible change is coming, and it's going to destroy all of us."

She waved her hands in a dramatic move, and the waves grew with the gestures. The deck began flooding beneath her. She could swear the edge of the waves was beginning to form spikes, unlike their usual flowing shape, but she had to focus.

Marin coughed awake, their expression painted in surprise as they stared at their soaked pants. He quickly stood and tried to run, but Paddy still held tightly despite being wary of the water coming up around them.

"What... what else do they say?" Paddy managed to spit out while making sure he wouldn't be dragged into the water itself.

"Seven of Swords." This was the confrontation that could change everything. "You have something that doesn't belong to you."

Risala perked up and exchanged a look with the captain and Paddy. Josey began to sign to the crew, frantic about what was going on. Iris felt the performance from Appius below was over the top. The water spirits were having their fun, and an almost mocking jingle rang through the sky.

"You have a caemi on this ship," Iris confessed, holding up the card she had previously mentioned. "And it will be the cause of your demise."

"How did you know that?" Risala demanded. "You must have been trespassing as well!"

"It was the cards and spirits, I've already told you this." She had to raise her voice to get her words through. The waves became loud and thrashed against the wooden ship and soaked each crew member.

"You're lying to us!" Risala was desperately trying to keep her grip on the deck while helping Josey, too. As if calling her bluff would save them. It would not. "Take the rat to the plank!" She called to Paddy, who tried his best to do so amongst the chaos.

A large body emerged from the lower deck, revealing himself in slivers of sunlight peeking through the violent waves. "Risala, Captain!" The chef had arrived as requested.

"Mikael!" Risala called as the crew looked on with gaped mouths and wide eyes. As Iris suspected, it was a sight to behold when the chef showed himself. "What are you doing here?"

"Believe the little one. She told me of my family. She knew I had a wife at home with my little boy and girl—just from her cards." He held his hands in a pleading motion, playing the moment as the most important of their lives. If they wanted to live, they would listen.

"Iris, help!" Marin was trying to claw away from the plank, having to clench it to avoid the spirits snapping up to grab at them as a shark would.

Risala growled, baring her teeth. Iris could tell there was an obvious struggle between the vengeance she wanted and the lives of her friends. "What other cards are there?"

This was the one Iris was looking forward to showing. Part of her was embarrassed to admit she was utterly thrilled to be presenting her cards in such a way, that her talent could be used for such a flashy plan. She had never felt this way before in her usual readings, blood pumping and adrenaline rushing. Would she ever be able to do this again? Would she ever get another chance?

"Death." She added a fun inflection to the word—as to even further scare the pirates—and held up the card showing a skeleton knight riding a white horse, murdering anyone in their path. The card that scared her clients the most, usually assuming it meant actual death. That was her intention this time.

Gasps were heard across the ship, and Risala froze for a moment before she frantically turned to Paddy. "A sacrifice! Let's sacrifice the kid to the spirits, and we'll be saved."

Iris flinched. "Wait, that's not—"

She was too late on the draw when Paddy forced Marin into his arms and tossed him overboard without a second thought. The spirits of water were threatening to turn the ship upside down.

Marin's body hardly caused a ripple amongst the rifts and miniature tsunamis around them, and Iris prayed to Ter and Mian that Marin would remain safe in the grasp of the spirits. Appius would do something about it, right? She didn't just get her friend thrown overboard, did she?

She had to remain focused.

The waves didn't stop, and Risala's face dropped.

Crates smashed into the mast and away from the splinters came rusted chains, coins and jewels. A barrel rolled towards Iris, barely missing her and crashing into the captain's chamber door, revealing leather journals, hats, clothing… where did they get these from? Others they'd captured before this?

"Look at what you have done." Iris tried her best to make her voice boom while her words were being eaten by the surrounding spirits. At this point, she was getting desperate, too. "Do you realise the relationship between a caemi and spirit? They want their caemi to be safe and you have gone against nature itself to capture a caemi. We will all pay for this now."

"Okay, OKAY!" Risala screamed, forcing the sword away from Josey's hand and tossing it away. "Look, we aren't going to hurt anyone. We just need this to stop, make it all stop. I'm not going to get my friends bloody killed for a damn caemi. It's not worth it, dammit."

As Risala raged, the time came for Iris to clean up this mess. She stood as close to the hatch down to the lower deck as she could, knowing Appius was below and could hear her.

"Mighty spirit of water, mighty spirits of the sea. Please show us mercy as the ones who have gone against you will amend their ways!" Iris yelled her formulated prayer to the skies, hoping to the gods everything would be alright.

And just like magic, the waves calmed not long after and the ship was still again. The deck was still flooded, but hardly so now—with the rocking allowing some of the water to slip away and back to the sea.

"Go get the stupid caemi from the bottom deck." Risala pinched the bridge of her nose, taking a breath and then turning to her captain to sign what was happening.

Mikael went to retrieve Appius and brought them up. Fortunately, with the crew recovering, they didn't question the speed of the chef's work.

Leaving the safety of the caemi to Mikael, Iris rushed to the edge of the ship in panic. Marin was still down there. Surely he wouldn't have drowned in the chaos, right? Surely he was still alive.

"Marin! Can you hear me?" she called in desperation, scanning the waters for any sign of their survival. She had one job, and it was to save her travel companion. If she had failed, she wouldn't know what to do with herself. "Marin?" she cried out again, tears welling up in her eyes and making her vision blurry.

Suddenly, there was a low rumble from underneath the ship. Risala screamed in an obvious fear of the chaos starting again. Paddy was holding his head, his mind fried from what had just happened with the spirits.

"What the hell is that?" Risala yelled.

Iris didn't bother to look as she kept praying and praying for the safety of Marin. Then her eyes were forced upwards. A giant wave towered over her.

On top of the wave was a hollering Marin—obviously tired and beat, but alive nonetheless.

"Thank you, patrons above and spirits of the water!" he sang into the skies before the wave began to dip and dive into the deck, dropping them onto the soaked wooden floor.

Iris scurried over to the short senti and wrapped her arms around them, ignoring how their clothes were sticking together from the damp aftermath of their performance.

"Oh, thank gods you're okay. I wasn't ready for any of that." Iris rested her cheek on top of Marin's drenched hair.

"I'm okay, Iris." A soft chuckle came from them. Even when they almost drowned, they were making light of the situation. "I'm still here."

The crew made their way below deck to dry off and recover. Most of them sat on crates, while Iris and Marin sat at the small table in the room. Pegs remained above deck, volunteering to sort out the crates and barrels that were caught in the mess.

"We knew we were screwed without caemi in Kyross anymore. We would lose our blessings and favour from the spirits, at least, our advantage." Paddy looked down in shame.

"And you decided kidnapping a caemi was a good idea?" Marin bothered to question, ringing out their vest and unbuttoning some of his dress shirt to allow himself to dry.

"It was so easy to do just that. We didn't want to spare the money, food, and supplies for another crew member, also having to hide them while we were near Kyross. It was easier to keep them hidden away in the first place," Risala explained, as if it were the most obvious thing in the world. "Scouring sunken and washed up ships is dangerous work, and we need luck to find treasure worthy to selling off."

"Caemi are people too," Iris interjected. "They need water and food to survive, and you saw what just happened. You're better off making friends with them and treating them properly to earn the ocean's favour. You've done the opposite of what you wanted." She never knew that people had to go to such lengths for survival, and it explained the obscure amount of items they had for such a small group.

The crew looked down in shame, and Mikael returned with a plate of warm food and a tall glass of water, setting it on the table and gesturing for Appius to eat. After being starved for who knows how long, Appius devoured the food.

Josey took her hat off and placed it on her lap. She signed to Risala to translate what she wanted to say.

"We apologise, Appius, Sybil, and Marin. We were wrong, and while an apology cannot make up for what we did, we will do our best to make up for it and accommodate all of you." The crew bowed their heads low. "Appius, we would like to offer you a place on our ship. Your own room, new clothes, money, food, water. We just wish for good fortune on our travels."

Appius waited to swallow what they were eating before replying. "For that, I would like some time. Provide me with what you listed until we help Sybil and Marin safely get to Excava. From there, I will decide whether I will take that offer."

With a fair negotiation, the captain and Appius shook hands.

"I'm relieved that's sorted." Paddy sighed. "Though I am very interested in learning about your cards, Sybil."

Iris perked up, grabbing her cards from her pocket and shuffling through them. While they had some water on them, the cards were sturdy enough to withstand it and just needed some time drying.

"It would be my pleasure to explain and read for you."

As she interpreted the cards as she had to Mikael, Marin left the room. They reassured the crew they were just going to get some fresh air at the top. Iris noted to check on them afterwards.

She figured the readings may reveal something to gain more trust from the crew members and, by chance, disclose something that could help them in any future situations. She didn't have control over the crew, but she had the cards in her hands and the cards were always right.

First, she did a reading for Paddy, which confirmed his passion for researching spirits. He only ignored it because people in his old life claimed he wouldn't get anywhere in life that way. That was the reason he resorted to sea travel and errands.

The cards said that if he were to attempt making something bigger out of his interest and research, he would be supported by those around him and finding a mentor would be most useful to him. This was shown through the Three of Wands, Three of Cups, and Three of Pentacles. She found it interesting that three was a repeated number and noted looking into number meanings as part of her tarot studies.

Second, she did a reading for Risala. Her reading revealed she was holding herself back because of the expectations she had. Her opinions of herself were deeply rooted in the mindset of her old village, where negative influences were prominent and forms of expression weren't seen as positive.

She admitted to being interested in exploring sexuality from a young age, and that she had no control over how her community restricted her. This led to impulsive decisions in her life, such as becoming a thrill seeker on the ocean. The solution presented was to surrender herself to discovering new perspectives instead of keeping to what she knew.

This was shown through The Devil, King of Wands Reversed, and The Hanged Man.

She also did a quick reading for Pegs, but Pegs only asked about what to eat tonight. The answer was fish—the Page of Cups helped show that.

Last was Captain Josey. Iris felt hesitant about reading for them since she didn't know how to communicate the answers to her. Risala offered to sign what the reading was, and so that was settled.

"What would she like to ask the cards?" Iris began gently shuffling the cards as she awaited a translation from Risala.

"What is blocking me from my full potential? That is what she wants to know."

It was a well-worded question for someone who hadn't done a tarot reading before. Iris often enjoyed completing readings for these kinds of questions because they meant her client could work towards improving something of theirs.

She handed Josey the deck to cut, to which she tried to split the cards evenly. Then she was prompted to draw three cards from the top of the deck.

The Hierophant Reversed, Queen of Wands Reversed, The Sun.

"The cards have a clear message for you," Iris spoke with intention so that Risala would have time to sign what she was saying to the captain. "Beginning with The Hierophant in Reverse, this indicates you sought external approval for what you did in the past. You wanted others to reassure you that you were on the right path. This card is showing you don't need to hold yourself to that anymore. You can be the one telling yourself what you're doing is correct."

The captain nodded along, a thoughtful expression on her face. She leaned forward with her elbows on the table, her hands clasped together as she waited for more.

"He is encouraging you to examine the way you do things around here and align them with your values. What do you truly think you should be doing? You're losing your sense of freedom."

She could see the captain was sceptical about the reading, her eyebrows furrowing and then signing something to Risala.

"She's saying this card is too on the nose about what we were dealing with before. How does she know you aren't rigging the cards?"

"This is part of why I get the client to cut the deck." Iris smiled smugly. She had a feeling she would be questioned. The cards were always right. Of course, she couldn't prove the meaning of the cards without some sort of source, but with everything so accurately read, it was difficult to further question. "The captain chose those cards herself. Really, this is a reflection of something she should be thinking of, not me giving her my personal advice."

The captain pondered for a moment before gesturing to continue.

"Next comes the Queen of Wands in Reverse. She indicates you are reaching a point of self-respect and confidence and you need to let this happen in order to get through your barriers. You know what you stand for and the meaning of success for you isn't the same as to the others. If you ever feel lacking of confidence, bring your energy and attention inwards to focus on rebuilding your sense of self. Figure out who you really are."

The captain didn't have anything to say to this card, but there was thought behind her eyes. The cards were truly pointing to what values the captain held and how they saw themself. It was encouraging a lot of re-evaluations.

"The Sun is a really nice card to pull in a reading. It is success, radiance, and abundance. Combined with the other cards, this indicates the path you take from here will be successful and fulfilling. You will be able to spread positivity to those around you and within yourself."

As Risala signed the final sentences, the reading was concluded. The crew sat in silence for a while, all of them mulling over what they were told. Well, except for Pegs, who was eating a fish in the corner.

"Thank you, Iris," Paddy said, breaking the silence. "I think we all have something to think about now."

Making her way up to the top deck once again, she looked around as she popped her head above the ladder hole. She tightened the hood around her neck as the cool wind blew into her face, and spotted Marin on the other side of the ship, leaning against the railing and just staring at the sea.

It was quiet except for the splashing of small waves hitting the side of the wooden ship, and she sought to not interrupt it, softly stepping onto the deck.

The sky was orange and pink rather than the blue from earlier. She still wasn't used to having any clocks around compared to back home, where she had multiple clocks to ensure she was working correctly, following her routine. She assumed it was approaching late afternoon now.

"I guess that's what I get for trying to be the hero, huh?" Marin said without moving as Iris approached them.

She stood beside them with her hands folded in front of her. She looked between Marin and the sea, wondering what they were staring at or perhaps what they were trying to find in the endless blue ocean.

"It was incredibly dangerous to give yourself up like that, and even leave me to save you," Iris replied. "Who knows what could have happened to us?"

They sighed, running a hand over their face. "I know, I know. But what was I expected to do when I found that caemi and then dragged you into it? Get all of us caught and thrown overboard?"

She pursed her lips. She was starting to realise that sometimes they did have to make a sacrifice to save others. It was admirable of Marin, but it still irked her to think they could've drowned. "I don't know."

Iris reached into her cloak pocket and pulled out a few bandages. While she'd never experienced injuries herself, her siblings' stage tasks sometimes resulted in cuts and tears.

"Bandages?" Marin gave her a quick side glance before looking back at the ocean. From here, she couldn't really see their face properly.

"Yes. I haven't needed these before, but I asked the chef what was best for sores such as yours, and he gave me these." She held them up and waved them a little. Even if she didn't need to use them, she could probably assume how to apply them.

Wordlessly, the senti held their arms out towards her and rolled up the sleeves, revealing some of the bruising from being held in the air and some she wasn't quite able to see earlier due to said sleeves over them.

She began to unravel some of the bandages and held one end against the side of his wrist, which caused Marin to let out a small

149

whine. She quickly apologised and tried to cushion the end in a spot without a visible bruise.

At first, her wrapping was rather clumsy and loose, and so she had to undo her work a few times to make sure the bandage was wrapped nicely enough. Marin didn't seem to mind as they quietly waited for her to finish one arm before she walked around to the other side and wrapped the other.

After the bandages were used up, the short senti let out a small 'thank you' before flexing their hands and wrists a little to test the constraints. Iris felt a small glow of pride inside for being able to help Marin in this situation, even if it was the least she could do.

Marin finally turned to Iris and looked up at her. Their eyes were tinted red and there was a frown settled on their face. They had been crying. "I almost died, and I could've gotten you stabbed by that sword. And then what would've happened to the caemi? I risked so much for Appius, how can I expect to save Kalaya?"

Iris avoided eye contact, playing with the cards in her pocket. "I expect we will have an actual plan when it comes to saving her. We also won't be bound by these travellers. There will be guards, yes, but you know how to get past guards."

She hadn't known Marin for long, but they did demonstrate enough for her to know that breaking into somewhere was one of the things they were good at. They weren't exactly breaking in anywhere on this ship. Really, they were trying to break out. That must've made it more difficult for the young senti to get anywhere.

Marin sniffed and wiped their nose on their sleeve, turning away again. She was glad they had gotten more shirts. "Thank you, Iris. Even though we met yesterday, I'm glad you're here."

The sentence made her feel warm inside again, though it wasn't something she was familiar with. It didn't feel extreme, but it was new. When was the last time she had felt a feeling like this in her chest?

"There is something I've noticed," Iris began, now placing her hands on the rail and leaning forward. She was trying to reflect on the feeling, comparing it to how she felt around people at home. "When I'm around my family members nowadays, it feels a bit… cold, if that makes sense. Like where I'm standing is not quite right, and I have to think really hard before I say anything."

Even with customers, she didn't experience the warmth despite them being different from her siblings and mother. "When I work, there is only a neutral feeling. No warmth, no cold. It's hard to really pinpoint anything in that case."

She placed a hand on her chest, trying to feel the warmth on the outside. She couldn't, but she could imagine it there. "Being around you gives me a subtle, warm feeling. It's the opposite of when I'm home. The last time I felt like this was… when I was practising tarot with my brothers. That was years ago."

Marin took a moment to think, bringing their fingers to their chin. "Hmm… have you ever had friends before, Iris?"

She tilted her head and turned to Marin. "Is this what friendship feels like?"

"Well, that's what I think. Friendship is when you can spend time with others and you feel happy doing it. When you enjoy spending time with someone. In comparison to…" It sounded as if Marin wanted to continue, but stopped themself. "If you want, we can be friends."

"But I haven't known you for very long." The only people she knew were her family members, and she'd known them for either her whole life or their whole life. It was a large shift to calling someone a friend.

"When it comes to friends, it can be a day or a year before you feel like you're friends. It all depends on how you feel inside while you're around them," Marin explained. There was a hint of excitement in their voice, which she was glad of. Their mood was improving. "So tell me more, how do you feel?"

Just in a short time, she had already made many memories from spending time with Marin. From when they first met at her booth, to them breaking into her room, to the talk they had, to running out of the gambling house in a chaos they formulated themselves. There was also their walk to the market and their experience of buying new clothes. She had gotten new books, and they ate at a nice café. They rescued a caemi from a guard and met this crew. This was her first time on a ship. She also had to save herself, Marin, Appius, and everyone else on the ship with all she knew, which wasn't very much when it came to the outside world.

"I knew I wanted to protect you and do my best for you. Even though I tell you off for being reckless and leaving your clothes everywhere, I do it because I'm concerned..." She turned away and diverted her eyes. It was difficult for her to reveal this to Marin. She wasn't used to revealing her thoughts like this outside of readings. "When you said you were glad I'm here, that made me feel warm inside. Like... acceptance. It was a feeling of acceptance."

It clicked in her head. Being around Marin made her feel like she was exactly where she needed to be. It was different from being told tarot wasn't much, that she needed to be better, or that she had to consider what others felt before her.

"Then we're friends." Marin gave her a thumbs up with a determined expression, eyes beaming.

Iris smiled—a small smile, since she still had a lot to process, but a smile nonetheless. "We're friends."

For a little while, they just listened to the water splashing, little spirits occasionally dancing above the water, and watched the orange and pink sky turn to a darker shade.

"You knew that was going to happen, didn't you?" Marin broke the silence.

"What was going to happen?" She couldn't pinpoint anything particular that had happened during the last day. A lot happened.

"Me getting in trouble. You knew. I know you knew." She could see a smirk dance on Marin's face. "Well, you couldn't have known exactly what would happen or what to do to prevent it, but it's one of your specialties. Your plan was impressive, playing into the minds of the crew, using your talent, as well as using Appius and Mikael. You're a quick and thorough thinker."

She didn't have much to say about that. She did consider her tarot reading a talent of hers, but it seemed Marin had something more on their mind. She wasn't able to comprehend what they were saying, and she wasn't willing to push for now. However, she was slightly proud of how she got them out of the situation and ensured their safety to Excava.

"Maybe I did know. The cards are always right."

For the rest of that evening, they enjoyed the sunset and night sky, taking in the sounds and smell of the ocean and each other's company.

The rest of the trip to Excava was as peaceful as it could get with play-fighting that was a bit more competitive this time around between Marin and the crew now, but play-fighting nonetheless. Iris was able to get through more book reading, absorbing more each day on witchcraft and tarot. It was before long that they arrived in the heart of Kyross.

Chapter 12
the hanged man

Ringing bells awoke Iris on the day of their arrival at the Excava docks. As it had been a few days at sea, she was now slightly more used to her temporary bed and not wondering where she was. She had also gotten used to the smells in and around the ship, as well as waking up to Marin coming back from his morning walk around the ship or seeing them stretching in the middle of the room. They were a morning person, or so it seemed.

"What's that noise?" Iris mumbled as she rubbed the sleep out of her eyes and sat up.

"Bells." Marin chuckled.

"… I understand they are bells. I'm wondering where they're coming from."

From the other side of the room, a flurry of clothes was thrown into her face. It surely shocked her, and Marin earned a glare from her.

"Get ready and meet me on the top deck. I've already packed everything." They were already out the door by the time she had neatened the mess on her bed into a folded pile.

Iris got herself out of bed and changed into linen trousers and a lace up shirt, bringing her thoughts together with each pull of the drawstrings. So they had finally arrived at their destination. She would have to get used to yet another location, imagining Excava Kingdom would be vastly different from Vestirr.

Her hand froze as she reached for her tarot cards. She only had a couple days until the end of her week, as her mother declared. And she had wasted it travelling on a boat while not earning anything to her name.

For several moments, she remained still, running through both sides in her mind. Her mother would understand right? But she wanted Iris to earn her money fairly through work. But this way she was being creative and her mother was always clever and creative with her solutions. But she ran away with strangers without her mother knowing.

She blinked, her room coming back into focus, and glanced at her cards again. With a deep breath, she flipped the top card. Four of Swords. A man laying upon a platform—peaceful, and golden. A sign that she had to relax and let the opportunity come together.

While she didn't feel secure in her heart, she knew to trust her cards. When had they ever failed her?

Once she tidied up the rest of the room, such as her bed and Marin's, which they had left unkempt for the entirety of their stay, she made her way to the top deck of the ship.

Pinewood and a sweet aroma floated in the air. First impressions proved this city was much more decorated than her own, the trees neatly trimmed and kept in designated plots rather than along the paths, and beds of flowers welcomed townspeople as they walked by.

Despite Vestirr being the trading capital, the number of ships found at the Excava docks put her city to shame. Ships, large and small, appearing to be of different purposes, were docked at the port.

The bells had stopped ringing by now, but Marin was staring up at something a short distance away. She followed their gaze to find a tall tower with a point at the top and a clock face.

"That's where the ringing comes from. In Excava Kingdom, they have a clock tower which helps everyone keep track of the time."

"Huh. So I suppose we'll be hearing that throughout our days here?" Iris didn't particularly like the sound of that. She wouldn't want to be woken up by loud ringing each night.

"Honestly, I don't notice it anymore. It might need a bit of getting used to, but I just wanted to let you know where the bells were." They turned to Iris with a beaming smile, almost like they were proud of showing her the clock tower.

"Oi, kiddies!" Risala called to them from the port. The group of pirates were gathered around, similarly to when Iris and Marin had first met them in Vestirr. "You two going to grab your stuff?"

She turned to find where Marin had placed her luggage but, by the time she had, Marin was already hoisting it onto their back and was ready to go.

"Doesn't that get heavy for you?" Iris was thankful she didn't need to carry a suitcase full of their clothes, but she was slightly concerned for Marin's back, especially when they practically sprinted down the ramp from the ship to the dock, and almost overshot into the ocean.

"I've carried heavier things. Ever carried a drunken man larger than you out of a bar?" Marin laughed. Iris hadn't, so she had no idea what that was like. "Anyway, I know a place we can settle and piece together our plan."

Iris approached the crew, who were chatting and singing amongst themselves. If she didn't know better, she would still assume they were just sea travellers who delivered goods. Despite treasure hunters who sold off the belongings of the ocean's deceased, they kept a friendly exterior. It made Iris wonder how many other people like her asked for a ride, only to be caught off guard and threatened to be thrown off the side of the ship.

Perhaps that was what the caemi back in Excava was going to tell them before Marin sprinted off.

Marin bowed toward the captain. "Thank you for escorting us here. And…" They straightened up and looked away shyly. "Sorry for the trouble."

Risala signed what was said to the captain. Josey signed in return with a smile. It didn't seem like there were any hard feelings.

"Well, from having you on our ship, we've learnt a lot. We still gotta do what we gotta do to earn our living, but… now we just hope for the best." There was a pause as Marin looked at them with hopeful eyes. "You know, Appius let us know about their answer first thing this morning. They're pretty content hanging out with us on the ship as long as we look after them. We will, I assure you!"

Marin cheered and roughly embraced the captain who chuckled and pat Marin on the head.

Paddy walked up to the two and gave them a handshake. "Good luck with whatever you get up to here. Can't guarantee we'll be around for when you need another oversea trip, but you know who we are now."

Iris and Marin said their goodbyes to the crew, thanking them once again for the trip. Before they made their way off the dock, she felt a tug on her sleeve. She turned around to see Pegs standing in front of her. She was unsure why Pegs got her attention until she noticed the golden pocket watch in Pegs' hands.

"You're giving it back?" Iris slowly reached out to take it in case this was a trick, but there wasn't any resistance from the little person. "I thought it was payment for the trip."

The mute traveller shook their head and gave Iris and Marin a thumbs up before heading back to the ship and disappearing.

Marin clapped in excitement and grabbed the watch from Iris, holding it gently in their hands and staring at it.

"My watch! I gotta admit, I was rather sad when I had to give it up." They pocketed it with a smile before stepping forward, now entering the bustling kingdom of Excava. "Come on, I'll lead the way."

There were many similarities in Excava to Vestirr, and Iris assumed it was because both cities were rather popular in their markets, entertainment, and for tourists. It was one of the reasons why the Galacia Gambling House was so popular and got a lot of traffic.

She did notice that in Excava, royal banners and crests were much more common. They were often seen hanging from flag poles standing in front of large buildings, and even on smaller banners on market stalls. Perhaps it was the kingdom's way of honouring the royal family. In Vestirr, this tradition was not unfamiliar, but much rarer.

The city was built on the side of a monstrous mountain, the castle in its grandeur sitting at the very top. From down here, she could see that the higher you went on the mountain, the fancier the buildings were.

The architecture was also more sophisticated in Excava, even the ones closer to the bottom of the mountain, compared to the older, worn buildings of Vestirr. The buildings didn't show much wear—evidence of constant care and maintenance—though something about it reminded her of the caemi. This much perfection had to be the work of magic or something else otherworldly.

"How do they maintain their buildings so well?" Iris asked as she followed the short senti in front of her. She admired the buildings along the way, though, due to her airheaded appearance in the moment, attracted a few salespeople in an effort to sell her something. Marin had to pull her away from them.

"Excava Kingdom was known for using magic to keep their appearance in top shape. This meant they employed the assistance of caemi to do so."

So she was on the right track with her assumption.

Marin paused to look around before letting out an 'ah' in recognition and making a left. The streets were ever busy, so Iris had to pay careful attention to Marin's spontaneous navigation. A lot of the streets looked the same despite housing market stalls and shops for different purposes. They came across the occasional building that would stand out against the rest for their colour and size, as well as alleyways that looked unusually broken down compared to their large counterparts.

"So... what would that mean for the kingdom now that—"

"I don't know," Marin quickly said. "I mean, the deportation of caemi isn't a small thing. We..." They looked around again and then continued. "The caemi had a big part in how things worked around here. Not only the care of the buildings, but their presence assisted magical flora and fauna. Over time, you'll notice there will only be mundane wildlife found here, as everything else will either move to Syriphia or die out."

"Oh." Iris had never properly seen any magical flora, considering it was only a week ago when she first left her home. The only animals she really saw were birds, especially crows, hanging around the windows. Sometimes people would ask for readings about pets, but she couldn't recall if any of them were particularly special creatures she would categorise as magical.

"So..." Marin turned to her with a smile. "I want to ask you something since we're making progress towards saving Kalaya."

She shot a glance at the senti. What were they up to? "What would you like to ask?"

"Well, you didn't want to come on this rescue mission until I went more into who Kalaya was. You know, someone who did similar things to you. I want to learn more about why you followed a stranger like me."

She tilted her head, mulling over the question. "Why do you want to know?"

"It's actually a good way to find out more about another person. It reveals your motivations and what you value. Maybe what you struggle with as well."

What she struggled with and valued? These things were kept between her mind and cards, never to be revealed to any customers or strangers. At the same time, Marin wasn't a stranger anymore, but a friend.

As they spoke, she watched the flowerbeds they passed by, flowers that were trying to reach the sun as well as those content with remaining where they were, spreading their petals out, decorating the path they walked.

"I haven't explained this to anyone before," she admitted.

"Take your time." They gave her a gentle nod.

"I suppose… I want to meet someone like me. My family members aren't very interested in tarot reading like I am. My brothers used to humour me and spend time looking at the cards, but eventually, they learnt business was more important. I was lucky enough to turn my passion into something I could earn from."

Marin nodded along, letting Iris continue. Usually, she spent her day working, attending meetings and sorting out papers. Those precious few hours she had for herself were reserved for essential care, like hygiene and eating. There was never time for talking about feelings in the Galacia family.

"The lack of interest from my family, and even my clients, despite them wanting readings, left no connections. Maybe that's why I didn't make friends while I worked. I was waiting for someone."

Her heart was hit by a pang of sadness and realisation. Talking about this out loud was harder than she expected, and tears were beginning to well in her eyes. She wiped her eyes before Marin could see.

"Kalaya may be that someone. Even for a short while, I will find someone I can see myself in."

"Can I hug you?" Marin asked quietly, continuing to watch the path ahead of them.

She flinched, coming to a stop where she was. Would she be okay with it? Her mother wasn't a hugging person, and neither were her siblings, as they were too busy. She did enjoy the hug from Mikael, so maybe this would be alright. "Yes, you can."

Marin stopped beside Iris and suddenly wrapped their arms around her. The force of the embrace almost made her fall over, but she stumbled into balance and made sure she wouldn't get in the way of other townspeople.

"There's an obvious reason I'm on this trip. I care for my friend, and I'm willing to give everything up to make sure she's safe. I went all the way to Vestirr and back just to get you so you can help." Marin sniffled into her top.

If there was one thing Marin was truly passionate about, it was other people.

"We'll be alright." Iris patted their head a few times. "Thank you for sharing."

They nodded before letting go and looking up with apologetic eyes. "I'll make this trip worth it for you, okay?"

Their walk brought them to a more 'local' part of the kingdom, suburban houses more prominent and off from the main road, and only a few small businesses dotted around, such as tailors and bookshops. Market stalls were scarce, and benches and patches of grass to sit at took over. She couldn't take her eyes off the architecture of the city and the attention to detail.

Not much was said as they continued walking, but she noticed Marin was staring at the sky. The sky was empty except for the clouds floating by, so she didn't quite understand, and she only became more concerned when they walked right into another townsperson.

"You need to watch where you're walking," Iris warned, as if she hadn't almost been in a few accidents herself.

She pulled an apologising Marin aside and looked around. The incident reminded her of the horse-drawn carts in Vestirr, but at least the ones in this city kept to the side of the path instead of riding through the crowds, a more solid system in place.

"I'm just cloud watching—nice turn out today." Marin feigned innocence, batting their eyes at her.

Iris blinked. How do you watch clouds? "I have no idea what you're talking about."

"Really?" They paused and grabbed her arm. "Come with me, we'll be quick."

They led her to a nearby patch of grass, one of the many communal spots of the area. Despite how many people were around, Marin took off the suitcase and fell onto the grass, laying on their back.

"Now you lie down too." They lazily raised their arm and waved at Iris.

She pursed her lips, not wanting to get grass in her clothing when another outfit caked in sea salt was already in need of a wash. Marin insisted, and so she carefully laid down next to them.

"If you look up at the sky, there are clouds."

She looked up. "There are indeed clouds."

"Here's the fun part. You can use your imagination to make shapes out of the clouds. It's like they're telling a story!" They waved their arms about, then let them fall. "There's a dog right there."

Iris squinted, but all she saw were normal clouds. There was more variety in shape than the ones outside her window—longer clouds, ones that weren't very dense, and also fluffy clouds—but she couldn't pinpoint anything.

"Am I doing it wrong? I can't see anything." She frowned. As much as she wanted to see what Marin was seeing, she was just staring at the sky.

"Hmm... well, it can be hard to imagine something if it's been a long time since you've done something like this. With all that work you say you do, I wouldn't put that theory past you."

Marin hummed for a few moments until they let out a small 'ah-huh!'. "How about this? Usually, when you're reading your cards, you let the stories and pictures come to you in your head, right?"

She nodded, but it didn't prove very useful when they were lying down and not doing very much. "I do. I read that's called visualisation with a mix of... some sort of psychic ability. Clairvoyance?"

"It's just like that. Looking at the sky like your cards, and using them like your cards. You stare at them and let the pictures come to you."

She quite liked that advice. It made sense to her how it could apply similarly. With the newfound perspective, she took a deep breath and closed her eyes, then opened them. She focused on one cloud and looked for the shapes. Suddenly, a crown appeared.

"Oh, there's a crown."

"Where?"

"Right there." She lifted her arm and pointed.

"That looks more like a... shell!"

"Does that mean I did it wrong?" She wanted to make sure she got this right in front of Marin.

The short senti chuckled, sitting up. "You can relax, Iris. Cloud watching doesn't have its wrongs and rights. More like... each person sees different things."

Slowly, she was able to spot more shapes, and her understanding of cloud watching was forming into a complete puzzle. She quite enjoyed the stillness of the moment, smiling as she watched Marin burst into laughter about some of the pictures they saw.

They returned to their walking trip, satisfied with their cloud-watching session. Only a few minutes had passed when they slowed to a stop, a spark of recognition in Marin's eyes as they approached a large wooden structure.

"Here we are!" they announced, trying to enter at the same time as a few people that were exiting.

As they held the door open, Iris glanced up at the hanging sign which read 'inn', a symbol of a key underlining it. Just from having the door open, she caught a whiff of firewood and soup welcoming her into the building.

She took a glimpse inside, seeing a few wooden tables scattered about with a varying number of chairs at each—perhaps patrons who sat down in the dining area moved to accommodate numbers. Along the side of the room, close by a staircase, there was a counter set up with a till, keys hanging from a box behind the counter, and also steaming dishes that were quickly taken to be delivered to tables.

Just as she was going to enter behind Marin, a voice from the other side of the road caught her attention.

"Good sirs, I understand my presence may be threatening to you but I am—" *quite interested to see what the future has in store.* His voice echoed in her mind.

She whipped around and, standing on the steps of the city library, on the other side of the road, was the man she had given a reading to all those days ago. Two guards stood on alert, their weapons in their sheaths, but ready to be drawn at any moment.

The man's curly, frizzy hair was tied into a neat ponytail, and his outfit was much nicer than what she saw him in previously—form-fitting leather pants, a large belt with a silver buckle, an orange tunic fit with a brown cloak.

Iris grabbed Marin's arm, making her way to the other side of the road. "Look over there! It's the man who paid me these coins so we could go on this trip."

The short senti turned around, their eyes widening as their gaze settled on the man. "Wait, Iris, where are you going?"

"We should talk to him, maybe even thank him."

The blurred faces of clients were usually forgotten by the time a reading concluded, but this was different. It was difficult to get the man out of her head after how much he gave her, and he also facilitated her and Marin to go on this trip so they could save Kalaya. The least she could do was say thank you.

"I don't think that's a good idea," Marin quickly interjected, pulling back on her arm. "We should get inside now that we're here."

She managed to join the small crowd of people gathering to watch the guards and the man, though Marin's pulling was proving to be a nuisance as she tried to listen in.

"If you want, you can go back to the inn, and I'll meet you there. I'll be quick," Iris said, sparing a glance at the desperate senti.

Before Marin could contest, the booming yells of the guards made them both jump and spin to where the commotion was happening. Somehow, the situation had escalated enough for the guards to draw their swords and hold them at attention.

The man showed no signs of fear, a blank slate. All he did was tighten his grip on the short stack of books in his arms. It truly made her wonder, what were the chances of coming across this man again, in another city at that?

"Under the queen's orders, we are to investigate suspicious activity from those in the great kingdom," one of the guards stated. The demand was recited with no pause and a level tone of voice, familiarity surrounding it.

The man hardly flinched in the presence of drawn swords, opening his satchel and sliding the books in. He held his hands up. "If you are to call the simple action of borrowing books from a library suspicious, I'd say some self-reflection would be in order. Is this what you are spending your time investigating in the name of your queen?"

In a swift movement, the man ducked between the two guards and positioned himself behind them, catching them off guard and tripping them on the steps. The small crowd gasped and murmured, and Marin was fixated on the action too.

As the guards were recovering, the man turned to the street with a pleasant smile, offering short bows of apologies, until his eyes hovered over to where Iris was standing. At first, she thought his attention was on her, but his eyes weren't quite looking into hers.

Following the man's gaze, Iris turned and found Marin staring back, their eyebrows furrowed.

The staring contest was broken as the man bowed and an arm flew right above where his head just was, the guard missing his hit. This time, the man spun his satchel and hit one of the guards in the chest while kicking the other.

His moves wouldn't manage any damage through the guards' armour, but it disoriented them enough for the man to scamper down the short flight of stairs and establish some distance.

He prepared to make a run from the guards when he approached Iris and Marin. "You know where to meet me, Marin."

With a final look between them, Marin sending an irritated 'tsk' in his direction, the mysterious man bolted into the crowd of people, the guards chasing after him.

"You didn't want to go across the street because he's someone you know. Isn't that the opposite of what you would do?" Iris crossed her arms, not even bothering to look around the room Marin led her to before splaying out on a bed.

"I told you I didn't think it was a good idea," Marin said with a groan. "Now we have trouble."

"You're trying to hide something from me." She couldn't wrap her head around Marin's actions. The man was so generous with the money she was given, and he was even a friend of theirs. What weren't they telling her?

"I panicked!" They held their arms up in the air. "You might've done the same if you were in my shoes."

She sighed and walked over to the bed, sitting on the edge. "Perhaps it would be more useful if you told me the truth next time, okay? I didn't see why I couldn't just walk over."

They sat up and started picking at their collar and sleeves. A moment of silence passed before they replied, "I'll explain myself better next time, thanks for telling me. But this has thrown a rogue fox into my plans."

"How so?"

"Give it a few moments," Marin simply said with a knowing tone.

Curious, but patient, Iris began unpacking their luggage into the set of drawers that sat by a cheap vanity—some bandages strewn about the top. The room indicated use; a pair of boots sat in the corner with a vest hung over a chair.

How did Marin end up in Vestirr in the first place, considering they stayed in Excava?

Her thoughts were interrupted as Marin got up from the bed and walked towards the door and, as if on cue, there were three thorough knocks. The young senti swung the door open to reveal the curly-haired man, still carrying his satchel of books, but looking slightly dishevelled.

"What in Ter's name was that, Myst?" Marin demanded as they moved aside and gestured for the man to enter the room.

"Not even a friendly hello, dearest Marin?" Myst chuckled and gently tossed the satchel of books towards another bed. Some of the books slid out, and now Iris could see the titles on their spines. A couple were about caemi history and some on studies about caemi. Why such an interest in caemi, especially in these times?

"You even got new clothes again. Did something happen to the last set?" Myst looked them up and down.

"You can have your hellos after you explain what stunt you were trying to pull there." Marin walked over to the bed to take a look at the books as well. "What's got you looking into caemi?" They had taken the question right out of her mouth.

"Just borrowing some books for safekeeping. You can never be too careful around these Excava guards. Wouldn't you agree?"

Marin rolled their eyes, and it appeared to Iris this was the first time they were genuinely irritated. Their previous restlessness would've been due to a caemi in trouble, or because they needed to use the best of their time to get Kalaya back. Judging by the way these two were conversing, they weren't on the best terms.

"Could I get an explanation for what's going on between you two?" Iris asked, breaking their attention away from each other and immediately directing the man's attention to her.

"Dearest Sybil, it's good to see you again." Myst bowed to take her hand, though she pulled it away as he did.

"I know we've met before, sir, but I don't consider us close. What was your name? Myst?" She sounded it out, slightly off-putted to see someone she didn't expect to see again in front of her eyes.

"Myst it is. You can call me that if you wish, and masculine pronouns work best for me. It must come as a surprise to you that we're meeting again. I wasn't certain how well you'd travel here."

"So you know each other." It was more of a statement than a question. "And you knew I was going to be with Marin."

Upon taking a good look at him, Iris established the clothes he wore right now were much more fitting than what she first met him in. Perhaps her initial assumptions about him were wrong, but it still didn't answer why he presented the way he did in the gambling house.

"Unfortunately, we know each other," Marin said in a flat tone, moving the satchel of books aside and splaying out on the bed once again. "Myst is a friend of Kalaya's as well."

Myst shook his head with a laugh and shrugged. "Marin and I are friends too, but they're being a bit of a baby right now."

All Marin did was grab a pillow and toss it at Myst in response, only for him to catch it. Despite the way the short senti was speaking to the other, it did seem like they were friends deep down.

"And of course I was going to get her here safely. I wasn't going to rely on you coming to save the day, considering a couple of guards were on your tail about freaking books."

"Now, now, Marin. No need to get your own tail twisted." Myst chuckled and Marin let out a soft 'shut up'. "Anyway, care for some reading, Iris? These books could be of interest to you while Marin and I have a bit of a catch-up. I'll even escort you to the room Kalaya was using for your comfort."

Iris was unsure about the prospect, though she couldn't tell if she was worried about leaving Marin alone with Myst, or that she didn't want to be without Marin to guide the way.

"Will you be alright with him, Marin?"

Marin perked up. "Oh, I'll be fine. If he tries anything, I can handle him." They flexed their arm.

It didn't completely reassure her, but she had to trust they would be fine, and that she would be, too. After all, they would need to catch up if they wanted to proceed with their plan to save Kalaya.

Chapter 13
temperance

After Iris was taken to Kalaya's room further down the hallway, she couldn't help but stand by the doorway as she held a pile of books to admire the interior view. If she didn't know this was an inn, she would've mistaken the room to be one of someone's house rather than one for renting out.

Instead of a cheap vanity, in the right corner was a dark wooden desk, customised with an oval mirror and a fancy patterned frame. There were also a few dressers around in the same style that had round flower pots decorated with white roses looking as healthy as ever on top. Did roses normally stay as healthy without someone to tend to them?

She almost felt uncomfortable entering the peaceful and homey room, though the only other place she could stay was Marin's room, and that was occupied.

Stepping inside, she saw the bed was neatly made against the far wall, a tapestry of the moon displayed behind the bedhead. Sitting on the bed was an instrument case.

She approached the case, the clasps on it loose, and slowly lifted the lid. Inside was a violin, a sheer cloth laid on top. Perhaps it hadn't been touched in a while. Iris didn't want to change that, so she shut the case once again and took a few steps back.

Inspecting everything around her, she began to piece together an image of Kalaya in her mind. There weren't any exact details, as there weren't hints to the actual appearance of the caemi anywhere in the room, but she could imagine her gentle playing of the violin, each time taking a soft cloth and wiping the instrument after playing.

She could imagine the female caemi sitting in front of the vanity and brushing her hair to get ready in the morning. She had also spotted some jewellery and accessories, complete with small gemstones, sitting upon the vanity, which were of beautiful taste.

Alongside one of the flower pots, there was a pointed gemstone attached to a short metal chain. While Iris hadn't seen something like this in real life before, it reminded her of the witchcraft book, mentioning different forms of divination, including a pendulum. The picture in the book looked similar to what was before her.

Iris inspected the pendulum. What did Kalaya do with this divination tool? Was she also offering advice and guidance, like Iris did, or did she do something else, much more impressive?

Her eyes hovered over a large book full of pages and paper sticking out of its edges. It was open to a page of writing, though she wasn't quite able to make out what was written, the curvy handwriting being elegant but mostly illegible to her.

Bringing her attention away from the caemi she was yet to meet, but already admired, she sat at the vanity to give herself some room to place the books down.

During her time at the gambling house, she could only learn about caemi when they became her clients, and even then, she didn't note their race. It wasn't much of a reference as she wasn't allowed to talk to the patrons outside of work per her mother's rules—it was unprofessional to make friends with the clients.

Now, with these books, she could learn more about this untouched area of knowledge.

She placed the books in front of her and inspected them one by one, looking at the covers and the titles. With no better guide on where to start, she hovered her hand over the books and picked one at random—a compilation of caemi studies by different authors.

The first few pages went over diagrams of caemi anatomy, which she noticed was similar to senti. Some of the differences were, of course, the animal ears and tails, and occasionally, the caemi would have other body parts to match their animal counterpart, commonly legs.

She also learnt the animal was chosen by the caemi's aura, explained as the manifestation of a caemi's soul through magic, and an animal spirit would appear in a smoky, transparent form when summoned.

Different caemi had enhanced reflexes or senses, depending on what 'clan' they originated from. Fox-based caemi were more agile, rabbit-based caemi had stronger legs, cat caemi were nimble and proficient in high places… the list went on. What would life be like if she were a caemi? Though it wasn't like she had much use for physical abilities.

Reading about this explained why caemi were assigned tasks such as maintaining important buildings and other hard labour jobs as they were more physically equipped for the tasks compared to senti. This left senti with less magical tasks caemi still participated in, which were regarded as more mundane tasks.

Since Kalaya was a caemi, how different was she from her friends? What kind of caemi was she? What was her job and did it involve her caemi abilities? If Marin was capable of scaling walls, running around with a heavy suitcase, and breaking doorknobs as he did, what could she do?

Iris rested her chin on her palm. Marin would be even more powerful if they were born a caemi, and she didn't know whether that was impressive or scary. She still had a lot to learn about

Marin, such as what they were doing before Kalaya got captured, and even how Myst and Marin met in the first place. She knew they enjoyed travelling, but what did they do to travel, and how could they afford it? Where did Marin learn to do the things they did? Why did they like cuffs on their sleeves? How come they liked eating so much, yet they still bound around as if they were as light as a feather?

And in the end... once she got back to Vestirr, would she see Marin again? She would go back to her everyday routine and business, completing readings for people she hardly remembered the faces of, taking in their problems and hardships each day and providing advice, only for it to be thrown back into her face half the time.

When she went back home, would she be able to leave again without someone like Marin helping her out?

She took a deep breath and went back to reading to take her mind off questions she didn't want to find an answer to. It was still a while before the end of the trip, so she would think about that when it was time. Even if the occasional thought about Marin entered her mind, she kept reading until she finished the first book.

A knock on the door woke Iris up with a start. Her blurry surroundings couldn't have been her home. Where was she again?

With a look at the vanity in the corner and the view outside the window revealing a city she didn't recognise very well, she remembered she was in Excava Kingdom instead of her hometown, Vestirr.

She also remembered that after finishing one book, she grabbed another and moved over to the bed, as the vanity chair was getting uncomfortable. She must have fallen asleep in the middle of reading the book and didn't get very far.

"Hello? Is this room occupied?" A familiar voice came from the other side of the door and some shuffling made her ears perk up. Footsteps—ones she had grown to know in her time at the Galacia Gambling House.

It was her eldest brother. Was she still dreaming or somehow hearing things? Another knock answered her question.

"Apologies, but we were told this room could be used as it hasn't been occupied in a while. The door is locked, so perhaps there is some sort of mistake?"

No, that was her brother, and she also heard the whispers of a higher voice alongside him. What was he doing here? True, he was staying in Excava for the business guild meeting. But she was honestly caught off guard by his sudden appearance in the very inn she was staying in with Marin and Myst. Also, it was a little upsetting the innkeeper wanted to rent out this room. Kalaya still had a lot of her possessions around.

She was unsure what to do, feeling a sense of dread at the idea of opening the door and having to explain why she was so far from home and how she managed to leave in the first place with no real business-related reason like he had. She also didn't want to explain Marin, a stranger she had followed and made friends with.

But knocking rapped on the door again. She knew her brother was insistent on double-checking things. It was like him to make sure this room he was told he could use wasn't actually being used.

"Just a…" she began quietly, scampering off the bed and towards the door. "Just a moment, please!" She strained her voice, unsure whether to use her real voice or try to hide her identity.

"Ah, my apologies. So this room is being used? It would be most helpful if we could talk face to face to sort this situation out."

Her brother was also better at speaking with people when seeing them, which was how she reasoned his habit of holding meetings at the Gambling House with investors rather than writing letters.

She reached towards the doorknob and placed her hand there hesitantly. Did she have a choice? No, he was likely to get the innkeeper to get her to come out and sort it out. Or Marin could come by and check what the commotion was about, only to reveal she was behind the door.

Feeling like there was no other choice, she twisted the knob and opened the door slightly.

On the other side, she saw her brother waiting, as well as a woman she hadn't seen before holding onto his arm. She didn't want to assume anything about her brother, but it seemed like a partner of sorts. The woman was as tall as her brother was, which seemed like a good match, and she was pretty as well.

"Hello," she said, staying as still as she could, as if it would mean her brother not looking at her. "I'm using this room."

"I understand, I can speak with the innkeeper to organise another room for me." Her brother turned to apologise to his companion before turning back to the door and looking right at Iris.

A moment of silence fell upon them, and recognition grew in his widening eyes. She did not doubt the same thoughts were running through his mind—why was his sibling here? What were the chances?

"What's wrong, darling?" the woman asked in a soothing voice.

"Iris."

She didn't like when her brother used that voice. It meant she was in trouble or was doing something wrong.

"What's iris?" the woman asked, following with a chuckle.

She quickly shut the door and turned her back to it. Maybe they would go away, maybe something magical would happen and her brother would suddenly forget she was there. Maybe this was a dream, and she was still actually on the ship and they were just arriving at the Excava Docks.

But instead of any of that happening, there were more knocks on the door.

"I know you're still in there. Open the door so we can talk."

There was more whispering from behind the door, and she could only assume it was him explaining who she was to his companion.

Now would be a good time for Marin or Myst to come out of nowhere and see what was going on, bringing the attention away from her. Perhaps they would think of a solution to help her. But there was no way for her to get their attention or their help in a situation like this. This was her problem.

"What do you wish to talk about?" she answered, as if they were back at home.

"I'm sure you can figure the answer to that one out." He knocked again.

She sighed, and a whimper escaped from her as she grabbed the doorknob again and opened the door a bit wider this time, revealing herself to her brother.

"Hello, Taelyn." Iris avoided eye contact with either of them.

"Hello, Iris." Her brother greeted her in his ever-professional voice. "What are you doing in Excava Kingdom?"

She felt that no matter what she answered, it would sound silly. Going on a trip with a friend? What friends did she have back at home? Travelling to meet another tarot reader? Why would she meet someone she had never met before? Rescuing a friend of a friend, except she'd just met this friend a week ago? That was a horrible answer.

"Must I be honest?" Iris took all her courage to look up at her brother. It was only respectful to do so.

"Considering I'm seeing my baby sister in a city across the sea, away from home by herself in a nicely furnished inn room and avoiding her older brother..." Taelyn took a peek into the room as he spoke, then shifted his weight onto one side while crossing his arms. "Yes, I expect you to be honest."

Iris sighed and took a moment to get her thoughts together. "I was approached by a senti who needed my help to rescue a friend who was falsely captured."

"How did you get to know this person?"

"I... didn't know them when we first met, but they knew about me. Their friend told them to come to find me because I can help."

She watched as Taelyn's face turned from disappointment to concern. "Are you sure you weren't scammed? I mean, we do work in a *gambling house*, but you aren't being kidnapped, right? Where's your friend now?"

"They're talking with another friend, catching up before plan preparations..." Was he going to believe this even though it was the truth?

"Iris, a lot is going through my mind right now. For one, does our mother know you're here? Has she met your friend? You shouldn't be leaving the house unless you're leaving for business. It's a big world out here for a young girl like you."

Iris was starting to have second thoughts about everything she was doing. Even if she had justification relating to the business for her choices, she felt they would fall flat in the eyes of her older brother. She didn't know much else she could say about her case.

"You aren't going to send her home, are you?" the woman spoke up, wearing an expression of concern too.

"What else am I supposed to do? She isn't meant to be here."

"As if you were meant to be sending me letters and coming on dates with me during your business trip." The woman arched an eyebrow and looked at him teasingly.

Taelyn sputtered, speechless. He turned away and scratched his chin, thinking of what to say next. "I just… I do care about you, Iris. And I don't know how else to show it—especially in front of our mother."

She was reminded of that swirl of sympathy during their last meeting. Did he want to keep her safe? Even after all those years of letting their mother take the lead in decision-making and knowing what was best?

Her brother remained quiet, and so the woman moved her brother aside and faced Iris. "Hello, dear. My name is Nora. I'm assuming yours is Iris?"

She nodded, not knowing what to expect from this person, though she seemed to be defusing the situation for her.

"Did you choose to come here by your own choice? You weren't forced to come?"

This time, Iris shook her head. "No, I wanted to come for my own reasons, alongside helping my friend."

"Then you can go home when you want. Your brother has written about you and your siblings to me and, as far as I'm aware, one of his sisters is of an adult age. You don't appear to be the young teenager he also speaks of, so…"

She drew out the syllable and turned to Taelyn, prompting him to finish the thought.

"So, my sister can make her own decisions…" he mumbled, then cleared his throat. "What she's trying to say is that if you chose to come here, and since you're old enough, you can take responsibility for your own actions. I mean, I want you to go home so you're safe, but…"

She watched as her brother stared at his companion for a short while. He was giving her a gentle look she didn't recognise, one she had never seen her brother wear before. What was the feeling that prompted that kind of expression?

"While I'm here for the business meeting, I'm here for selfish reasons as well. I'm not going to explain right now because I need to sort out our room for tonight, since *this one* is being used. Perhaps when we meet again, I will explain more."

"I think you're just a little embarrassed," Nora added with a giggle.

"No, I'm not." He huffed and began walking back down the hall. "I'm going to speak to the innkeeper about this mishap and get our room!"

Once he disappeared downstairs, Nora burst out laughing and shook her head. "Don't worry about your brother too much. He's strict, but incredibly protective. You seem like a strong young woman."

"Thank you, Nora." She bowed as a formality. She'd never met any siblings' partner, so she was relieved it was a pleasant experience. Nora seemed like a down-to-earth person who was able to balance her brother out. It was refreshing to have a buffer between the two of them and someone to voice out what she found herself not able to say.

"No need to bow, but you are most welcome. Good luck with your rescue, and we may see each other around."

With a farewell, Nora left her to the room once again, joining her brother downstairs to sort out the inn room mix-up.

Chapter 14
the moon

That encounter with Taelyn and Nora didn't leave Iris in much of a mood to read anymore.

She took some time to look for some pieces of paper in the room, assuming Kalaya wouldn't miss a few sheets, and made a record of things she found in the books of caemi. Notes on spirits were also added to the collection.

By the time she gathered the books, slid her memos into her pocket, and made sure she left the room tidied for Kalaya's return, it had been a few hours since she arrived.

"Finished with reading?" Myst's voice came from the doorway, which made her jump.

"Myst." She turned, finding him leaning against the door frame and holding the satchel from before. "Do you want your books back?"

"Oh, no. You can keep them for now, though this satchel will make it easier for you to carry them around." He walked up to Iris, took the books from her hands, placed them into the satchel, and then handed it back to her.

She wondered if she would get another chance to sit down and read with the plan to retrieve Kalaya coming closer, but she agreed nonetheless and looped the strap over her chest.

"Anyway, still have that coin?" Myst gave her a knowing side glance with a smile.

Oh! She had forgotten about it along the trip but she didn't skip on bringing it with her, ever curious about why she was given it and what it meant.

She reached into her pocket, pulled out her deck, and from the same pouch the cards were held in, the coin fell into her hand. "Of course. Now that you're here, can you tell me what it is?"

He blinked, peering over at her hand and arching an eyebrow. "Why, it's a coin."

"I understand it is a coin, Myst, but I was wondering why it's different from the others. Why it gave me little sparks of… energy and made me want to carry it around. Is it magical?"

"That depends on what you consider magical, little Sybil." Chuckling, he walked up to her, took the coin and held it up. "This is a gold coin from the lands of Syriphia, where the caemi come from. Perhaps it is magical because it is touched by caemi, but it is a coin nonetheless."

Confusion struck her. She took the coin back from Myst, flipped it back and forth and rubbed it between her fingers. Was it really a normal coin? Was she just imagining the sparks of energy? Why was she so obsessed with it?

"Is there nothing else you can explain?"

"Well, I didn't give it to you without purpose. I knew it would be unfamiliar to you. Typically, people have to change their coins to Kyross currency if they plan to gamble. Think of this as the placebo effect. I wanted to give you a symbol to indicate freedom, having fun… finding family, even friends."

Her mind was brought back to the reading she gave to Myst in the first place, unknowingly meeting someone she would meet once again in another city and a friend of a friend. In that very reading, she outlined the pursuit of an adventure, not overloading one's plate, and also finding connections outside of a traditional family.

How ironic and coincidental. It made her wonder if her reading truly did resonate with Myst. If anyone were to be considered his family outside of his own, it would include Marin and Kalaya. It was evident he found issues with Marin before she and the short senti met, and with Kalaya missing, it would break apart their family. They were all technically on a fool's journey, having to save someone from a castle, not knowing what the plan was just yet.

Perhaps her cards were sending messages to more than just her clients.

"How did your conversation with Marin go?" She peered behind Myst to see if Marin was by the doorway as well and was waiting to come in, or maybe standing outside, but they were nowhere to be seen.

"Ah," Myst began, putting his hand on the back of his neck. "As well as I expected it to go."

He walked further into the room and sat on the bed. Iris quickly rushed over to move the violin out of the way. She didn't want Kalaya to return to a misplaced or broken violin.

"What is that supposed to mean?" She took a seat at the vanity, keeping her distance from Myst.

"He's still on edge from something that happened before all of this. They weren't the happiest about talking to me alone." He paused, and she stared at his face, attempting to read what he was thinking. It was easier when she was giving a reading to him. Now that she knew who he was, he seemed more hesitant to reveal anything. "They keep secrets they shouldn't."

"Such as?" Part of her didn't want to know. There was a lot she wanted to find out by herself, and in her own time, rather than through Myst, but she couldn't not be curious.

"They're so incredibly... selfless. They want to keep things to themselves despite being close friends of mine, as well as Kalaya's, so much that it ends up hurting us all in the long run. In my eyes, it ends up as being selfish. He wasn't willing to discuss much with me. He walked out on me to do something else in preparation."

Was there something Marin was keeping from her? They were rather clear on where they were heading and even included her in situations such as the caemi on the ship. Despite her being just a tarot reader, they still trusted her to be part of the plan, even when it went wrong.

Perhaps Myst misunderstood something, or he assumed she didn't know what was going on. But what was Myst's place in this rescue, as well as the relationship with Marin and Kalaya?

"Surely they have a reason for keeping to themself, right? What would they be hiding that could affect me?"

Myst chuckled solemnly. "Ironically, more than you may think. I know them better than you do. This is why I'm talking to you about this—I can't hide the lies of who I see as a brother."

Iris kept her composure and face neutral as to not reveal anything to Myst. They weren't close, after all, and at this point, she needed to ask the right questions to make out what was real or not. She still needed more answers. "Why did you come see me before I met Marin? Did you plan that?"

"Kalaya instructed us to reach out to you. You were the closest person she could think of for... whatever reason she had in mind. I didn't understand why, but Marin was adamant about finding you. I was in charge of retrieving funds for you to use on the trip here. No doubt because he would rather have anyone else but me in his partnership to rescue her..."

Her heart dropped. It came as a surprise to her that this was being revealed now. There weren't many signs Marin was arguing with someone else in the first place.

But she wouldn't let his words get to her now. Not until she knew more.

"I know that isn't what you want to tell me. There's something else." Her eyes narrowed and pierced the side of the senti's head. Was he drawing this out on purpose, or was he afraid of something? In any case, she would find out what he was hiding, too.

"Frankly, I think Marin is just using you. He isn't your friend."

The room became quiet, the birds outside the window chiming down and the mumbling noise from the lower floor coming to an ill silence. At this point, she could hear her own breathing and heartbeat. She could even hear Myst's fast-beating heart.

It wasn't as if she hadn't entertained the thought, but why did it surprise her so much to hear it was true? It made her numb. It made her angry. It made her feel like Marin didn't trust her despite what they had been through and what she was doing for them.

Why place her trust in someone for it to blow up in her face? She had left her home and business, in hopes of returning as someone her mother would be proud of, and now she had to put up with more than she signed up for because she overextended and decided being friends with a stranger would be *okay*.

"I am sorry for this, Sybil, but I don't know how much you can trust what Marin has told you. I mean, I'm their friend and look at where I am. Who knows what they're hiding from you? I just wanted you to know before you got into any trouble with them. I'm guessing they haven't told you they're a—"

Iris took a deep breath to maintain a professional appearance, but the effort was futile.

"I think I've heard enough."

She left without saying goodbye, shutting the door behind her and leaving Myst in the room. She didn't know if it was a way to separate herself from the young man or because she didn't want him to see the tears that were beginning to run down her face.

Crying wasn't something that was permitted in the Galacia family. Her mother liked to tell her *'Galacias don't cry'*. It was unprofessional and didn't contribute anything to the business. She would say they were only feelings and she could get over them. It worked for her brothers, as she hadn't seen them cry in years. Though she could swear some nights she could hear sniffling coming from some of the rooms down the hallway.

In this instance, she tried her best to take her mother's advice. Why did someone who was still basically a stranger deserve her tears? Why was this happening now that she was all the way here in Excava?

Her efforts to question herself, like she usually did, didn't work this time. This situation meant a lot to her because she was following a hope she had as a younger girl. Because she believed in something.

Marin wasn't a stranger. They were a friend, but they both still had a long way to go before they knew everything about each other. And really, she didn't feel like she needed to know everything to care for Marin. They were a fun person who cared a lot about their passions and was willing to go on an adventure with her so they could both benefit.

And so the tears fell, making her vision misty and blurry as she made her way back to Marin's room. She recalled Myst saying Marin went out to do preparations so the room would be empty, anyway.

She didn't bother to wipe her face as she began to sniffle and shake, the tears continuing to flow. She didn't know what to do or feel when her world was unbalanced.

On one hand, she wanted to reasonably speak with Marin, professionally, to get an understanding of this, but on the other hand, every part of her was telling her she was only lying to herself. It was hard to convince her mind that what she knew right now wasn't the truth.

Swinging the door open, not realising how hard she had pushed it, she shuffled into the room. It felt like the only right choice now was to go home. What was she supposed to do when Marin and Myst obviously had things covered? Maybe her family was right: the business was the only thing she needed on her mind and to focus on. It was a trusted routine and made use of what she was good at.

Making her only friend outside of her family cost her tears—not to mention travelling overseas and going through all this trouble only to hear Marin was just using her.

She went straight to their luggage and finally wiped her eyes and nose so that she could see the items before her. Her and Marin's clothing were mixed up, and she didn't want to leave Marin without clothes, so she began to sort them as she felt her body curling up on her.

Is this what it felt like to be sad about something she cared about? Is this what it was like to be betrayed? She had only heard stories of this feeling from her clients.

She could take the rest of the money and make her way back home, on a ship that wasn't full of pirates and captured caemi. She could undo everything she had learnt and thought on her way here and just go back to what she was doing. She had experience getting here so she could just as easily go back by herself, right?

It would only bring what she was inevitably going to do closer. She wasn't going to see Marin again after they and Myst were reunited with Kalaya. She wasn't part of their group. If Kalaya was also a tarot reader, why would they need another one?

She couldn't begin to imagine what her mother would say to her.

Pulling the last clothing items from the luggage, she noticed a piece of paper sitting on the bottom. Something was drawn on the other side.

She picked up the paper and turned it over. It was a drawing of a young woman with wavy brown hair, a blue cloak, white gloves that covered any remaining skin, and a ring on her finger. Looking up at the cheap but usable mirror in the room, she compared the drawing to herself. It was a drawing of her.

After checking the suitcase again, she found a couple more pieces of paper, one more worn than the first one. She pulled those out as well and took a look. There was another drawing of her, but it was much rougher, and there were notes scrawled on the page. The handwriting was beautiful cursive and she could only make out some of the notes that read *'find this person in North Vestirr. She is around the same age as me. She can help'*.

Iris could only assume this was a drawing given to Marin by Kalaya before they couldn't see her again. Myst did say they were both asked to find Iris, but she didn't expect there to be a drawing of her as well. The more detailed portrait didn't have any signs of Kalaya's handwriting, so where did it come from?

The last piece of paper seemed the freshest of the group, the handwriting a neat print. She suspected it was Marin's but couldn't bring herself to read it. Not only because it had much more writing, but because it could reveal more than she wanted, just like the conversation with Myst. There was no point anyway if she was leaving now.

She stuffed her clothes into the suitcase, leaving the pieces of paper amongst the pile of clothes that were Marin's. The suitcase would be a pain to carry, but perhaps it would distract her from what she was leaving behind—including the very person who got her and her suitcase there in the first place.

She had hoisted the suitcase onto her back and was about to head out when she heard tapping from the window behind her. She passed it off as birds, since it happened all the time when she was at home. Though, the voice coming from the other side of the window and another tap a second later told her it was something else.

"Iris? Can you open the window, please? I can't keep myself on this sill for very long. It's also rather high up…" Marin's typical rambling filled her ears and she quickly turned around to see them holding onto the window.

Marin… they were back. Her hand twitched upwards—it'd only be courteous to let them in. But at the same time, if they weren't so happy-go-lucky and stayed more grounded, then they wouldn't find themself in these situations. Who said he had to climb walls? Why did they have to act as saviour, as if they never needed saving? It only reminded her of their second encounter, breaking laws in the name of saving their friend—breaking into her life without permission.

She did a final check of the room, tapping her pocket to check for her tarot cards, and started walking out of the room. If they got themself up there, then they could find a way in. This wasn't her business.

She only looked back once, to see Marin's nervous smile fading as they watched Iris leave. She shut the door.

Marin was smart, Marin wouldn't let themself fall, Iris repeated to herself. She didn't have to feel bad for leaving them behind. They did well all on their own and didn't need her.

She hopped down the stairs, trying to balance the suitcase on her back. It proved harder than she expected. One would assume that removing half of the load would make it easier. She stumbled off the last step, almost running into a chair that was left untucked from its table.

Temptation to kick the chair in frustration struck her. A coin flipped in her mind, one side that blamed Marin for everything. For getting her here, for making her feel this way. The other side knew it was her fault. She trusted a stranger in the first place, and she disobeyed her mother.

As she passed more scattered tables that were beginning to fill up for lunch time, waiters dancing around to collect orders and the innkeeper shouting commands from the counter, she spotted Nora sitting in a corner, drinking from a cup on her own. Where did her brother go?

Before she could sneak past, Nora spotted her and waved, calling her name. She didn't want to make a sour impression on her brother's partner, and so she reluctantly shuffled over, avoiding laughing patrons and those swinging their arms to the music drifting across the room.

"Where do you think you're going with all that?" Nora had a smile on her face, jutting her chin towards the suitcase. Her face told Iris that it was merely a fun poke, but she couldn't help but feel a pit of shame digging into her stomach. Could she really do this on her own?

"Where's my brother?" Iris tried to change the subject, playing into an urgent expression on her face to counteract the casual conversation.

"He's just upstairs, checking things out after…" She pointed her thumb towards the innkeeper. "Did something happen?" she insisted.

While Nora seemed trustworthy, she didn't want to make her problem someone else's burden. She had to focus on getting home and once she was on the ship, she'd have to prepare to face her mother. What would she say? *Mother, I was dragged away by a scoundrel. They broke into our house and took me away, making promises of riches and adventure. I was a fool to trust them, and for that I've learnt that you know best…*

"Iris?" Nora snapped her fingers. Now she wore a look of concern and inched her hand towards Iris'. "You don't have to tell me but—"

Iris ripped her hand away and bolted for the inn door, taking a chance to slip through a gap as a group of travellers entered. She bumped into them and her balance was thrown slightly, but she forced herself to breathe and ignore the touches, to ignore the sounds, to ignore the sudden change in temperature as she reached the sunlight after a fan-cooled stay.

She attempted to gain her bearings, struggling as she didn't recognise the road and couldn't figure out which way to go. She only knew the paths of the gambling house, and even then there were some areas she had never been.

Her only solution was to find *up*. With a skip to the middle of the path, a few people murmuring as she spun around, she spotted the castle in the distance, which meant she had to go the opposite way to find the port, and her way home.

She wanted to run as fast as she could, far away from everything that would remind her of her mistake. But her legs felt like jelly and her hands were shaking as she took the path back. The buildings around her blurred, the details disappearing. She felt enclosed, like everything was shrinking onto her. Birds stopped tweeting and people became shadows.

Eventually she passed a small alleyway and dove into it, ignoring the eyes of the shadows staring at her. She shrunk against the side of a building and brought her knees to her chest. She wanted to cry and sob, but she couldn't. She shouldn't.

So much happening, too much feeling. Why did she feel so much? If she kept going like this, all of the sadness and anger and fear was going to make her explode.

Before she knew it, tears were streaming down her cheeks. She couldn't do it, she wasn't strong enough. Why did she think it was a good idea to leave in the first place?

She felt each second pass in the way her heart beat deeply in her chest, like it was stabbing at her and forcing her to acknowledge what was happening.

What were they going to say about her now? Marin and Myst were going to find Kalaya on their own, and how disappointed would Kalaya be? And now she had lost her chance to meet another tarot reader, someone to learn from, someone to relate to.

The walls around her were starting to fall apart, and she wanted to let herself fall with them so she didn't have to experience this anymore—then someone grabbed her, and she screamed.

"Iris! Iris, it's me! Stop screaming, it's okay." The person shook her and she kept her eyes closed. She stopped screaming but she could hear her own whimpers filling her mind.

"Get away from me, get away from me," she repeated, rocking into the person's shaking.

"Oh Mian, what have I done?" the voice said, and it only made Iris' tears feel heavier. "Okay, okay, uh…"

Through all the noise, she could hear the person shifting and then taking a seat besides her. Their hands trailed onto her shoulders and unclipped the suitcase. She was too weak to fight them off, so what if they robbed her? These clothes weren't even hers. But at least now, her shoulders relaxed and things weren't as heavy anymore.

The person moved closer, so their arms were touching, and they started breathing deeply. What were they doing? Iris continued listening to the breathing, and soon she copied them with deep inhales and shaky exhales. Her heart was better now, not thumping as much, not as threatening.

"What are five things you can see?" the voice asked.

She didn't want to open her eyes. "It's dark, it's all dark."

"I see you, Iris. And I see a wall in front of us. There's a rock over there. Can you tell me two more?"

After a few more deep breaths, she opened her eyes to the wall in front of her. Then she looked to her right. Marin sat with their knees up and forearms resting against them. They stared upwards. How did they find her?

"Marin…" Then she turned her head, avoiding the possibility of meeting their eyes. "There are people over there." The shadows she thought were staring at her earlier were gone.

"Great, and four things you can touch?"

"My fingers." She touched her fingertips together. "The ground, the wall, my shirt."

"Three things you can hear?"

"Your voice, there's a horse somewhere. A baby is crying?"

"You can hear that? It's so quiet to me." They picked up a small rock underneath them and threw it towards the street. "Two things you can smell?"

"I can't really… smell anything?" She sniffed, her nose was blocked.

"Okay we can skip it. One thing you can taste?"

She licked her lips and picked up the aftermath of her tears. "Salt."

Once she took another deep breath, she brought her gaze to Marin again, and they turned to her too. He wore a small smile, but it only made Iris sadder. Why were they trying to make good of this situation?

"Thank the patrons above that I could find you… I mean there aren't many paths back to the docks so I figured that you would've just went down and—"

"Marin, I'm going home." Iris picked at the hem of her shirt, then shuffled on her bottom to find the straps of the suitcase again. "Don't stop me."

"Wait, home? But we're almost there. I just drew up a map and everything…" Their hands lifted and hovered over Iris' arm, but they didn't place them as Iris secured the straps and tightened them.

"Myst told me why I'm here and I don't feel like being here anymore. I was only here for the money, anyway. I needed it to please my mother." She didn't want lies and hope anymore when all she needed was at home.

However, the whole reason she agreed to leave with Marin was *because* she wanted to find something she didn't have at home. Was she even lying to herself now? The overwhelming wave of confusion, uncertainty, and sadness made it difficult to act like herself, and she couldn't pry herself away from the thought of curling up in a ball at home, just dealing with what she had to.

For a brief moment, Iris looked into Marin's eyes and saw the concern in them—they were sad and scared. The way they stood showed they were ready to grab onto her. Their breathing was uneasy, like they didn't want to believe this was true. But it wasn't going to be enough to stop her.

She burst up and pushed past the short senti, holding her hands close to her stomach. *Push away the feeling, push away the feeling.* She was a Galacia.

She used her tactic, finding the castle and began heading towards the sea again. Her senses attempted to focus on what was around her, but all she could hear were Marin's footsteps following her.

"Iris, you need to let me explain. You aren't going to leave with just one side of the story, are you? Are you not going to stay to listen to me? I'm your friend, not him."

She was frankly getting annoyed at both Myst and Marin telling her things to make her trust them instead of what she wanted to hear. It made her feel like she was just a toy between the two of them and a reason to take a stab at each other rather than work things out.

"I just want to leave. There's just too much." Too much feeling, too much to explain. Too much to do, too much money to make.

Marin fell into stride with her and she put some distance between them. She just wanted clear answers, like the ones she got from her cards. They didn't lie or make things confusing. They weren't like people who would treat her as a replacement.

"You can't leave, I need you to do this, need you with me. I want—"

"All this time I was only a means for you to get what you *want*. I should've known from the start, Marin!" She whipped around and stepped into their space, causing them to take a step back. "I was never part of your group. You never wanted to be friends with me."

"No, that's not right. You've got it all wrong!" They waved their hands and attempted to smile again but Iris wasn't having it.

"Don't tell me what I think. You can't make assumptions like that." Frustration bubbled inside her and she just wanted Marin to leave her alone. She had no place here, why didn't Marin just admit it?

"It may have started that way, but things have changed. We've made memories, we've had moments. We've worked together. You are part of our group now!"

"It all started during that damn reading." Iris stomped her foot and tears were threatening to fall again. If only she didn't entertain her curiosity. If only she didn't want to trust Marin. Their charm really did work on her, and she beat herself up for it. "You lied to me, and I believed you."

With a huff, ignoring the flash of hurt over Marin's expression, she continued her walk. The blue of the ocean came into view and now not only did she taste the salt, she could smell it. She couldn't hear Marin's steps behind her anymore.

"I can tell you the truth, I can!" Marin yelled. A few people in front of Iris spun around to the commotion. "I can even show you the truth."

As much as she urged her curiosity to stay buried in her heart, for her to forget their voice and to only look forward at the passenger ships waiting to leave the dock, to leave for her home, she couldn't. Deep down, she wanted the truth.

She stopped walking and turned around to see Marin running after her, almost smacking their face into her chest but stopping short of it.

"Please, Iris." They looked down, and she couldn't tell what they were thinking. "Draw a card, and you can tell me whether you want to come back with me, and I'll tell you everything."

They were right. The cards would always tell her what she needed.

Iris finally lowered her shoulders, letting the straps of the suitcase sag down her arms. She didn't realise she had tensed up so much.

An overhand shuffle later, a card popped out from the pile and landed on the floor in front of her. *The Star*.

With that, she knew she was ready to listen.

Chapter 15
the star

The forest was never-ending, dense layers of trees generating with each step and the tall branches looming above like the gods casting their judgement. The spirits whispered ancient secrets in the leaves, but Marin didn't have time to listen.

They dodged and weaved over fallen branches and thick trunks, and the wind rushing past was slamming into their chest. It felt like their lungs were about to burst from how much they were taking in.

The night sky was nowhere to be seen, with a thick canopy stopping any moonlight from shining through. There was only what they could make out in the limited light, and the snaps of branches behind them.

"Do you even know where we're going?" Myst grunted as he attempted to keep up.

Marin would've chuckled at the fact they were faster than their friend despite being shorter, but there wasn't time for that.

"Shut up," Marin hissed, the sound of clattering armour chasing them in the distance. They had to get out of here, and soon.

The rocks of the forest floor dug into their soles as they forced their sprint to a stop and leaned against a tree to catch their breath. Their chest was burning and each breath only caused the fire to spread across their body, legs stinging and arms feeling numb. They hated feeling this way—there was only so much rush they could handle.

Myst stumbled to a stop as well, but swung his arm into Marin's collar with the remaining force he could garner, pushing them against a tree. The rough bark of the tree dug into their sore back, but they bit the inside of their cheek to silence any verbal reaction.

"Answer me, Marin. What the hell are we doing?" Myst's voice was hushed but laced with poison, the heat of his quick breath brushing against Marin's face.

They held their breath, looking at Myst with pleading eyes. Silence was a priority in this moment, as the commotion that was following them came closer and closer. No matter how badly they wanted to reply to Myst, it just wasn't the time for it.

Two orbs of light could be seen from the corner of their eyes, revealed to be lanterns carried by a group of guards. Their swords were drawn and ready to slash anything that made a movement towards them.

"Did we have any eyes on their whereabouts?" one of the guards called out to the others.

Marin doubted it, having implored Myst to get away from the guards the moment they could. Any distance they created was an advantage. Even though they stood in the same area at this moment, their location was unknown.

"No, sir," someone from the crowd answered. "The only information we have at this moment is that there were two others. The third is currently being held captive. They were seen running into these forests but... following them is proving ineffective."

Marin couldn't help but grimace, reminded of the disastrous fate of their friend. Every part of them was screaming to go back, to risk it all so they could at least tell themself they tried. But it was no use. Every bone in their body told them they had to run—run as far away as they could for their safety, and the peace of mind of their captured friend.

And so they waited, the blistering pains of their escape and mistakes eating at them as the guards tried their best to clear the area, but missed them entirely. Marin could feel their companion's arms shaking from the weight of lifting them against the tree, and so they tried to grip onto the tree to lighten the load.

"What will the captain say about this?" a guard asked, moving away from earshot.

"We'll just have to wait and see."

Only a few more moments passed before the sound of leaves crunching under armoured boots disappeared amongst the trees, the story of their presence only to be told by the spirits.

Myst released Marin from his arms, dropping them on the forest floor to be stabbed by the rocks and twigs. At this point, his limbs must have turned numb to all the pain.

"God and Goddess above, why in Kyross are you so heavy?" Myst shook his arms out.

"Is that really what you're going to complain about after you decided to push me against a tree?" Marin shot back, sending a glare in Myst's direction. Now that the lanterns were long gone, it was hard to see.

"Alright then, I'll complain about something else. Like… the fact we're just leaving Kalaya to get held captive? What kind of friend are you to leave her in the hands of Excava royalty?"

"Do not bring friendship into this," Marin replied sharply. "We both know it has nothing to do with friendship and do you honestly trust ourselves to retrieve her without, you know, *her* help?"

Before they continued, Marin swung the satchel looped across their chest to the front and pulled out a few pieces of creased paper, then threw the almost empty satchel into Myst's stomach with more force than they'd like to admit.

"What are those?" Curiosity overtook Myst's urge to retaliate. "Neither of us packed… sheets of paper?"

"Kalaya did," Marin explained. "I think she was more prepared for this than we were."

They crouched down and laid the pieces of paper on the ground, flattening them and picking rocks out from underneath. Now, they needed light to read the pages.

Feeling the ground, they picked up a few sticks, only to throw them further away and search for more. Myst joined their efforts and began searching for certain sticks as well. As the two brought a few chosen sticks together, Marin lit a small torch to hold between them, illuminating the surrounding area. It was enough to see the pages and each other's faces without exerting more effort than necessary.

"Thanks," Marin offered half-heartedly before bringing their attention back to the pages.

Kalaya had given them the papers before they split up during their mission, as if anticipating her capture. Some of the papers were blank, which caused a small pit of disappointment to settle in their stomach. Flipping through, though, they found two pages filled with Kalaya's handwriting, which earned a sigh of relief.

A location was mentioned—North Vestirr—as well as a description of someone they didn't know. The page read as a sort of stream of consciousness, thoughts flowing on the page as they came.

This young person is the same age as me. She can help get me back, and help us. She is identified by the name Sybil in the Galacia Gambling House. You will find her on a Sunday afternoon a week from now, reading cards for herself. The last card she reads is VIII Strength in Reverse. This card is about inner strength, self-doubt, low energy, raw emotion. Reciting something along these lines will grant the attention of this person...

The paper continued to recount a day as if it was going to happen in that exact way. It provided as much as the person's hesitance to speak to Marin, and also ended with the note:

Marin will locate this person after the first rejection. In what way is up to the discretion of Marin.

The rest of the document was unintelligible, covered with scribbles.

"I don't understand," Myst mumbled, tracing a finger along each line to reread it. "Who is this? Why did Kalaya write this?"

"It must be another one of those spirit things," Marin concluded, shifting to the next piece of paper which, rather than paragraphs of writing, was a rough sketch of a young woman—perhaps the two papers worked hand in hand in identifying this 'Sybil'.

"You know how Kalaya asks the spirits for guidance? This might be another case where she did and… seems like she knew about this."

"So she knew she was going to get caught?" Myst tsked in frustration, slamming his hand on the tree next to them. "If she knew, this wouldn't have happened."

Marin furrowed their eyebrows, folding the papers once again and pocketing them. "Listen to yourself. We've both been told time and time again that just because she knows, doesn't mean she can exactly change the future. If she could've helped it, she would've."

They sighed, running a hand over their face. It was very like Myst to blame everyone but himself for something that happened. Yes, he was charming in how he spoke, and he was clever in some areas, but reading the room wasn't his thing.

Just because the two of them hadn't learnt witchcraft didn't mean they could brush off the magic altogether. Myst didn't say much else and tugged on Marin's collar as if to signal getting a move on.

They picked up their speed once again, not sprinting like they were before, as they had shaken the guards off their tail. The sooner they got out of the forest, the easier it would be to regroup and convene about what had happened that evening.

"We need to find Sybil," Marin said suddenly into the darkness a few minutes after they began trekking.

"What? You mean the person Kalaya was writing about?"

"Of course. We need to trust her and find this person, even if she is on the other side of the sea, and we need to travel to Vestirr."

"Are you honestly going to trust a bunch of spirits talking to Kalaya? You do realise it takes almost, if not more than, a week to get there and then we need to get back here with this person. She will be stuck in the hands of the horrid guards for two weeks at least, and who knows what they will do."

They took a moment to think, considering what their travel plans would be limited to and what could result from their unsuccessful mission. It seemed their chances of getting help on rescuing Kalaya from fellow caemi in Excava the very next day would be more hopeful than tracking down this person, but…

"I'm not letting Kalaya's efforts go to waste. Clearly, she wanted us to know this, and she would've wanted this."

"Now you're spouting nonsense. I'm better off staying here gathering help than going on a scavenger hunt for a stranger."

At this point, Marin wasn't able to feel their legs anymore, but seeing thin strips of light coming from between the trees ahead gave them a reason to keep at it. While the forest wasn't any more forgiving at its edge than it was in the middle of it all, being able to see the rooftops of Excava Kingdom was a welcome sight to their tired eyes.

Their knees buckled from beneath them as they trudged a small distance further from the forest to ensure they had fully escaped it, then collapsed on the lush green grass illuminated by the moonlight above. They had never been happier to see grass.

"Listen, Marin, I will help in one way. Funds. I will get funds to this Sybil in any way I can, but after that, it is up to you to make your way back here. Once I complete my task, I'm returning to do what I can. Understand?"

"Understood," Marin managed to get out before the comfort of the ground took over and they fell asleep to the sounds of leaves rustling behind them and the calls of morning birds in the distance.

Chapter 16
the chariot

"I suppose you know what happens from there, considering you were directly involved…" Marin chuckled nervously as they finished the story and glanced at Iris, who was staring, not at them, but in thought.

The two of them sat on Marin's bed, having returned to the inn after a silent walk. Nora wasn't downstairs anymore, perhaps back in her own room, and for that Iris was relieved. She didn't want to deal with explaining to her right now.

The room was a right mess upon Iris entering again, and she wondered if she left it that way through her blurry vision, or if Marin had a part in it, trying to work out what was going on.

From what Myst said, to Marin's side of the story, plus everything she still had to work out about those two, it was a lot to take in within a short time. She would need to reflect and process when things weren't as hectic, and they weren't so close to rescuing Kalaya.

Iris picked up the piece of paper she couldn't quite read before and looked over it again with her newfound knowledge, finding it easier to make out the words now that she had heard the story. It surprised her how detailed and accurate it was to what happened. Kalaya knew all this just from spirits? She would have to ask Kalaya about this one day.

"What did Myst mean about coming back here to do what he could?" She had only seen Myst with the books on caemi, and that was it. Was that meant to help?

"It's a little unfortunate. He intended to get the help of other caemi, but right before our plan was enacted, the queen pushed the order to deport all caemi. From there, he couldn't do much without the two of us."

Quite a lot of things went the wrong way for the trio, from Kalaya being captured to the caemi being deported. She hoped to try her best to help them reunite.

"What about this drawing?" She shuffled through the papers and pulled out the more detailed drawing of herself.

"Oh." Marin's face flushed red, and they took the paper into their hands, holding it away from Iris. "That's my drawing."

"Really? I didn't know you were an artist." She found their reaction a little funny, but she didn't let it show as to not further embarrass the senti. "When did you draw this?"

"I drew it before I approached you at the gambling house. When I saw you, I knew Kalaya's sketch didn't bring you justice, and so I took a few moments to draw it out properly. I was thinking I could give it to you or Kalaya when we get her back as like… a souvenir."

"You captured my work appearance rather well." The attention to detail in the drawing made her smile.

"You are aesthetically pleasing. I mean, I don't get romantically involved with anyone, but I do know when someone looks nice."

Iris nodded. She wasn't familiar with focusing on another's appearance much except for a few people she had come across on her journey. Bea wore her greens well, and she remembered Risala was good at coordinating her tops and jackets with the bottoms she wore. She wondered what Kalaya looked like.

Iris ignored the thought for now and instead reflected on the situation they had on their hands. "We need Myst here, too. It doesn't help that we aren't on the same page and keep sharing about each other without the other person. Does that make sense?"

Ever since Myst had arrived and joined the two of them, the lack of communication between all of them was straining the team and putting a stop to their plans.

Marin placed a hand on their chin with a small 'hmm.' "Yeah, you're right. When Kalaya was here, she usually had to bring us together when it was time to discuss things. Since I often liked to prepare in my way and Myst had his methods, too."

"Do things like this usually happen amongst the three of you?" Iris asked. The three seemed like good friends, but there were also some differing opinions.

"We've known each other long enough that these petty moments rarely happen these days. Instead, the three of us play into each other's strengths well and can support each other. Really… it's why we need someone like Kalaya to bring us together again, I think. Maybe that's why the spirits told us to find you. Because you're filling in the gap."

Iris tilted her head, thinking back to the earlier conversation. "Am I a replacement for Kalaya?" At least this time, she didn't feel any overwhelming feelings coming over her and was only curious.

"No. You aren't a replacement for anyone because you're different from us. You just happen to share some significant qualities with Kalaya that will help us reunite. Don't let yourself compare." Marin looked at her with a stern look, as if they were trying to burn their message into her mind. After what had happened earlier, she couldn't blame them for wanting to make sure.

She nodded wordlessly. She would remember this, and she was glad to get Marin's side of what was happening with a proper explanation behind the situation as well. While the thought of returning to what she was familiar with was unnervingly comforting, her memories of home were still cold and without the friends she so desired.

Perhaps this mission was meant to be. With each passing day, she was putting the pieces together from the dreams she had and it made her realise the three figures in her dreams may as well match the trio of friends she met on this journey or was yet to meet.

Though, there was something she cut Myst off from saying earlier that she was curious about and a factor that was unexplained in her dreams. The ears that belonged to the hooded figure. The caemi ears that belonged to Marin Boudreau.

She turned to Marin and placed a hand on their shoulder hesitantly. She wasn't used to initiating contact like this, but she felt that this moment was important enough for it.

"There is something I want to ask now that we cleared that up. Is there anything else you want to tell me right now before we go off to find Myst?"

She trusted Marin could judge what they were comfortable telling her at this moment. It hurt to be left in the dark, but from what Marin demonstrated, they were willing to thoroughly explain and talk about it as long as she was open to listening.

"Do you have anything in mind?" Marin asked, looking at the hand on their shoulder and placing their own hand on top of hers.

She opened her mouth, then closed it to think. She figured it would sound quite silly to just guess Marin was a caemi based on a few blurry dreams she had. If they were only vague connections she was making just because she had met Marin in a hood, it would humiliate her and lead to more questions.

But… there was more. There was more than the dream and she knew that, and was only pushing away the evidence at the thought of not doubting her friend's words.

"I do have some things I'm curious about." Iris sat up straighter. She couldn't sit with her questions forever. If she wanted answers, she needed to ask.

"And what would those things be?" Marin gave her a welcoming smile. There was the warm comfortable feeling again, where she felt acceptance of what she was doing.

"Well, you scale buildings, burst through windows, you broke a door handle. You have this particular drive when it comes to caemi, as if you are protecting your own kind. It's something I can't quite pinpoint. Also dreams. I had dreams you were in, except… you had a few extra features."

Marin remained quiet, listening on and nodding, taking in what Iris was recounting. She grasped for words, to place into a question what she had been wondering. Only now would she know the truth as she sought it.

"I'm wondering, who are you, Marin? And maybe…" She paused. "What are you?"

"I'm a senti, just like you," Marin replied a bit too quickly.

While she wanted to believe what was being said, she felt that something was not being disclosed. She did want to give Marin the space to reveal what they needed to in time, but at this moment, she wanted to press on a bit more.

"You don't have to hide this from me. I'm only wondering because I was reading some of the books Myst gave me and…"

She pulled her papers from her pocket and showed them to Marin. Written were different passages from the books and then comparisons to Marin. Looking at it now, she didn't realise how much she had written about Marin themself instead of caemi in general.

"You got a good amount of information just from those books…" Marin mumbled, reading the notes closely. "I bet Myst set this up on purpose."

"What do you mean?"

Marin sighed, standing up from the bed and stretching their limbs as if preparing for some physical activity. Iris couldn't guess what they were about to do, and it made her unsure if she was prepared for what was coming, but she patiently waited. She would trust her friend.

"He wanted to make this happen, but I suppose it was coming in due time."

As Marin said that, the air around them felt lighter, like a weight was being lifted from the room itself and the walls creaked into a relaxed state. It felt refreshing, like walking into Bea's shop all over again.

What made the situation strange was the fact that Marin started glowing. People weren't meant to glow, were they?

The light emitting from them was bright, but not in a way that blinded her. She was able to watch as the light surrounded them in the form of small dancing orbs—almost imitating the spirits of earth she knew of—and Marin took a few deep breaths.

It was like a galaxy of stars manifested around them. Stars she could hardly see when she was in her room every night, looking out the small window in hopes of something new. This was more than she could ever imagine.

She couldn't tell what was going on, or if this was a bad thing. She hadn't seen anything like this before, and it was too fascinating to tear her eyes away.

Some of the orbs started coming together at the top of Marin's head as well as their backside. It wasn't until they started forming the shapes of cat ears and a tail that she realised what was happening. Marin had caemi features.

As fast as the features had arrived, the light dimmed, and the room returned to normal. The air wasn't as light anymore, but she could feel magical energy lingering.

Marin remained silent, standing with their back to her with their newly formed tail moving side to side. The ears and tail were a beautiful dark navy that went well with the neat outfit the young person was wearing. Did they intentionally match?

"Marin?" Iris said quietly, getting up and walking around Marin to face them.

As they lifted their head, she noticed one of their eyes was navy while the other was brown like their eyes had been in their senti form. It looked different, but also alluring.

"You got me, Iris." They chuckled, reaching up to scratch one of the ears sitting on the top of their head. "I'm not a senti…"

She had her suspicions, but she wasn't quite sure what to think now that they had revealed the features that debunked her entire reason for thinking Marin *wasn't* a caemi. She hadn't considered the features could be magically hidden. How many more caemi were hiding right in front of senti's eyes?

This also explained how Marin was physically capable of the things she was confused about. A cat caemi would be good at scaling walls as well as landing if they were to fall. At least, that's what one of the books said in a study about actual cats compared to the caemi counterpart.

"Wait, is this why you're an advocate for caemi? Or why you tried to save those caemi? Or how you knew about caemi magic being used on the buildings and animals?" Iris blurted out the questions circling in her mind, forgoing her usual desire to keep a professional and collected appearance. With something as magical as this, it wasn't the time to keep her composure.

Marin laughed, a smile appearing on their face, which was a welcome expression. "Yes, but anyone can be an advocate for caemi. Yes, but who wouldn't save someone in trouble? Yes, it's something even senti know, but since I am a caemi myself..." Their voice trailed off as they turned away in embarrassment again.

"That is... quite amazing." Iris smiled as well, staring at the tail and ears in awe before she diverted her attention. "Sorry, I don't mean to stare. It's just different to see caemi features on you. I've seen caemi before."

Looking at Marin's eyes, she could see they were thinking again. At the same time, their ears twitched every few seconds. Caemi feature added another layer of mannerisms to analyse.

"I'm a caemi. Born and raised in Syriphia. I'm sorry I didn't tell you sooner." Their tail dipped lower.

Now that they had revealed this piece of information, she was more okay with finding out sooner rather than later, and it didn't stop the flurry of questions in her mind. "How did you hide your features? Why did you hide them? Is Myst a caemi as well? So the three of you are caemi? Is that why you were running away in the first place?"

Marin gently grabbed her hand and petted it. "I can answer all your questions, but you're going a bit fast. I hid my features using magic, as you may suspect. It's not an easy magic because we used to not have to hide our features until the queen... did what she did."

She nodded along. "You were hiding them because appearing as a caemi in Kyross and especially in Excava Kingdom would cause you to be captured too, is that right?"

"That's exactly it. I have to be a senti for the rest of the world so I can organise this plan to save Kalaya, but it also meant I had to hide it from you to make things easier."

She nodded again before Marin continued, "Myst is... also a caemi. You're right. You'll find out what kind when he reveals it, but I don't know if he wanted me to tell you. But he started this, so he deserves it." The short caemi's lips formed a playful pout.

She didn't suspect Myst was a caemi as well, but, at the same time, she hadn't spent as much time with him as she did with Marin.

"In terms of running away, the guards already knew we were caemi. If we were caught, they'd keep all of us in that prison and have their way with us until they finally let us go to send us back to Syriphia. Whenever that would be. They don't exactly hold the most ethical guidelines, that rotten Excava royalty."

She didn't know why, but it made her chuckle when they said things like that. Perhaps it was the small fire she could see in their eyes, or the love they felt for others, even if it meant getting through guards and royalty.

"I understand." She moved one of her hands to pat Marin's head. It was a little harder with their ears in the way. "And… I'm glad you did tell me now. I know there's a lot we still need to learn about each other, but I want to feel included if we're doing this together."

They sighed in relief and leaned into Iris, resting their head on her chest. "I'm just happy I can finally tell you. It takes a lot physically to maintain the senti appearance and also to keep it from you."

"What? So all this time you haven't even been at your best ability?" Iris was even more shocked now. Just how powerful was Marin, or caemi for that matter?

"Oh trust me, what happened with the pirates would've gone much differently if I didn't need all that power to hold my looks." Marin gave her a wink, though something clicked in their mind as their cat ears started twitching and they looked at her with a frown. "You're not going home, right? Are you going to stay for the plan?"

She sighed into a smile, taking a look at the mess she made on the floor from Marin's clothes. "I'm staying. We still have to rescue Kalaya, of course."

"Well, this is a happy sight to see."

Marin and Iris turned to the doorway to see Myst watching them, leaning on the doorframe with an eyebrow arched.

Chapter 17
the fool

The three of them stared at each other until Marin burst out of Iris' embrace and charged at Myst, grabbing him by the collar and holding him up against the wall. It was quite the sight to see, as Marin was considerably shorter than Myst, and Myst was even taller than Iris, but she imagined they were only able to do this with the strength given back from revealing their features.

"You're such a liar! Why did you lie to Iris about her place in the plan?" Marin swung his hand towards the doorway and, without having to touch the door, it shut with a slam and locked with a click.

It took Iris by surprise, but after what she just witnessed with Marin revealing themselves as a caemi, these actions were probably expected from now on.

"What are you talking about, Marin? You know no one can replace me or Kalaya. You're just lying to yourself."

"I'm the liar?" They let go of Myst, letting him fall to the floor with a thud, then grabbing his face roughly. "Tell me, what did you tell her? What did you tell her that you're calling the truth? What is this nonsense about replacing?"

Myst bared his teeth. "'It's not nonsense. From the very moment we stepped onto those grounds with Kalaya, you didn't want to work with me. That's why she got captured."

Iris could feel the tension in the air rising in the room, Marin and Myst pushing each other to reveal their faults. Staring at Myst, she could see pointed teeth in his mouth which she overlooked earlier. Was his disguise slipping as well, with Marin pressuring him?

"We're a team, Myst. You'd think after so many missions together, I would've gotten past any thoughts of not working with you. I'm not trying to sabotage our team, but clearly, you are by making Iris leave."

"I'm not the one who tried to intrude on someone else's role. I'm not the one who keeps secrets. I'm not the one who stopped following the plan just so they could try to save me when I didn't need saving."

From what she could piece together, Marin, Myst, and Kalaya were a team who completed unnamed missions together, though she couldn't quite pinpoint the nature of them. Each one of them having a role meant plans were organised in detail beforehand and it was expected for each of them to follow the plan.

Marin and Myst were very different people who held their values. Myst was right: Marin was a self-sacrificing person and they tended to hide things, but they did it for good intentions and because they didn't know better. Marin being upset at Myst was justified, but Myst must have been tired of being kept outside of the thought process or being confused about what was happening.

She understood uncertainty and confusion could lead to frustration.

"I jumped in so I could protect my friend. What other reason do you need? I wasn't going to leave you to be taken, Myst."

"You left Kalaya to be taken," Myst hissed at Marin despite his face being held firmly in their hand.

Silence fell on the two of them as they panted. Marin let go of Myst's face, took a step back, and turned away. The thought of Kalaya being imprisoned was a quick way to dampen the mood, but it at least de-escalated the rising tensions.

After moments passed without another word, Myst was sitting by the wall with his knees to his chest, and Marin was over at the bed, staring at a scroll sitting upon it.

Iris approached Marin. "Is everything okay?" she asked, but could already tell the answer.

"I tried, Iris." Marin sniffled. "I wanted to save her."

"Why couldn't you?" It was a part of the story she didn't know, and there was still more before that. For now, though, she needed Marin and Myst to be on better terms so they could get their plan to rescue Kalaya in motion.

Myst shifted from behind her, standing up and walking over to them. Turning to him, she could see the tears he was fighting back. "The plan involved separating. Her task required an amount of stealth that wasn't possible with the three of us together."

"It was either you or her," Marin interjected, throwing up his arms. "I couldn't save you both."

"A choice between the two of us is an easy choice, Marin. You know who you should have chosen."

Marin sighed and ran a hand over their face, then drew in a sharp breath. "And you say I'm the self-sacrificing one." They reached down and grabbed the detailed paper and drawing from earlier, shoving it in Myst's face. "Look at this, Myst."

"What about it? We've found Iris now." He pushed Marin's arm away with a side glance at Iris.

It wasn't a look of distaste, but it seemed his feelings of distrust and perhaps even jealousy were showing now that Marin was revealing the truth.

Iris watched as Marin backed away again, their low-positioned tail swinging slowly, and took a seat on the bed and stared at the papers. "I can't tell the future, Myst. It was a split-second decision I had to make between two of the friends I care about most in the world."

"No matter if you can't tell the future, I still think you should've chosen Kalaya's safety, and you know that, too." His voice was strained, reaching for the possibility the other caemi could've been saved.

"That's not the point, Myst. I can't tell the future, but Kalaya can. She knew this was going to happen and let it happen. If she was meant to be the one saved over you, she wouldn't have left these papers for us to find Iris in the first place."

Myst opened his mouth to respond before he stepped forward and took the papers back to take another look. As he read over them, his expression changed from one of frustration to sadness. Myst let his arm fall, letting go of the papers which fluttered down to the floor. "I see," he said simply, avoiding eye contact with Marin.

"I know you're upset Kalaya isn't with us right now, and that the plan went astray. I'm upset as well you know. That's why I'm making all this effort."

Myst nodded, going to sit beside Marin. He wrapped an arm around the cat-eared caemi and pulled them closer. "I'm sorry, Marin. You're right, I just want Kalaya back, and it's taking us longer to do all this. I just hope it's worth it in the end."

After Marin rested their head on his friend's shoulder for a few moments, Myst stood up and approached Iris, fixing his curly hair and adjusting his tunic.

"Iris," Myst began, "I'm sorry for the trouble. I caused a rift between Marin and yourself when you're just trying to help us get Kalaya back."

She gave him a small smile. She was yet to get to know him more, but she could see he did care for his friends. "Times are tense and to have your friend locked away is... scary. Perhaps frightening. I've never had a friend who was in the same position as Kalaya, but I imagine if I did, I would feel the same as the two of you."

"I do hope we haven't forced you to stay." Myst gestured between himself and Marin. "After all this, I'm surprised you are still here."

"Admittedly, there were a few mishaps along the way here and I was going to go home but…" She was reminded of the conversation she had with Marin just before they reached the inn. Life wasn't only about work. "I left home to earn some money. I needed some to make up for my misconduct at work and to prove myself to my mother. But as I've been on this journey, Marin showed me friendship, Bea and the pirates showed me magic, Myst, you've shown me knowledge through books and…"

She stared at the pile of clothes on the floor again, and her suitcase, packed and ready for her to leave Marin forever and never look back. She was ready to go back to what she had and put up with it if it meant always being with what was familiar to her.

"For the first time, I was afraid I was going to lose it all. When I was told the plan may have gone ahead without me, despite joining for money in the first place… I didn't want it to be true. I wanted to be here with the two of you and save Kalaya."

For a quick moment, a flash of light surrounded Myst and, just like with Marin, a pair of orange animal ears and a tail appeared in place of the glowing orbs. Once Iris was able to get a better look, she noticed the ears were a bit taller and pointier than Marin's and the tail was bushier. It looked similar to fox caemi features, as demonstrated in one of the books she had read.

"Even if I don't fully understand Kalaya's abilities, I'm grateful you care to help us find her. It does mean a lot, and it means we'll have better success with the plan." Myst stretched his arms up, his tail following suit.

"Speaking of the plan..." Marin hopped up from the bed and quickly grabbed the scroll. They walked over to the table, unrolling the large scroll and revealing a hand-drawn map. "Look what I got."

Iris walked over, taking a look and noticing it was labelled as the Excava castle grounds. It included different rooms, and though some sections were missing information, for the most part the entire perimeter was covered. There were notes on guard patrols as well.

"Where did you get this?" she asked.

"Well, you know how you said I was an artist earlier? You were close. I draw plans, blueprints, maps—it's one of my specialties when it comes to my work with Myst and Kalaya."

The details of the map were far too impressive to ignore. This level of skill must've taken years of practice.

"Incredible work, as usual, Marin." Myst patted them a few times on the back, leaning over the map to take it in.

"Is this what you were doing when you left?" Iris asked, then thought back to Marin hanging out the window. "Wait, if you were doing that, why were you scaling the wall?"

Marin looped to the other side of the table and took a seat. They leaned back on it with their feet resting on the table.

"I took a trip to the castle, which didn't take too long using the rooftops. I managed to take a few high vantage points in the trees, though it wasn't long before the guards caught me trying to climb the wall to get a sketch of the courtyard. This is one place we lacked in our original plan... only relying on vague assumptions of the castle."

Being able to hang out in the tall trees seemed like a perk of being a caemi, and it helped Marin could view the layout of the castle from different points high above.

"Let me guess, you had to make your way to the rooftops to get back here, too?" Myst arched an eyebrow, poking at the fact they were caught. Marin replied with a shy nod. "Anyway, any idea where Kalaya is?" Myst pointed at the map, nothing indicating the whereabouts of the caemi.

"This map is of the ground floor, but the prison is said to be underground. Unfortunately, I can't be underground to see the layout of the prison." They leaned forward, the chair's front legs returning to the floor, and pointed to the staircases on each side of the throne room. "These lead upstairs, not downstairs. I don't know where the stairs to the underground area are. I imagine special access would be a royal secret and the guards would have their way through the barracks."

"The barracks are always too guarded to get through," Myst mumbled, looking in the left top corner of the map where the barracks were noted.

"For now, I've written some plans," Marin said, dragging their finger across the map. "From an entry point we decide on, we will have to make our way to these unnamed rooms. We haven't been able to scout an obvious staircase before anywhere else, and we know what these rooms are."

"What you're saying is there may be an entrance in one of these rooms?" Iris asked, gesturing to the empty spots on the map.

"There are a few buildings of prestige designed like that," Myst chimed in. "For example, some temples are known to have secret passageways for the priestesses to travel through. I imagine it is a similar case for the castle. There are bound to be secret tunnels all over, but they are secret for a reason."

Marin and Myst shared a look, but then returned to the map. Iris hoped she could keep up with everything going on to help as much as she could.

"There may be a secret entrance from the maid's quarters as well, which is at a slightly lower level than the ground floor, but not low enough to gain immediate access to the prison. If it did, we would need to spend quite a bit of time down there searching amongst the traffic of the maids themselves. We probably won't try this, too much time," Marin continued to explain as they reached behind them to the drawers, grabbing some writing tools and rolling them onto the table for the three of them to use.

Iris took a pen and located the maids' quarters, which were marked along the outer left edge. *Between the underground floor and ground floor, maids and valets are expected.*

Further along, she noticed there was an entranceway surrounding a garden. The indoor portion was drawn on the map as an outdoor patio. Connecting to it was a hallway with unnamed rooms and one marked as the library.

"Is this entrance not a viable one? I understand we can't exactly walk in without any other plan, though, depending on the day, this area of the castle could be unoccupied," Iris suggested, hovering her finger along the map as she spoke.

"I suppose if there isn't an event scheduled for the outdoor area, it would be unoccupied for some time. The only problem with having to find out what these unnamed rooms is that they are… unnamed. We don't know their uses, and so we can't judge the traffic of that area well." Myst grabbed a pencil and started tapping it on the table as he looked at the other entrances on the map. "This may mean entering a familiar area and making our way to the unknown parts."

Having so many potential people around the castle, aside from the residents and guards, proved to make planning trickier. They only knew the patrol of a few guards, and focusing on the schedule of the royal family themselves would already be a tedious task.

"When were you planning to enact the plan, Marin?" The time of day would narrow down their options.

"We usually plan for the night. It's easier to be unseen in the dark and while the castle is asleep." Marin paused, their ears twitching for a moment. "The last time we tried a plan like that, it got Kalaya captured."

"Even with the night on our side, there were a few unpredictable factors that got us caught." Myst's pencil tapping quickened. "We didn't even have enough time to observe what went wrong. Usually, Kalaya would be able to answer these things."

"Why try at night again, then? If it opens you to the same mistakes of the plan you've already tried." The Four of Cups came to Iris' mind. It was a card that typically represented ignoring what was being blatantly offered in exchange for sticking with familiarity, even if it made the situation worse. Sometimes what they needed was the most obvious answer. "Maybe the solution is to blend in during the day."

"I don't think that's a good idea," Myst responded, though he sounded unsure. "What brought you to suggest that?"

At first, it was the card, but she mulled over it more. The idea had to come from somewhere, not just the image of the card.

When it came to her usual job, it was busy no matter the time of day. Marin used this as an advantage when trying to find her, and it also helped Myst sneak through the formal environment despite wearing poor attire. Additionally, Marin and she had an easier time leaving home with everything else going on at the same time.

To sum it up, it was the art of acting in broad daylight—to act when others would least expect it and deceive them in such a way. It only meant it would take more effort to fit in.

"My home is always busy," Iris began to relay her thoughts. "It meant anyone could blend in if they put in some effort. Why notice something slightly out of place when you have other things to focus on? This may apply to the maids and valets we have the potential to come across."

"Are you saying we should disguise ourselves as a way of entry?" Marin asked, contrasting Myst's scepticism with a hint of excitement.

"It's an option if we want to try an outer entrance to find the tunnels you speak of. There must be a way to know…" It was difficult to be sure if her plan would work or not, considering she hadn't done this before.

She simply had to take from her own experience at home. Of course, learning from her mother throughout her life meant the knowledge wasn't exactly applicable to breaking into a castle to rescue someone, but she wanted to try her best for her friends.

A cheeky smile grew on Marin's face, and they walked over to one of the drawers to reveal it was full of paper. At a glance, she could see the plans, blueprints, and maps Marin had mentioned just earlier. Somehow, the young caemi was able to dig their hands into the mess and pull out something with a look of confidence.

They brought back a small pile of papers and spread them across the map. Each piece showed different levels of wear with different ink colours, though a consistent style of scribing. The imagery on each paper seemed familiar, and it wasn't until Iris reached into her pocket and pulled out her tarot deck that she realised what the drawings were of.

"That's the Five of Cups," Iris said, shuffling through her deck to find her own Five of Cups and placing it next to one of the sheets of paper. "Except it's only a rough sketch of it."

"Exactly right. All of these papers are analyses of cards Kalaya pulled before we went on our missions." Marin beamed with pride.

She picked up the pieces of paper and read over them, looking back at her cards when they were referenced. The writing provided insight into locations, outlooks, and even people who may be present on the scene. The Five of Cards indicated the need to cross a bridge at the unnamed location rather than the side they were originally planning to go from. It made sense aligning to the meaning of the card of moving forward and past the cups that were knocked over and not of use anymore.

"So you're saying, I can use my cards and tarot to analyse the plan ahead, and give us insight into what we are missing." She had never thought to use her cards in such a way. Before this, and as she knew it, the cards were used for guidance and not particularly answers. Though from what she had read and had seen demonstrated by Kalaya, with enough knowledge and practice, she could pull even the path into a castle she never would've stepped in otherwise. She supposed it was similar to her knowing what she shouldn't have about her clients.

"I remember this." Myst held out a hand to take one of the pages. "The Six of Wands. We didn't know the calendar of the city we were in, but apparently, there was to be a celebratory festival over a few days. We could've figured from the location on the day, or by chance hearing it from someone. But it was just that, by chance. Kalaya's cards helped us plan."

The process didn't seem too complicated, though Iris had to admit having such responsibility was nerve-racking. Kalaya must have much more practice than her in this scenario, but obviously, they couldn't approach her about that at this moment.

"I'm more versed in… what I like to call storytelling readings." Iris began to shuffle her cards in preparation for a reading. "I like to lay out a sequence of cards that tell a story rather than what Kalaya has done with individual cards."

Marin nodded, gesturing for Myst to grab some new pieces of paper. "Maybe that could help us even more. You can try your best to imitate Kalaya but, in the end, do what you know best."

And so Iris took a few deep breaths, bringing her attention to the shifting cards in her hand, rhythmically landing in her palm, and going in the same cycle over and over again. As usual, she felt the familiar flow of energy from her hands dancing around the cards. It was reassurance, each time she did this since she left home, that she still had her flare.

As with each reading, she knew when to stop shuffling and then cut the deck herself. She took another deep breath and closed her eyes, picturing herself at home at her table, the soft velvet cloth decorated with crystals that enhanced her connection to the reading topic at hand and a few decks from her collection she could select from to appeal to the present client.

In the peace of her mind and still silence of the two sitting around her, she asked the cards what they would need to know about the next day.

Then, she picked up the top card and flipped it over.

Justice.

Just based on the associations with the word itself, it seemed to Iris a law and justice related event would be happening at the castle on the day of their attempt. Pictured was a seated man, though the crown gave her reason to believe it was indeed referring to the royal grounds.

Hovering her hand over the deck again, she flipped another card over.

The Chariot.

With a town in the background of the card and besides the Justice card, it was possibly a sign a chariot-like vehicle would be approaching the castle on this day with the figures involved in this event. It presented itself as an option. Perhaps they could use a chariot as a form of transportation alongside the others, blending into the group. Alternatively, it was a point of distraction that could allow them entry to the other side of the castle while the arrival was happening.

A final card was chosen to wrap up the reading, revealing itself to be *The Empress.*

An image of the queen formed in her mind—she was likely to be present during this event, which eliminated her from being in other parts of the castle.

Hesitation racked Iris, unsure what to share since she hadn't read about something like this before, but she had to trust her intuition if she wanted to get anywhere. The cards were always right, she had to trust them.

"What do they say?" Marin and Myst asked at the same time as they watched Iris look up from the cards.

"Tomorrow, the queen has scheduled a meeting with… I'm not quite sure who, but they're involved with the law and justice. Nobles come to mind. A meeting about the recent caemi changes with important figures. They may be arriving in a vehicle similar to a chariot rather than by foot."

She said it with as much confidence as she would to her usual clients, and that was with pure confidence. Despite her nerves, the newfound use for her tarot readings sent a buzzing excitement through her. This was a feeling she had last felt when she was still new to the practice of tarot.

"You *are* like Kalaya…" Myst mumbled under his breath, though Marin had a much more excited response coming with claps from the young caemi.

"That's incredible. I had a feeling this was what we needed you for, but I wasn't able to confirm it until now!" Marin stared at the cards in awe. "Can we ask the cards more questions?"

Iris recently discovered Marin's excitement for her cards put a smile on her face, and she enjoyed that feeling. It was just as well that she, too, would be excited at this moment. "Of course, but remember this: they don't like repeating questions. I will say that much."

With that statement, she shot Myst a knowing look, which was returned with a small smile. The plan would soon come together with the talent of Marin, the thoughts of Myst, and the tarot in her hands.

Chapter 18
the tower

Being so close to the Excava royal castle was daunting for Iris. It was infinitely larger than her home, and she thought the Galacia Gambling House was huge.

Walls of thick stone bricks that didn't allow for any climbing shenanigans stood tall, protecting the outer perimeter of the castle, with only one main entrance watched by a group of guards and a metal gate that had to be opened on request.

Although the castle was sitting on the same land as the upper-class district, it felt like it was on another level, with its grand towers watching over everything. It was right between early afternoon and evening, and so the sun was resting above, but slightly west of the castle, the towers casting shadows into the forests.

Despite having planned what they would attempt today, buying new clothes for their disguises, having backup entry plans to their backup entry plans, and also reading for the day ahead, Iris found herself shifting her feet and picking at her clothes.

The question of *are you sure we'll be able to find her?* came from the mouths of all three of them, even if they encouraged each other with reassurance and confidence. In the end, they were all anxious about the fact things could go astray again, or that somehow Iris' interpretation of what the cards were saying could be wrong.

As far as they knew, they wouldn't know if they would be able to find Kalaya until they tried.

"Did you make sure to bring the notes?" Myst turned to Marin, who was adjusting the cuffs of their shirt.

"Of course I did, it was the first thing I did this morning." Even with saying that, Marin swung the messenger bag around and checked inside to find the scrolls of paper they had finalised their plan on.

The three of them carried individual bags so as to not give Marin all the responsibility, and it was easier than trying to hide one larger bag. They had to prepare for separation if it was required—at least it would put them in a different position than the last plan they had.

They didn't look out of place, though, with tailored, colourful clothing they wore, and expensive golden jewellery decorating wrists, ankles, and necks. They had taken the effort to dress the part and blend into the upper district of Excava Kingdom.

The trousers of Marin and Myst were replaced with ironed slacks. Marin was able to wear their usual vest and dress shirt combination, but they were grouped with a blazer decorated with brooches and chains. Myst wore a jacket, swapped his tunic for a neater shirt, and added some golden jewellery, even if it was fake.

"Nothing I would usually decorate my clothes with. Chains aren't good for constant movement," Marin had said when they visited a shop selling accessories the previous night.

"They're lying, they love this stuff, but I've told them to dress more appropriately for our missions." Myst shook his head as he had tried on a jacket that suited him well—a complimenting cream with dark orange hems to his dark complexion.

Iris only smiled, happy her outfit was made of a dress that reminded her of home, and a shawl that sat over her shoulders. It was fancier and more expensive-looking than what she usually wore, which made her feel special. She just hoped the outfit wouldn't be ruined during the rescue.

She took a deep breath, shifting her mind back to the plan. While this was her first time attempting anything like this, she had Myst and Marin by her side to help. It was an adventure of a lifetime compared to her usual home routine of waking up and working until the sun went down.

Myst was found staring past the gates every so often in a way that only appeared like he was looking around and curious about what was inside, and not because he was watching for the patrol of guards.

Then a scream cut through the air and so began the next predicted part of the mission. Iris herself had read this phenomenon on the cards last night, lending some warning, but still startling her. Marin pulled Iris to the side as the scene changed before them.

From the rooftops and alleyways came a rush of senti and caemi, all of their clothing a patchwork of colours and patterns. Their hands grasped wooden signs and a show of light, fire, water and earth rose from the crowd. Iris could only assume it was the result of magic.

Chanting rang through the street. *Free the caemi! Caemi are not our enemy! Down with the queen!*

At the appearance of animal ears and tails, the guards launched into action to contain the commotion. They stared at the magical display in awe, but showed their loyalty to the crown by equipping their spears and threatening the group to stay back.

A fair number of the protesters started to charge the gate and shake it, alerting the guards on the other side. Iris could only watch on with a gaped mouth, only having seen the chaos from the gambling house as a comparison for something like this.

Even small children with a variety of caemi features from ears to tails to paws to limbs clung to the legs of older senti and caemi, hinting that perhaps these were the offspring of both—*a caeti*. The ones most in danger from the queen's changes.

Some caemi and senti linked arms and started to sing, contrasting the intense outcry by the gate.

From the heavens came the messenger, who delivered us a blessing

To form two halves, to grant us humility, to make us powerful together

Here and there, top to bottom, lend us a hand.

For Ter and Mian were kind and bound us forever.

The music and yelling and dancing and magic overwhelmed Iris and she turned away just in time to catch a glimpse of... a flying caemi?

Before she could even process anything else, Myst pat Iris on the back. The signal to get moving.

The three of them made their way to an alley on the right, stepping through leftover confetti and streamers. What was going on? Why did the caemi appear so openly in front of the guards?

"Iris," Marin said. She couldn't see their face as they continued to squeeze through the path in front of her. "Try to clear your mind from what just happened."

"But what *did* happen? All I read yesterday was a ceremony, some sort of celebration..." It irked her to not know what the cards truly meant.

"A protest. It seems an association of caemi and senti have gathered to repel the orders... Ter and Mian bless them, but they may be in over their heads for something so dangerous."

The conversation dwindled as Myst slowed down and used his hand to signal the next phase.

"The Two of Wands," Iris recited, taking Marin's suggestion to clear her mind. Marin began digging into their bag and wrapping a length of rope around their hand and arm. She continued, "There is a guard stationed at each cardinal direction of the castle walls. The one stationed in the west takes a break at each hour, leaving that side of the castle wall unwatched, at least along the top. He returns after ten minutes."

From the alleyway, they emerged to a small clearing with a pathway typically used by the employees of the castle to transport supplies. It was a well-worn gravel path, but the morning cart had already passed, needing to be prepared hours before the royals woke up. At least, that's what Marin said.

The beginnings of a forest outlined the right side of the path, the castle wall covering the left side. Other than the murmurs of the public in the distance, it was quiet. The large trees provided cover for them to duck behind and discuss the next few steps.

Marin tightened the rope around their hand and looked at Iris with a determined smile. "Once the bell rings, we're going to start making our way up the wall. I'll climb up first since I can manage it and then I can throw the rope down so you can climb up too. Myst will remain on the lookout before he joins us."

Iris nodded, reaching into her bag for a pair of gloves Myst had given her. They would supposedly help with holding the rope and not hurting herself. As she secured them, she recited the next part of the plan. "From the wall, we should be able to view this side of the outer courtyard as you marked on your map. The opposite side of the castle grounds is where the most maid traffic would be, and the outdoor patio is on that side, which is a possible meeting spot for the nobles today."

The bell tower a short distance away began to ring, and on the third ring, the three of them emerged from their hiding spot in the forest and Marin started climbing the wall. Remaining hidden, Iris could see a figure at the top of the wall making their way to the northwest tower, supposedly to take their break.

Her thoughts were interrupted as a rope dangled in front of her, ready to grab onto. Part of her was conscious her weight could cause a mishap, with Marin being smaller than her, but she had to trust their strength if they were going to have enough time to get all of them up.

Being mindful of her clothing, she took the bottom of her dress and looped it between her legs and behind her, then brought two handfuls of fabric back in front of her and tied them.

After pulling the gloves at the wrist to make sure they were tightly on, she grabbed onto the rope and followed what Marin had instructed her during their planning. She steadied one foot on the wall and, with the strength of her legs, she pushed off to get both feet up. Slowly, she scaled her way up while holding onto the rope.

It proved to be a little difficult given her lack of arm strength, or really any physical strength, but she persevered. This was to save Kalaya and, after this initial climb, there weren't any more climbs like this in the plan.

After a few minutes, she made her way to the top of the wall and was pulled onto the path by Marin. Using the most of her minutes while Myst was climbing, she took deep breaths to compose herself. Even for Kalaya, she didn't want to do that again.

"Hm." Myst brushed himself off as he steadied his feet on the ground again. "You were right. No one came by the path. I'm a bit surprised."

Iris had pulled the Three of Wands. The imagery depicted a man with his back facing the card and also a barren land ahead. Both were possible indications that their climb onto the battlements would go unseen.

"It was good to have a lookout in any case, but I'm glad we made it up here with no trouble." Iris looked around to make sure she didn't have to eat her own words. Luckily, the guard hadn't returned yet.

"That guard is probably going to come back by the same tower, so let's take the southwest tower. There are only a few rooms here we don't know of and can check. Based on the rest of the castle, I'm going to assume they are living room areas or studies. If we're lucky… we'll find a passageway on this side without needing to go near the meeting," Marin rambled on as they looked over the battlements.

The outer courtyard was located there and, from up here, they could see the gate opening for a few carriages. If Iris' predictions were correct, that was the party of nobles and the event that would be used to their advantage. She didn't see any of the caemi or senti from earlier… she only hoped they were okay.

Once Marin cleared the lower entrance of the tower, the three of them were on the move. As they travelled, she undid her dress, letting it flow and embracing her formal look once again.

The wooden door at the end of the battlement path leading into the tower was locked, but it was no issue when they had Marin on their team to break their way in.

Leaving the doorknobs behind, they hurried their way down the spiral staircase encased in the tower, every few steps lit up by the small windows dotting the exterior.

As they neared the bottom, she announced the next part of the plan. "The Seven of Pentacles and the Ten of Wands. We will come across a royal gardener once we reach the outer courtyard. Most attention will be drawn to the front of the castle with the guests' arrival."

"A bored gardener at that," Marin recalled. "Funny how a job watering flowers all day for the queen can get boring."

Iris emerged from the tower to see some stable keepers and a few other castle workers scattered around the area, but they were too focused on their jobs to notice herself and the others. They had purposefully chosen to sneak their way in, even with the disguise plan, as it was less likely attention would be drawn to them away from the main entrance—as well as the fact their disguises probably wouldn't work in front of the people they were trying to avoid.

"Let's go this way." Myst gestured towards the back of the castle, where the people would remain scarce and would be a good starting point for their search.

Acting in broad daylight meant they had to be assertive. Iris found this to be easy, adopting her usual work attitude of false confidence and blind trust in what she did. Myst also reflected the same familiarity, holding his head high and leading the group along the way.

Marin followed closely, constantly looking around for anything that could help their plan. As Marin was the most passionate and reckless of the three, it was important she kept them by her side until they all found their key to the castle. While there were gaps in their plans, they had to follow what they did have.

As they walked through the hedged path, admiring the tall blooming trees of the royal grounds and blending into the image they were going for, Iris could feel the natural spirits around her, just as she did in Bea's shop. The energy was much more overwhelming, likely due to the large increase in both size and quantity of natural features in this area. It did help to take a few deep breaths, which helped her stay in the moment and focus on the plan.

She remained attentive as the group turned the corner in their noble get-up. The backside of the castle was indeed full of gardens and pathways, leading to even more places to gather for meetings or spend time outside. A few gazebos were placed around the area, and everything was neatly boxed into a tall hedge.

In the distance was another building that contrasted the intricate architecture of the castle, a thatched roof covering a wooden structure. According to Marin's map, that was the barracks.

Her attention was brought to Marin as they tugged on her dress. What were they doing? But her questions were answered when she spotted someone amongst the rose bushes.

Almost exactly like how it was depicted on Iris' card: a young garden keeper held his tool by the top of the pole, resting his head on his hands, staring at the flower bushes growing around him. Even knowing her cards were right, they were scarily accurate in knowing what to show them.

The fox caemi whistled in an impressed tone. "Alright, we've located him, what's next?"

The Lovers.

The garden keeper would be useful to their plan to get into the castle. Though when asked how they would get the keeper on their side, The Lovers had appeared. With little thought, the group concluded that some charisma from a certain group member would be required.

Marin cleared their throat and adjusted their vest and blazer, rolling their shoulders. With a final touch, they brushed their hand through their hair and fluffed it up. Despite having no interest in a partner, being charming really was useful here.

The young caemi took the lead now, while Iris and Myst followed close behind. In this situation, Marin just had to be themself and that was something they were good at.

"A fine-looking boy amongst fine-looking flowers," Marin began, a shining smile overtaking their lips. They let their hand run through the flowers as they approached the gardener, holding a single rose in their palm to examine it. "What has you so down, mister?"

The gardener perked up, quickly holding their pole by their side and then bowing to the group of them. It seemed like a trained response to the presence of the usual residents. "My apologies. I didn't realise the meeting was to be held outside. I can take my leave—"

"Oh no, stay." Marin shook their head and stepped forward. The gardener stayed on the spot but slightly leaned back. The caemi then held their right hand out as an offer.

The gardener hesitantly took Marin's hand. "Oh, okay…"

"You needn't apologise. We aren't part of the meeting, just the children of the nobles who are gathered."

Their pre-planned disguise—to be the children of the nobles scheduled to meet today—was not incredibly suspicious, and their attire, aura, and presentation supported the disguise enough for unaware employees, such as the gardener himself, to play right into their plans. As long as they didn't run into the actual nobles, everything would be okay.

"You… you were not catered for? Usually, if the guests' children are here, the maids and valets organise a—"

"No need to stress yourself." Marin smiled widely, gesturing to Iris and Myst, who gave the gardener a small smile and bow. "My companions and I enjoy the outdoor breeze, though… would you care to be our guide inside?"

"Your guide inside? I don't understand." Confusion laced the gardener's words, which prompted Iris to speak, her lies the most convincing in situations like this.

"You have a lovely garden." She didn't have enough time to look carefully, but at a glance, it was more beautiful than any garden she had ever seen, so she wasn't entirely lying. "I'm sure your work in the castle itself is also impressive. We don't have a guide, as they have been appointed to other roles. We would enjoy your company if you could show us around."

"I don't think I'm the best person for… for such an honour as this." Pink dusted his cheeks as he looked at Marin, who was keeping their eyes on the gardener. "I-I would love to, but as I said…"

"We may not know the best person, but surely you're familiar with the layout of the castle with your watering and tending schedules and such," Iris insisted.

The garden keeper took a few moments to think, taking a look around the garden and also at the tool still in their hand. "Okay, I haven't much left to do for the garden, so…"

"Wonderful," Marin said, taking the tool from him and letting go of the gardener's hand, though lingering for a moment by the fingers. "Let us make our way inside."

Marin passed the tool to Myst, who placed it against the wall. The gardener stumbled towards the entranceway, pushed it open, and stood aside for Iris, Myst, and Marin to enter.

It was unlocked, and that they knew. It was easy enough to enter and search the rooms themselves, having a reason why they were in a castle at hand, just like they had explained to the garden boy, but there was an essential part they were missing.

Someone with a role of a gardener who traversed daily through the castle to water the flowers was the best person to tell them about each room, help them get directly to the rooms they needed to, and to better fill in the map which they could use later for clearer navigation if the gardener had to leave. It was just like having a member on the inside without having to fill that role themselves.

And so they began the tour, the gardener telling them a short story every so often. Iris could tell Marin had to hold back from laughing whenever a dismaying story of the royals came up, and on the occasion, she would send a small kick into their shin as they 'admired' the room.

So far, there were no signs of secret entrances. Iris never actually knew of the different ways entrances could be built into castles, never having any at home or hearing it from anyone. They were secret for a reason. Fortunately, before they arrived, Myst explained the different methods of secret entrances nobles liked to use.

No statue was left unmoved, and each fireplace had their contents poked and gates shifted. Paintings were investigated for hidden doorways and switches when the gardener had turned their back to either of them.

One of them usually had to strike a conversation with the gardener to have the time to check what they needed in each room, which so far were a variety of living rooms and empty rooms that were just for displaying pieces of art. Most of the conversations were shallow small talk, though now it was time for Myst to converse and ideas were beginning to wane. He decided to bring back a topic from earlier.

"So tell me, young gardener…" Myst started. Iris personally found it amusing Myst would use young for the gardener when they appeared to be a similar age, but perhaps it was part of the disguise. "Why did you appear so sad, so bored, when we met? In such a lovely place, what could get you so solemn?"

The gardener hummed for a moment. Unlike the other questions asked, they took longer to think of their answer. "When you start work each day looking at the same beauty over and over again, it begins to lose its beauty. Many have told me it's their dream to work in such a pretty place, but… I lack the adventure others receive in their occupations, no matter that I'm working for the royals. They probably don't even know my name."

It occurred to Iris that they hadn't introduced themselves properly or asked the name of the gardener yet. It wasn't really necessary to the success of the plan, but mentioning it… it was the least they could do for the poor gardener, who was willing to leave his post to show them around.

"Can I be so curious as to ask your name?" Myst asked the question she was thinking, but went so far as to take a seat on one of the couches available in the room and led the gardener by hand to sit as well.

While Marin was checking another painting, Iris turned back to look at Myst. There was a look behind his eyes she couldn't pinpoint. Something like recognition, or maybe nostalgia. Perhaps a feeling of familiarity he couldn't quite admit.

"My-my name?" the gardener stammered. "Oh, it's not very important, it was just an example—"

"My name is Myst." Just like when Iris and he had met again, Myst held the gardener's hand and bowed his head, this time able to go far enough to rest his forehead on the top of the gardener's hand for a moment before straightening up. "Please, tell me your name."

"Yori…" the gardener managed to get out, taken aback by Myst's intimacy and sudden care for his name.

"It's a pleasure to meet you, Yori. I'm sorry to hear the royals don't pay you attention."

The gardener blinked before snapping back into the conversation. "It shouldn't be a concern of yours, sir. I am just a gardener, and they are queens, princesses, princes, nobles… like you."

"It shouldn't matter," Myst replied sternly. "A noble, a merchant, a peasant in the slums—it is a simple practice of respect to know another's name if they are to be around me."

The last time Iris heard Myst so passionate about a topic was when he was arguing with Marin. It made her wonder why Myst held such an opinion, and what had happened previously in his life. She still didn't know what he did or what his life was like, which was understandable, given the short time they had to get to know each other, but it did remind her of the first experience they had together.

Myst and Yori continued to converse as Marin approached Iris. She had just finished readjusting a head statue.

"Gods above, this room doesn't have anything either." Marin sighed, placing a hand on their face. "I don't want to go near that side of the castle. If we didn't find any guests here, it means they're over there."

With such a nice day, Iris wouldn't be surprised if the meeting was taking place on the outdoor patio she had pointed out yesterday. "There must be another clue. We did pull more cards on this yesterday, we just haven't been able to link them to possibilities."

The Hermit, The High Priestess, and Three of Pentacles.

She took some time to close her eyes and imagine The Hermit in her mind, the cloaked figure standing amidst an empty landscape with only a lantern in his hand to light the way. She was yet to come across anyone like this since she met Marin, and it only made her more curious as to how it could apply to something like a castle.

"What are you thinking?" Marin asked, placing a hand on Iris' arm to bring her back to focus.

She opened her eyes, turning to Marin. "The spiritual meaning of The Hermit isn't very helpful, we should look into the symbolism instead."

"How can we do that? The Hermit, the man with the cloak and lantern?"

Iris looked at Yori and Myst. The Seven of Pentacles was helpful in its meaning, but the imagery was almost accurate to how they found Yori in the gardens. "What if The Hermit is someone we can find in this castle? Someone who works here, who will lead us to the location we need."

"How are we supposed to find that someone out of all the people who work in this damn castle?" Marin huffed. She watched them cross their arms from her peripheral. "It may take us days to do just that."

It seemed like they had hit an obstacle again. They needed a way to find a person who fit the description of a lantern carrier without questioning each member of the castle staff.

As she was thinking about this, Iris approached the seating area and took a seat on an empty couch, with Marin following close behind. It would appear too suspicious to remain standing and staring at the decor of the room, especially with Myst and Yori not far from them, engaging in deep conversation.

"Do you have many close friends in the castle?" Myst tilted his head with an arched eyebrow.

"Not many. A good friend of mine used to work with me… but they're a caemi and you know what's happened to them." A caemi friend was taken away. That made three of them in the room who lost someone to the queen's orders. "I know of multiple staff members of the castle, but haven't established much of a relationship with any others."

Oh, perhaps the answer to their problems was sitting in the very same room as them. If they could get Yori to tell them about someone who carried a lantern, it could be their clue to finding the entrance.

"We would like your help with something, Yori," Iris interrupted, which earned a sharp glare from Myst that she ignored. "Do you know anyone in the castle who carries a lantern around?"

Myst's expression turned to one of confusion, though Marin gave him a look of reassurance. Unfortunately, they didn't have all the time in the world to get Kalaya back, and something could go wrong anytime now.

"A lantern? We have a few keepers around the castle who carry lanterns as they work during the night as well. I know a couple personally, since they also patrol the garden. Why do you ask?"

Iris opened her mouth to answer, but realised the only reason she had was to find a secret entrance to the underground to save a prisoner. That reason wouldn't pass very well with someone they tricked into showing them around the castle and thinking they were nobles. She hadn't prepared any reason for this.

She felt Marin touch the side of his hand to hers and leaned forward to overtake the conversation. "A curiosity of mine, actually. Out the front, we saw someone carrying a lantern in the day."

Myst chimed in, playing along. "As you know, it's quite obvious seeing a person in the garden with a gardening tool to know what they do. Or someone with a saddle and hay to understand they are a stable keep. Who knows what a figure with a lantern may be attending to?"

"Oh, of course. That makes a lot of sense." Yori nodded. "Well, there are a few reasons why someone would be carrying the lantern even during the day. There are places in the castle that are naturally dark, such as the cellar."

The cellar didn't quite fit any of the signs or messages they got from the cards, so it had to be someone else. "So, these dark places in the castle, are there many more?" Iris insisted.

"There's only one other place, but I've never been there before. In the library, near the back, there are castle archives. They contain encyclopedias and also what are considered sacred texts. Like, books written in the name or theoretically by the patrons above."

At first, this sounded like the average sectioned off area of a library, but the thought of bookshelves hidden away brought Iris to remember her own shelves at home. Perhaps a secret entrance could work similarly. In addition to that, The High Priestess card indicated sacred knowledge, hidden knowledge. It lined up well with the archives.

Was it possible that what they were looking for, their key to saving Kalaya, was in the castle library? Considering the library was located where the meeting likely was, she needed something more to confirm her suspicions, to justify visiting the library enough and risking their discovery.

"Can you tell us anything else about the library's lantern keeper?" Iris was hopeful.

"I don't see her much, but I've heard something from other gardeners." Yori tapped his chin. "Because of her job of guarding the sacred texts, she has quite a few titles we call her by. The keeper, the librarian and, the most prestigious-sounding, *the high priestess*."

And that was enough to settle their next destination.

Chapter 19
the empress

Once they had cleared the right side of the castle, it was time to confront the area they had hoped to avoid. To Iris, it felt as if this was inevitable if they wanted to be thorough in their search. Luckily, Marin and Myst saved the day with their explanation, which was enough to convince Yori.

"So at the end of this hall is the library and—"

Yori's guidance was interrupted by loud talking coming from outside as they got closer to the patio. Myst quickly grabbed Yori to ensure he wouldn't walk in front of the open entrance.

"What are you doing?" Yori frantically looked around to understand why Myst may have done that, his voice quivering.

All of them stayed silent as the meeting continued outside.

"Are there plans to locate the remaining two assassins?"

The voice of Queen Taelore emitted into the hallway, causing Marin to grimace and pull a face at Iris. She shook her head and placed a hand on top of his head.

"With one captured below, we have all we need to find the others. On the land of Kyross and in the hands of Excava royalty, they will not be missing for long."

Seven of Swords. It seemed one of the assassins was also kept underground alongside Kalaya. It made her wonder if Kalaya was okay and if there was any trouble having an assassin imprisoned in close vicinity with her. It would also have to be noted when going down there themselves.

"Myst?" Yori whispered, causing the three of them to snap their attention to him.

"Ah, yes? I mean, we…" Myst stumbled on his words. He looked at Marin with pleading eyes, who then looked at Iris.

They needed to get to the library as soon as possible so they could search it for the entrance, but they didn't want to risk the attention of the meeting possibly shifting to them, which would result in them getting kicked out, or worse, arrested.

With the circumstances, it was a good time as any to reveal the plan to Yori in case he could help more or at least understand their thinking.

"We need to tell him about the plan," Iris said. Marin nodded slowly, a hand on their cheek.

"Plan, what plan?" Yori interrupted, holding his hand out in front of Myst.

"We don't have a choice, do we?" Marin said. "With the library right there, but the meeting also right there, Yori is our best bet for getting there as soon as possible."

Iris spun on her heel and stepped away, creating a distance from the entrance. The other three followed, Myst gently dragging Yori along. It was far enough for them to have a discussion, but close enough to still see the library door at the end of the hallway.

"Yori, there's something we must admit," Iris started, looking at the poor gardener, who Myst held by the underarm. "We may not be who we say we are."

"What do you mean? Myst's name isn't Myst? What does this have to do with any plan?" Yori stared up at Myst, who stared back at him.

"No, that's not what she meant. I am Myst, but we aren't the people we say we are. We aren't the nobles' children." Caution was evident in Myst's voice, not wanting to anger or upset the gardener.

"Wait, who are you then? What are you doing here?" Yori jumped, taking a step away from the group. "You aren't assassins, are you? We've had three too many assassins in this castle recently, at least from what I've heard."

Marin lowered his hands in a downward motion. "It's okay, Yori. We aren't here to hurt anyone. We're trying to rescue our friend who was falsely arrested."

"Wait, so you aren't nobles…" Yori repeated.

"Yes, that's what I just said. We were pretending, to get access to the castle."

Yori frowned, looking down. "Were you just using me to get in here? You weren't interested in me bringing you around?"

Myst quickly went up to Yori and gripped his shoulders. "Don't say that. We may have needed your help to get in, but you really are a great person. Actually, I would like to extend an invitation to you. Perhaps we can visit the town together sometime after this—"

Marin cleared their throat and Iris tilted her head in confusion. That didn't seem like it was part of the plan or very useful towards it in any case. Had Myst somehow become attached to the gardener boy?

"Now isn't the time for dates. We need to get past this patio so we can check the library for an entrance." Marin crossed their arms and gestured their head toward the library.

"An entrance to what?" Yori was flustered by Myst's proposal, red rising to his cheeks. "You mean one to the prison?"

"Exactly," Iris confirmed with a nod. "Our friend is down there, but there aren't any obvious staircases that lead there. We think there is an entrance somewhere and the signs so far have pointed to the library, particularly the archives."

Yori hummed in thought for a moment, then quickly nodded. "I got it. You need a way to distract or remove these nobles and the queen so you can get through."

It would be difficult to distract them without revealing themselves first, only having Yori to leave behind to do the work. The most they could do was figure out a way to get their attention away from this area. With little thought of the situation they were in, Iris was quick to perk up.

"There might be a way we can use our lie to our advantage." Iris pointed between herself and the two caemi. "If Yori reports seeing a group of suspiciously dressed caemi on the other side of the castle, they would either go and check, or go and alert guards. Either would move them away from here, out of curiosity or safety."

Myst let out a small 'ooh' before digging into his bag and forcefully opening Marin's to dump the contents in.

"What in Ter's name are you doing?" Marin hissed, trying to pull their bag away.

"If we give him a bag to flail around as evidence of someone trespassing, it can make his lie more believable." While Marin thought the idea over, Myst quickly put the rest of what he had in the bag.

"You're right. And we can use flowers!" Marin's eyes lit up. They entered into a room nearby and returned with a bundle of flowers. "Are these from the garden?"

"Yes, usually we take flowers from the garden inside the castle. Why do you ask?" There was a look of wariness on Yori's face as he watched Marin handle the flowers.

"If it's quite alright with you, you can make these flowers look trampled and push them all into the damned queen's face, convincing her someone trampled her garden while they broke in, carelessly dropping their bag." At this point, the short caemi was chuckling to themself.

They equipped Yori up with the bag and flowers, which were looking rather sad, but Myst offered to buy him even nicer ones the next time they saw each other.

"And are you sure you can do this?" Myst looked at him with concern. "Will you be okay left alone?"

"Trust me, Myst. I spend a lot of time in the gardens with only the flowers and bees in my company. Even though you and your friends were tricking me, you're the most company I've had in a while."

The response reminded Iris of home. Despite the constant traffic and even personal clients who would come by for readings, she was still left to her own work without any friends or connections. Myst and Marin were also the most company she had since as long as she could remember.

"Is there no way we can take Yori with us?" Myst asked one final time.

"If we must, we would have to go all the way around again to avoid the ongoing meeting, and we've already taken too much time searching the rooms. The sooner we get to Kalaya, the sooner we get out and the less likely we slip up and get caught," Marin summarised.

Yori placed a hand on Myst's shoulder. "I'd love to go out sometime after this. Go get your friend, I'll handle the distraction."

Methodically, Yori wore an expression convincing enough to be about the appearance of caemi alongside evidence of their arrival, his hair ruffled and shirt untucked to hint rush and distress. Iris almost laughed. It was an ironic mirror to how Fleur usually prepared for a performance.

The fox caemi smiled. "Stay safe."

Yori gave them a nod before heading to the patio, calling the queen's name loudly with the bundle of crushed flowers still dripping water along the floor and the messenger bag they would have to say goodbye to. It earned a burst of joy from Iris before the three of them readied up to make their quick exit to the library doors as the guards came to take the nobles and queen to another, *safer* part of the castle.

"Smitten by the flower boy, Myst?" Marin teased as they entered through the library double doors.

Revealed was a series of tall bookshelves, in two columns on the right and left of a carpet path, almost touching the ceiling. They were a dark wood complimented by just as dark book spines that filled the shelves as far as Iris could see. There were also a few tables scattered around the area, though how neat the tables and chairs were arranged made her think the room wasn't sat in for very long or often.

"Oh, hush." Myst lightly pushed Marin away from him. "I've enjoyed his company so far, that's all."

"So much that you asked him out?"

This earned another push as they began walking through the library, checking in case anything appeared out of place, but they knew the archives were where they were going.

There were a couple of fireplaces that lined the walls opposite each other, though they were cold and unlit. There were small piles of ashes, and old wood that was dried out and thin.

"What should we do once we're in the archives?" Iris approached the back wall of the library with an archway in the middle of it, a sign hanging above reading *ARCHIVES*.

"As far as I know, bookshelf entrances work by moving certain books or finding something to trigger it from behind the books. Though, I feel as if it won't be that simple for something like an entrance to the underground prison," Myst answered.

"Did we have more tarot cards to go off of?" Marin dug into his bag and pulled out his notes to answer their own question. "Together with The Hermit and The High Priestess is the Three of Pentacles. How do you think that works?"

Iris peered into the archives, unable to see most of it clearly. "It's dark in there, I can't assume much."

"This is why they need lantern carriers... well, since we aren't going to run into anyone here..." Light orbs danced around Marin, revealing their caemi features once again. He then held their hand up and the orbs manifested in their palm, bobbing up and down. "We can use this as our lantern."

She stared at the light in awe as they entered the archives, darkness shrouding whatever Marin's light couldn't cover. The archive shelves were very similarly arranged to the ones in the main area, except these had much larger books and a thick layer of dust covered each spine. Some paintings were decorating the ends of each aisle, but they were worn and the details were unrecognisable. Perhaps this was where they kept paintings when they were replaced.

"Do you still have your deck?" Marin walked up to some of the shelves and shifted the books, but then almost immediately retracted their hand to shake the dust off.

Iris reached into her bag and carefully pulled out her deck from its holding pouch. Shuffling over to Marin, she used the light to flip through them to find Three of Pentacles. "I'm assuming you would like to see the card."

"Unfortunately, I don't have a memory of these cards like you do. Seeing the card might help us figure out what we should be looking at."

Iris held the card out to Marin, who took it gently and stared at it. The card featured three people standing under an archway with a pillar in the centre, three pentacles embellishing it in design. The three of them were staring at said pentacles.

"It looks like that's meant to be us." Myst peered over before returning to the middle of the path, which also had a carpet lining it. Though she couldn't see it very clearly, it did seem less frayed than the one found outside. "That detail may help if we find something like the card is showing in here."

Iris went off to explore more sections of the archives until she noticed that instead of paintings decorating the wall of the last two opposite aisles, there were small reading rooms built-in, with archways and pillars as part of the structure. While they didn't have any pentacles, they were strikingly similar to the card.

"Marin, Myst, come look over here." Iris peeked into the main aisle to call the other two over.

Myst walked over quickly while Marin followed slowly, once again shaking their hands off and bringing the light orbs back up.

"You found the pillar!" Marin clapped in celebration, but then looked to the other side of the room. "Wait, there's two."

"I believe there's a very simple way to figure out which of these is the one we want." She held her hand out to take the Three of Pentacles back, then turned it to show the other two. "There's a bench in this image, located on the left when looking at it."

Iris walked over to the right side of the room to check for a bench to find it was over to the right. Upon returning to the left side, the bench was in the correct position. "The bench aligns with the card."

She had to admit she was slightly proud of what she had just figured out, a beaming smile forming on her lips. Being able to gather the pieces of the puzzle from one tarot card was satisfying, but there had to be more.

"That's incredible, but…" Myst circled the pillar, looking around it and feeling along the cold stone. "Now what? There isn't anything we can really pull or move here that may trigger a doorway opening."

"Right…" For that, Iris was unsure. "What else do you two know about secret entrances?"

"There are many that work with sconces," Myst said.

"What are sconces?"

"It's a wall decoration, something on the wall that holds up lanterns or candles."

Ah, a fancy word for candle holders. "Considering you need a lantern to see in here, I don't think they keep sconces out."

"It doesn't appear so. Alternatively, there are hidden levers or levers disguised as other objects. I'm guessing they wouldn't keep the door handle to the underground tunnels in the open." Myst consulted the card again. "Remember what I said about the positioning on the card? Let's try that."

For someone hesitant about the use of cards in this plan, even while being friends with Kalaya who was a witch and caemi magic user, it was nice to see Myst trying to problem solve using the cards. She could also see why Kalaya, Marin, and Myst worked well together as a team. Their alternative perspectives and ways of thinking meant they could get a rounder picture or fill in the gaps others left in their plans.

Myst walked over to the bench and used the wall to steady himself on it, standing at the end of the bench as Iris and Marin stood on the other side, looking up as the people in the cards did. Nothing happened for a moment until Myst audibly gasped. "Something moved."

"What? Where?" Marin looked around.

"The bench. It wasn't enough to unbalance me, but I swear to Mian the bench just lowered." He jumped off.

With concentrated eyes, Iris did indeed see the bench move up and back to its original position. "I wonder what that does." She placed a hand on the bench, but it didn't move. Perhaps it wasn't enough weight. "Let's get both of you on the bench and see if it goes lower. It might be a part of the entrance."

They did as Iris instructed, and the bench moved even lower, now causing other mechanical sounds to emit from the walls, the sound of gears moving coming from underneath Iris. She stayed vigilant, attempting to follow the sounds to see what they would do, only for a final *click*, and a noise came from above.

The back of the pillar revealed a small compartment that was open now, and inside was a metal handle, a candle holder crossed with a lever. It was exactly placed where they would've been looking if they followed the exact imagery of the Three of Pentacles.

"Is this it?" Marin whispered, staring at the lever.

Iris was staring too, but between her card and the pillar. Not only did it bring them to where the mechanism was, but also showed them how to work it with the bench and where the lever would be. What else could her cards show them with the right questions?

Myst hummed, seemingly impressed with their efforts. "There's only one way to find out, isn't there? Pull the lever, Iris."

She lifted her hand and held the lever tightly. And then she pulled.

From further in the reading room, the wall began to shift and turn. It was loud, to say the least, and the stone against stone didn't make the most pleasant of noises, but it was nothing against the bubbling excitement Iris felt from the bottom of her feet and rising to the top of her being. They were so close to finding Kalaya, and they had gotten over a large hurdle with finding this entrance.

They all stayed silent, looking between themselves in disbelief. Marin got down from the bench, though took a moment to wait and see if the door opening would close. Fortunately, it seemed like the closing mechanism would be on the other side instead.

Myst hopped off as well, and the three of them approached the opening to inspect it. It was still dark in the next room, though

Iris could see the formation of a downward staircase. The entrance would bring them to uncharted territory, a mystery with each step.

Iris didn't have so much as a second to hold her cards up when a voice came from the main library. "Hello? Is someone in there? Prince, or princess, you know you aren't allowed in the archives…"

They weren't able to recognise the voice, and they didn't want to risk being found when they got this far. The mechanism was loud alongside the door opening, so she wasn't surprised someone heard them. But it meant they had to get moving and do the readings inside if they didn't want to get caught.

"We need to go," Marin said, as if he read her mind. "Quickly."

The short caemi pulled Iris along through the opening, and Myst followed closely. They searched for a way to close it, and this time, the lever was right beside the doorway. Marin pulled it as soon as they spotted it, and as the opening closed, the light of a lantern appeared around the corner.

"Gods above…" Myst panted, leaning against the now-closed wall. "And it's dark in here, too." He shook his head to reveal his features again and held up a hand with light as Marin followed suit. They needed as much light as possible if they wanted to navigate down here.

Their voices echoed off the walls, the round room they were standing in feeling cold and… unusually empty. It also smelled of rusting, despite nothing metal in their limited sight. Before them, as noted, the floor lowered into a staircase that appeared to go down far. Staring back at them at the bottom was only darkness. They needed to get down there.

Marin took a deep breath. "Well, let's go guys. We have a caemi to save."

The staircase seemed to go on forever and at this point, Iris' feet were beginning to hurt with each step down—she had been doing quite a bit of climbing and walking today, after all.

They continued down the never-ending staircase, and it was only at a brief moment somewhere along the line that the ground had flattened out and revealed two other tunnels on each side of them. The light coming from Myst's hand revealed a sign where one read 'waste tunnels' and the other 'armoury'. They had eliminated those tunnels in favour of the unlabelled staircase to be the one holding the prison they were searching for.

Myst and Marin made conversation between themselves to pass the time as they continued onwards.

"I don't think we should've left Yori behind." From the light in his hands, Iris could see a frown on Myst's face.

"As we said, there weren't many options. You can see your boyfriend again after we save Kalaya." It sounded like Marin was trying to be serious, though a small chuckle came from them after the second sentence.

"But what if something bad happens to him?"

"Please, he's a gardener looking out for the safety of his queen, and you were the one who had the evidence idea. I'm sure he will be okay."

She had to agree. "He's on our side too, so he won't reveal anything that will get any of us in trouble." At least she hoped so. Yori was nice enough to show them around and didn't immediately call the guards when they revealed their disguise.

"I hope you guys are right… Wait!" Myst held his hand out in front of Marin and Iris to stop them from walking, in turn putting out the light in his and Marin's hand. The two of them stayed silent, waiting for Myst to explain. "The staircase is ending," Myst whispered.

"What?" Marin whispered back.

Iris looked ahead. Further in front of them were a few small candles that illuminated a hallway with bars lining the walls. Perhaps those were the holdings of the prison they were looking for.

They must've been on the underground prison floor now, and ever closer to Kalaya, as well as the assassin. She had to stay on guard for that, and she was sure the others were, too.

"I put the light out just in case there were guards down here, but… I think we're here." Myst began walking forward, a hint of excitement in his voice. "She must be imprisoned in one of these cells."

Marin, being the reckless caemi they were, ran forward into the unfamiliar corridor, peering into each cell to discern the containments of each. She followed cautiously behind, wary Marin may stick their head into the cell of an assassin, but all the cells were unusually empty for a prison. She expected more dangerous people to be contained in these cells. There were also no guards down here.

She continued to check each cell until she heard the shout of Marin from the very end of the hallway.

"Kalaya!"

Both Myst and Iris ran up to Marin and looked in the cell they were standing before, finding a figure sitting in the middle with a small light emitting from one of their hands. From what Iris could see, long black hair cascaded over the figure and pointy purple cat ears sat upon the person's head. She noticed a similarly coloured tail was wrapped around them.

Without another word, they stood up, releasing the light that was in their hand, but instead of going out like Marin's, it started floating like it had a mind of its own and followed the person walking towards the group. She lifted her head and opened her eyes, sparkling purple eyes revealing themselves against the eerie darkness of the prison holding.

"Marin, Myst, it's so wonderful to see you two again." She had a strong accent Iris hadn't heard before, but she liked how it sounded.

And that was when she realised they had finally found Kalaya, trapped all the way underground in a lone cell amongst tens of empty ones, sitting in the dark with only a small being of light showing her any life in the darkness.

Iris stared at the caemi in the cell, finally being able to put a face to her name. Even with the ragged clothes the guards had likely given her and the dirt dusting her face from being denied time outside the cell, Kalaya was beautiful.

The purple cat caemi turned to Iris with a soft smile. "Sybil, it's a pleasure to finally meet you."

WHEEL of FORTUNE.

Chapter 20
Wheel of fortune

"Have they been feeding you?" Myst asked as Marin held Kalaya's face in their hands through the bars and examined it.

"Yes… kind of. They don't come here very often."

"We should get food once we get out of here," Marin mumbled, letting go of Kalaya's face and inspecting her arms. "A bit of dirt and dust, but no cuts or bruises, at least any new ones."

"Just the ones from before I got arrested." A small smirk appeared on her face, which made Iris hold her breath. How was she so positive after being in a prison for a few weeks?

"Why aren't there any guards down here?" Iris was both curious and wary of someone coming out of nowhere.

"They open a lock in the archives and travel down a dark staircase for a long while. About 1800 seconds? It's quite the time to spend walking." Kalaya was recounting her experience as if it were normal, as if it was just an everyday inconvenience.

"And then what?" Marin finished their inspection, now checking the cell holding Kalaya.

"They don't offer much food, because of how much effort it takes to come down here. Why spend so long each day in the dark only to feed a prisoner kept deep under the castle? It's also why there aren't any guards here. They also trust the darkness and malnourishment to keep me quiet." She lifted her hand and held the bar, but it was before long that she dropped it.

"So you don't have enough strength to escape. Can you still use magic?" Iris was still unfamiliar with the majority of magic and caemi, and what it entailed.

"Hardly. The only reason I have this light is a combination of witchcraft and caemi magic. I can call upon spirits of light with witchcraft and help maintain its light with energy supplied by my birth magic. This isn't nearly enough magic nor strength in me to break these bars or the lock. The guards also don't carry keys down here because why would they need to?"

The queen and guards had left Kalaya in such a weakened state, it was painful just thinking about it. She wondered how Kalaya had enough energy to even talk to them right now or how she lasted this long. It may have been a caemi thing, or maybe a combination of that and hope for her friends to return. Her willpower was admirable.

"Alright, let's get you out of here!" Marin gave everyone a look of determination as they balled their fists and gathered their strength. Then, they grabbed onto the lock holding the cell door shut and used both hands to deform the loop of the lock so much that it began to bend and break. Before it fully came off, Marin shook their hands off and took a deep breath. "Tough lock, but nothing newer than a doorknob."

As Marin was doing their thing, Iris wondered if the assassin was treated the same. Hardly any food and surrounded by darkness. She wondered if they would act violently in an attempt to get out of the prison and convince the guards to carry a key with them. If they were clever enough to attempt an assassination, surely they had an idea of escaping a prison, too.

"Have you seen the assassin down here?" Iris asked as the lock finally snapped enough to be taken off. The door swung open and Marin jumped into Kalaya's arms, causing her to stumble backwards, but she was able to catch herself and the excited caemi. "I heard they kept one of the three assassins, and it's something we should be wary of."

Kalaya lifted her head from Marin's shoulder, looking at Iris in confusion, then turned to the other two. A panicked look was exchanged between Myst and Marin, who lowered their arms and stepped away from Kalaya.

"We haven't told her yet," Marin mumbled.

"Told me what?" Now, Iris understood what it was like when Yori found out about their plan. Were they hiding something from her yet again? She was hopeful it wasn't too bad, considering they made it this far together to save Kalaya.

"I'm sorry, Iris." Kalaya stepped forward with an apologetic look.

"What are you sorry for?" She was starting to worry now. Just a second ago the group was celebrating the rescue of Kalaya and now they were all looking at her nervously, Marin's tail swaying slowly behind him and Myst's normally tall fox ears drooping down.

"I'm the assassin they're talking about."

Iris backed up to the other side of the hallway, which was only lined with more prison bars. The cold started digging into her back, which contrasted with her rushing heartbeat, blood rising, and adrenaline pumping through her.

If Kalaya was one of the assassins, it would make the most sense Marin and Myst were the other two yet to be captured. Dear Ter, she had been travelling with wanted assassins the whole time.

Marin had an obscene skill with opening locks and doors, not because they were a caemi, but because assassinations must've called for breaking into places with locks. He must've written maps and plans to kill people, not just as a hobby. Myst must've been a master of disguises as the one who chose the robes they were all wearing and somehow always had a change of clothes to be unrecognisable to guards he wanted to run from.

They had connections because assassins needed them to do what they did and get away with it, didn't they? Was that why Marin appeared so charming as well?

"Iris, calm down." Marin stepped toward her, but she held her hands out.

"Don't come closer."

Was the queen the right one all along? All those claims of violent caemi who were living amongst them all this time only to be revealed when they were unexpectedly caught? She had to admit she never witnessed anything the queen had claimed, but she knew Marin was more than capable of getting their way if they wanted. She also knew Myst was able to convince her to believe something that wasn't true.

Wait—with the timing of everything, the reason Kalaya may have been arrested, and the night of losing her to the guards… Kalaya was captured before the deportation of the caemi, and the three of them were why everything was happening to the caemi. They started all of this.

Marin paused on the spot, now standing in the middle of the hallway between her, Kalaya, and Myst. They held their hands up in surrender. "I'm not going to do anything, I want to explain."

"Explain? But you're all assassins. The assassins who were going to kill the queen." Her heart started beating even faster. Was she going to die now that she had helped Marin find Kalaya? "My brother was right, I should've stayed home. I don't know what I got myself into."

Her gaze skipped around, unsure how to remain still in this situation. Myst's hand twitched by his side and Iris grasped a bar behind her. He could've hidden a weapon in his belt.

"Iris, please. Breathe, close your eyes. I will not touch you. I will not come closer. I just want you to breathe and let yourself calm down." With pleading eyes, Marin took a step backwards to prove his point.

She pursed her lips, unsure if she wanted to listen. A part of her reminded her these were the friends she had made along the way, but maybe Marin was wrong. Maybe friends couldn't be made in a day or few.

But what if Marin was right?

She knew how easy it was to always prepare for the worst. Her mother reminded her that having a backup plan was better than just one plan. Yet… when she came on this journey, she had no backup plans.

With a deep breath, she told herself Marin tended to keep things to themself for a good reason. There had to be more.

Another breath. There was surely a good explanation for this. She could give them a chance to explain and think of a way to get out of there if the situation called for it. Deep down, she didn't want the latter to happen.

"Okay. I'm breathing." She lowered her arms to her side. "You promised that you were going to tell me everything last time… did you lie again to me?"

"I swear on my life and the life of my friends, I can explain this."

Iris stared at the three, who looked incredibly sorry. She didn't know how much truth there would be this time but she nodded for Marin to proceed.

"You're right. We're the assassins in question, the ones the queen wants to capture and likely sentence to death once she catches us. She only kept Kalaya alive since she planned to break her down so much to find the two of us as well."

She struggled to keep eye contact with Marin, not wanting her eyes to wander in fear that any of them would pull a weapon on her. They wouldn't do that, would they?

"But the queen twisted the story. We aren't killers. We weren't trying to kill her. She's had an agenda to get rid of the caemi for a long while now, and she used us to enact her plan."

"How do you know that?" Iris asked with squinted eyes.

"We're contracted by our own king and queen in Syriphia," Myst chimed in, stepping slightly forward but not more than Marin had. "The three of us are guild questers in Syriphia. Just like how you have your trade guilds and such, there are also quest guilds that exist on both continents."

She didn't have much experience with guilds in Kyross, but she was very aware of the business and trade guild that was located in Excava. It was the very guild Taelyn was having his meeting with. She had also only briefly heard about a quest guild in passing through the gambling house patrons who didn't spend a second looking at her. They just wanted to bet their earned money away.

"What business did they have for you here?" Iris pried, needing more information.

"A stolen artefact." Marin looked to their friends for a look of approval to continue. "The Excava family had stolen an artefact from the Rosell royal family years ago and our king and queen had tried to get it back through monarch-to-monarch meetings, but they never succeeded. Each time, the Excavas would threaten mass deportation."

Such as the one happening at that very moment. Hundreds of caemi were being arrested and dragged to ships, only to be sent to the other continent with hardly any notice or care. Did they kill off those of half caemi and senti like her brother said?

She didn't realise—couldn't have realised—all of this was happening so close to her. She didn't know anything about the ongoings between the two continents or the business the royals had. It wasn't exactly for her to know in the first place, but it was being revealed so quickly now that she had the three supposed assassins in front of her. Her mother was right, she needed to be better.

"I was captured during our escape. We had failed to find an entrance to the underground tunnels which would lead us to where they kept the artefact. Before we finished searching the castle in the dead of night, a stray guard patrol caught me."

From there, Iris knew Marin had to choose between saving Kalaya or Myst. She just had a location to place the scenario in now. The three of them had been in this very castle, where they all came today to save Kalaya. This first attempt must've been how Marin already knew some of the rooms in the castle.

"Marin and Myst managed to escape," Iris recounted. "They ran through the forest, even reaching to the opposite side from where we came in."

"That's exactly where we were. Myst and I had to run from the guards, who were also near the barracks on the east side of the castle. It was easy in the dead of night, in the density of the forest. As long as we were quiet."

"I suppose it didn't help that I was holding you up against a tree." Myst chuckled nervously.

"Unfortunately, this was the last thing they needed to set the plan into motion." Kalaya sighed, holding her head in her hands. "A failure to retrieve the artefact was also a failure amongst the caemi race. While we still have a place to go, having so many caemi return to Syriphia will cause a lot of trouble for everyone. And the half caemi and senti that have to be sacrificed because of us—"

"It wasn't because of us." Myst grabbed Kalaya's wrists and lowered them to hold her hands. "Listen, the queen was already planning this. She made our attempt to get the artefact back look like an assassination to justify her horrible actions."

"Are you able to do anything about it?" Iris stepped forward again, a trickle of confidence running through her. "You know the truth, you have to tell people so they can stop this."

Marin shuffled closer to Iris with a sniffle and placed a hand on her arm. "I asked myself that each day I was away from Kalaya, trying to find you so I could make things better in at least one way. I wanted so badly to shout from the rooftops that the queen was wrong and the caemi are dying for nothing. That the Excava family are horrible liars, causing the death and tragedy of so many." The small sniffle turned into several and tears started to fall from their eyes, their lips wavering and any words that tried to escape their mouth only came out as sobs.

Kalaya wrapped her arms around them and held them tightly, tears falling from her eyes. Myst placed a hand on Marin's shoulder and looked away, but Iris could see a stray tear falling.

"Marin, what can I even say? These are the sort of things I want you to tell me. I can't trust someone who keeps things from me." Even though she had a feeling telling strangers about royal plans were not allowed, but she was more than a stranger now.

"We're sorry for not telling you the truth from the beginning, Iris," Marin managed to say between sobs.

"The queen has too much against us and caemi-kind. We couldn't do anything to get our own artefact back, how are we to confront her about this?" Kalaya lifted her arm to wipe her cheeks though Myst pulled out a handkerchief before she did and handed it to her. "We can only do so much."

Iris had already started to see the effect of the queen on caemi through her conversation with Bea, the arrest at the port, how the pirates treated the caemi and the protest at the castle gates. To think that someone—the queen!—would falsely frame an assassination and have it lead to this... what else was happening in the world?

The three caemi wiped their tears and Marin had switched to hugging Myst instead, burying their face in his shoulder. Muffled whimpers emitted from the short caemi but they started to subside as Myst ran his hand through their hair.

Kalaya approached Iris and looked her up and down. It felt like a spark was running through her as she did. Without warning, Kalaya held Iris' hands, staring into her eyes. Iris held her breath, waiting for what was next.

"Now that you know the truth, you have a choice. We can either get you home and you'll never hear from us again..."

Despite her having wanted to return home when she'd first embarked on this journey, a part of her now discarded that option. She despised the idea of never hearing from them again.

"... or, perhaps you can help us complete our mission before we have to return to Syriphia."

In the past few days, a lot had been revealed about the three of them. Iris had never encountered anything like it before, even in her readings. These were her first friends, first betrayals, and first warm feelings in her chest. They were her first sparks that led her to wanting more from the world outside her destiny of forever being a tarot reader in her family business.

They had shown resistance to revealing everything to her, but they also shared what they could and were willing to explain the truth to her when it came to it. It wasn't like she was perfect or pure either, intending to travel for the money and eventually staying to help her friends.

This new part of the story didn't have to change her friendship with Marin, her developing friendship for Myst, and her, slightly hard to admit, adoration for the witch standing before her.

"I can help," she began, with Marin now turning to her and looking hopeful. "But I don't want to go through this again. I want your honesty, in exchange for my trust. I want to trust you all without being afraid something else is being hidden."

Marin nodded vigorously, jumping out of Myst's arms and skidding to Iris' side. "Can I hug you again?"

She opened her arms, let Marin run into her, and clasp their arms around her. Once again, she patted the top of their head.

"I can promise you honesty." Myst held a hand to his chest. "We all know there are some things we keep to ourselves, but the most important things will be shared."

Kalaya smiled, her purple eyes glistening. "If the three of us are going to drag you along, it's the least we can do from now on."

A wink from her sent blood rushing to Iris' cheeks. She didn't know what this feeling was, but it was warm and pleasant.

"Any-Anyway…" Iris gently held Marin's shoulder, and they stepped away, giving her a thumbs up.

She reached into her bag once again and lifted her deck from the mix of paper and writing tools contained in the leather satchel. While it was still rather dim in the empty, rusting prison, she only needed her cards and the will to read what she needed to.

As per tradition, she began to shuffle, a rhythmic thump felt in her palms with each slice of the action. It was like a beat of a drum manifesting in her ears, and she felt the ever-familiar strands of energy weaving through each card.

The three caemi stared intensely at her doing her thing, even though Kalaya was more than familiar with tarot. Perhaps, just like Iris, Kalaya enjoyed the thought of meeting someone like her.

The energy was flowing, and the cards were shuffling, so there was one thing she wanted to ask before they set off to get that artefact and finally get out of there.

"Tell me how it ends."

Chapter 21
the devil

Myst did what he could with the supplies he had to clean Kalaya up, taking the few handkerchiefs he was carrying as part of his disguise and dousing them with a bit of water he was carrying in his bag—now in Marin's bag due to giving his up—for the mission.

He gently wiped the dust from her face and some off of her arms. Marin dug into their bag and revealed a pair of cuffed pants and a tunic to replace the rags she was wearing. As Kalaya changed her clothes, Iris turned around, Marin and Myst following suit.

"It's what we can do for now," Myst noted to no one in particular. "Once we get out of here, we will get a bath running for Kalaya and a feast in celebration."

"I like the sound of that." Marin rubbed their hands with a small chuckle.

Iris bet Marin was only excited about the food and being able to dig into it, knowing the safety of Kalaya was in their hands now. She supposed she couldn't blame them for being happy about such a scenario, as she was looking forward to it slightly as well after all of this.

"Alright, let's move." Kalaya dusted her hands off and kicked the rags into the corner of the cell. She wouldn't be needing them anymore.

Two of Swords.

That was the first card that was pulled and it didn't take the group long to see the two swords pointing from each side symbolised the splitting path to the sewers and armoury. Where exactly, they didn't remember, but they didn't have anywhere to go but up.

Marin and Myst held out their hands and light started emitting little white orbs of magic once again, illuminating their way back to the long, winding staircase. Iris shivered. Back home, she had to walk up and down stairs every day, but this staircase would need more than half an hour to climb.

With each step, Iris thought about what she had been through in the last couple of weeks. The situation was much bigger than she imagined, and if she knew this would happen when she had first met Marin, she probably would've said no and stayed home. She was glad she didn't.

"So what is this artefact like?" Iris asked into the backs of Marin and Myst. There wasn't much opportunity to face each other as they all traversed up the staircase, the two light holders leading, and Iris and Kalaya following behind. She was surprised Kalaya was able to climb up the stairs after staying in that cell for so long.

"What do you mean?" Myst's voice echoed in the darkness.

"I understand it belongs to your king and queen, but what is it? Artefact is a bit vague."

"We haven't actually seen it before," Marin explained, their breath struggling slightly with each step up. "It's supposedly precious, meaning it was only seen by the royals and kept in their care until the senti queen had her own group take it for some reason. The Rosells didn't want to make a big deal, it wasn't worth a war."

"How will we know when we find it, then?" Having never seen it made it difficult for her to know what they were looking for, but the entire group not knowing? She found that slightly impeding on the plans if they had no map from Marin, a struggling direction for Myst to offer thoughts on, and a worn-out Kalaya. Most of their mission was an impromptu heist now, reliant on her, who did nothing to prepare.

"Intuition. As caemi, we were told we could sense it, since the artefact has an aura of its own," Kalaya explained quietly, steadily following behind the three of them.

"I didn't realise objects could have auras as well." Iris had a basic understanding of the caemi magic system only, but she knew caemi magic came from auras. It was like a barrel where the water was drawn from, and would replenish with time and rest. Based on what Kalaya had said earlier, she had a small supply, in which she had to draw from spirits for extra power.

"We didn't either, but it's true, and we're going to witness it once we have the artefact in our hands to bring back to our king and queen." Myst had an air of determination and leadership that helped Iris keep climbing. She was glad to have bought these new shoes back in Vestirr.

With several more minutes of stair climbing and conversation to pass the time, they finally approached the crossroad once again, this time the armoury being on the left and the sewer system on the right. Iris heard dripping in the sewage tunnel and, looking the other way, she was met with silence and darkness, the walls dotted with unlit torches.

"Which way should we go?" Marin leaned against the stone wall and slid down to sit on the ground, letting their hand fall and causing the light to go out.

"Perhaps we should split up if the cards are showing us two tunnels," Myst suggested, keeping his light orbs up.

While the suggestion was logical, no one followed up the sentence. Iris didn't feel like splitting up with the group in such an unknown location, and it seemed no one else did either.

"There must be more to the card, as usual. The Two of Swords, was it?" Kalaya turned to her to ask, to which she nodded in response. "A crescent moon is depicted on the right side of the card, above one of the swords. Maybe that's an indication of what direction we should go in."

"But that's the sewers… why would they keep it in the sewers?" Marin whined.

"Maybe there's something else." Myst held his hand out to take the card again. Iris handed it to him swiftly, as she had put the cards back in a way where she could present the ones she pulled with ease and speed. "I think it's important that her arms are crossed, or that her back is to the moon, like the symbolism of a different perspective." He took the card and took a few steps forward, past the tunnel entrances. Holding the card up with one hand, he gestured with the other arm to the armoury. "If we view the tunnels from the perspective of the lady instead of facing her, we can see the armoury is on the side of the moon instead."

Iris let out a small 'oh' in surprise. It was an impressive interpretation of the card, and she enjoyed how it made sense and came together. If the blindfolded lady was representative of their group entering these tunnels blindly, it would make sense they would be looking from her view rather than toward her.

"Okay, that seems about right." Marin got up again and dusted themself off. Perhaps they just preferred the dry tunnels, which she couldn't blame them for. "The armoury may be functional, but it is a potential cover up for the artefact. These sewers are likely exposed to the outside world, even if they are still hard to access and smelly, the armoury is the ideal choice of the two."

With the card Iris had drawn, Kalaya's recognition of the moon, Myst's perspective, and Marin's logic, they concluded the armoury was the best and most reasonable choice using the evidence they had gathered so far and began their trip down the unknown hallway.

There wasn't much difference between the tunnels as these ones were still made of cold stone bricks with the ground appearing as a large chunk of concrete. It wasn't like they had to focus on the aesthetics of an underground tunnel system in any case.

As the group travelled through the tunnel, Iris found herself slipping on the ground a few times, her footing becoming harder to manage and her balance being thrown off. Why was she suddenly slipping so much? A few laughs came from Marin until they fell right on their face onto the concrete ground.

On closer inspection, they found cracks within the concrete. Moss had made its way into them, making the path slippery. As they travelled, the cracks became more frequent, and the moss increased in density.

"Let's do this, Iris." Kalaya lifted her arm and linked it with Iris'.

Iris stopped in her tracks and turn to Kalaya. "What are you doing?" She didn't know what to think about the unexpected contact or the fact Kalaya was standing so close to her right now.

A small giggle came from the caemi, though it was quiet, perhaps due to the lack of hydration in her time down here. Iris reached into her bag as best she could with one arm to offer Kalaya the water canteen.

"Thank you. And this will help us not fall as Marin did." The statement earned a 'hey!' from the short caemi and Iris held back a laugh. "If we stay linked, it will be like having extra legs to keep us up."

What a curious solution. It wasn't anything she would've thought of herself, but she couldn't argue against it, and so they continued forward.

"Eight of Swords," Iris recited. "It seems there is a danger ahead, but nothing we can't handle. There will be things we should be cautious of, but it's not so overbearing that we won't be able to find a solution. The situation will be in our control."

"Well, there won't be any guards unless this is where they keep days of food supplies, but I doubt they would want to sit down here anyway," Marin theorised, scratching their cheek. "What else could be perceived as a danger?"

"A creature?" Myst suggested. "Like an animal, a big one."

"Would they even be able to keep such a large animal in these confinements?" Kalaya asked, to which Myst shook his head. There wouldn't be enough sustenance for a monster to stay alive.

"It could be something inanimate, such as the lock that got us into this tunnel in the first place. It could be a sign of feeling trapped within a puzzle, as such," Myst said, trying for another suggestion.

Iris thought it was a sound theory, though how likely was it that the royals would include a physical or puzzle lock on this artefact, considering they probably didn't expect anyone to find the library lock in the first place?

Apparently: 100%

The crew were met by two wooden doors, weathered and paint long deteriorated. Iris hadn't been paying attention to what was in front of them, and the ceiling had risen as well. Whatever was ahead, there was lots of it.

"Two doors for the armoury, genius!" Marin exclaimed, but Iris felt that it wasn't entirely genuine.

Myst walked up to the left door, the closest to him, and knocked on it. Iris didn't know what he expected. A guard to open it and greet them from the other side? Or the fabled creature they were theorising about to burst it open. Neither option was preferred, and that was what they got—nothing.

Kalaya shuffled to the right door and turned the handle, revealing it was unlocked. With that in mind, Myst tried the other and got the same result. Why would they have left these doors unlocked if they were trying to prevent anyone from entering the armoury without permission?

"What's inside?" Iris asked. Two doors for one room was strange. Something had to be wrong here, and she had a feeling they'd need to work it out soon to complete what they came here for.

Myst swung open his door, but none of them could see anything past the first few steps, even when he reached in with his hand lit up. Stone, dark and cold. A continuation of the floor they already stood on, minus the mossy growth. The other door was just the same. Now, this felt like a taunt.

"Time to split then. We can't risk one door not leading anywhere," Myst nodded to Iris, who was already standing on the left.

"No, what if the door we all choose leads all of us out? Then we won't waste time." Marin raised their eyebrows, challenging the orange caemi.

Both arguments were the same, so Iris didn't understand what the two of them were saying. Either way, it was a 50/50 chance, and it didn't matter what the actual answer was if they didn't find out. If Marin was correct, then it would earn them bragging rights, but if Myst was right, then they'd have to go back and try the other without any of them being able to scout the next room. None of them knew what was ahead of them, unless it was the armoury itself.

"We should still split up," Iris declared, earning an approving nod from Kalaya that made her smile. "Both answers have no meaning without trying both. By the time one pair gets to the end, the other will know what to do, whether that's to wait or try the other door. Let's not take up any more time with this."

The group agreed and set off.

Iris watched the back of Myst's head as he took the lead with his torch of a hand. His ears bounced around, and she remembered the rabbit caemi in Vestirr, and how their ears were even more prone to bouncing and flopping. It made her wonder how caemi slept and if their ears hit the headboard. And how did they wear hats? Her past dreams of Marin didn't provide a clear image now that she'd seen them in the flesh with their stout, pointy ears.

"Iris?" Myst called, not turning around.

She snapped out of her thoughts and blinked, taking a pause to gain her bearings, but not much had changed in the hallway of nothing they were traversing.

"Yes, Myst?"

"I was asking if you were okay. You weren't answering me."

"I must've been lost in my thoughts." Not that she would reveal what thoughts they were… silly ones, likely, in the eyes of a caemi and Myst no less. "Why do you think I'm not okay?"

"It's concerning you're asking that rather than answering, but mainly because of yesterday. We did clear it up, but you still cried and almost went home."

"That is what happens when you hurt someone's feelings." She raised her eyebrows in the darkness. "I'm fine, but I hope that won't happen again." Marin and Myst didn't have to make every conversation a fight.

"Sometimes it's like that, huh?" Myst chuckled, but the tight undertones of his voice acknowledged her point. "It hasn't always been easy, as they are a very different person than I am."

"But you still consider them like a sibling?" Iris was about to elaborate, but stopped short when Myst held his arm out. Then he turned around and put a finger to his lips, the light casting blobs of shadows on his face.

In a hushed voice, he said, "I think we were right about what's down here. There's something ahead of us."

Her shoulders lifted and eyes widened. "Something?"

His ears twitched slightly, like they were trying to turn towards this potential something. "I can hear…" A pause, more widened eyes. "It's alive."

Her smile was thin, and about to become a frown as she placed a hand on his forearm. "This must be a joke, right? You know I'm not like the others, I won't pick it up as easily…"

A loud *crash* confirmed her fears and Myst yelped with his tail jumping up with a frizz, the light going out as his hands turned into fists. Being plunged into darkness in the middle of nowhere caused Iris to yelp too. Now that thing was getting closer with heavy breaths being swallowed by a big mouth, going into big lungs.

Iris' instinct was to fumble and flip through her tarot cards, but they were no use if she couldn't see them. And with that, what could cards do against a beast?

Stomps and scampering bounced off the walls, as though the beast was accompanied by multiple large spiders with fiddly legs. Perhaps having no food down here was no issue… it probably ate the spiders and guards who found their way down here.

"Dammit," Myst cursed under his breath before an orange glow came from beside him.

His fingers were splayed on his side, and an object was starting to form. Then that object extended, like a rod, and then became two, which his hand tightened around.

Her gaze went between his hand to ahead of them, in hope, but also fear, that the glow would reveal what they were up against, but it was to no avail.

"What are those?" Iris stepped back, her voice wavering, unsure what was going to happen, but then a light breeze passed by her ear, a second before a loud caw of a crow sounded.

She whipped around, expecting to see the door open and a crow, but there was just darkness and... something moving in the darkness. Was that real, or was she just imagining things?

A crash came from behind her again. She spun to see Myst in a wide stance, the two rods in a cross above him blocking... she couldn't see what he was fighting, since there was nothing there, but the resistance in his planted feet told her otherwise.

She readied herself to run towards him, somehow his figure looking further away than only a moment ago, and then something grabbed her hand.

"Iris..." Her sister's voice. Fleur. She wasn't here, she couldn't be. Her little sister was still safe in Vestirr.

"Why did you leave, Iris?" Fleur's voice was a sickly song, combined with a screech.

Her hand was stuck in place, and she tugged only for it to feel like she was chained to the ground, with no room to move. As much as she wanted to keep her eyes closed, in disbelief, she opened one eye and looked to her right. The semblance of her sister's face was before her, contorted, crying, screaming.

"Please, stop!" She fell to the ground, her other elbow hitting the cold concrete, stinging and numb at the same time.

"My real name, Iris. Why don't you remember it? Why do you only call me by my stage name?" Her sister continued to cry before she screeched again and her ears started to ring.

Then she heard clinking. Ice in a glass. Liquid in a shaker.

"Iris." Aldo, her second eldest brother.

Slowly, she turned her head to the left. Her hand was released from her right, yet she found no motivation to move as her brother walked up to her, pushing his glasses up the bridge of his nose, and looked down at her.

"You're a disappointment. A bad example. An influence that taints the Galacia name." He continued to spin his whiskey glass, the ice clinking and clinking and clinking against the sides. "You're undeserving of Mother's mercy."

In a moment of silence, he opened his palm and dropped the glass. It shattered on the ground, and a thousand mirrors burst around her, the ice sliding towards her and leaving searing cuts on her calves.

"I should've never given her the idea of travelling." Taelyn's... Czar's voice echoed behind her. It took all her strength to grasp the freezing floor and turn herself around.

Nora held Czar's hand and shook her head. "It was a mistake to leave her at the inn. She isn't good enough for her so-called friends and she was better off at home."

The two stood together in the shadows, as if she and the others didn't exist. In their own world, speaking about her with regret.

"I should send for Mother to retrieve her. She will know what to do to put her back in her place."

"Yes, your Mother knows best. And it's for the best of the business."

"But what about her task? She hasn't a coin to her name. She has failed in such a simple assignment. What does that say about her work? Her place in the family?"

"Oh dear. It seems..."

Their voices became muffled. What were they saying? What was going to happen? He wouldn't leave her with their mother, would he? If she returned empty-handed, then...

"What's going on?" She pushed herself to her knees, hands shaking as she stood up. One hand reached towards her older brother and his partner. "Please, tell me what's going to happen." She shuffled towards them like a new-born animal, knees having to learn how to work again, feet unable to find their balance.

Don't leave me alone. Don't leave me alone. Don't leave me alone.

Don't leave me with her. Don't leave me with her. Don't leave me with...

Czar turned towards her, arms crossed, eyes narrowed and piercing. "Iris, Mother is here for you."

Thrown forward, her chest tight, velvet against her back, she sat with knees together, hands clutching the arms of a chair. Wind rushed by her ears and through her hair. She closed her eyes. Where was she going?

A crow caws.

My mother stands behind her desk, but her back is to me. Her sharp dark hair is neatly trimmed—it's always perfect, never bothered by the damp atmosphere, never a hair out of place from disgruntled patrons. Both of her hands are linked behind her and my gaze lingers on the gold and black beaded bracelet on her left wrist. I cannot see her face. I cannot see mother's disappointment.

"I give you one thing to do... and you can't even do that. And what do you do? Run off with these... despicable, stupid children who don't know better. Are you seriously putting them before your family? Before your mother? What am I to you?"

I open my mouth to speak, but my words don't even reach my tongue and everything feels so, so heavy. My feet are stuck to the carpet, where they usually line up with the pattern, the stars on the floor looking the same as ever, but never a comparison to the ones in the sky. When was the last time I saw the stars?

"I try so hard for this family." She finally turns around and slams her hand on the table, and I can't even bear to look at her face and so I stare at her fingers curling against the wooden desk, threatening to scrape and tear it apart. "I try so hard for you and this is how you repay me? I give you a home, food, a job. What more do you need?"

The chair begins to feel too small for me. It's too narrow for my legs, and my elbows can't leave my sides. My head is forced up to mother's gaze, but I keep my eyes closed.

"Marin Boudreau," she recites, and my shoulders lift. How does she know their name? "Marin Boudreau... Marin, Marin, Marin," she says again and continues. Where's Marin? Will they come save me again? Will they? "Marin, Marin... Little Boudreau." Where are they? Who are they... the sounds. They're sounds. The name is now sounds I can't recognise anymore.

Soon they're just syllables that have no meaning.

"Who is Marin Boudreau?" mother asks.

I shake my head. I don't know a Marin Boudreau. I don't know a Marin.

"One of your clients?" she asks.

"No," I reply, and shake my head again.

"Then he's not important."

She's right. The personal lives of clients only matter in the context of a reading.

I don't need to know the clients.

I don't know their names.

Who is Marin?

Two crows caw.

Three crows.

Four.

Will there be a fifth?

No.

I open my eyes.

And the window in mother's office breaks into pieces, like crystals falling to the ground. A song, a windchime.

A breeze.

I remember that the world outside is so beautiful.

And Marin Boudreau leaps through the window, catching themself on the carpet, not a shard of glass touching them, and they stare me in the eyes, a smile on their lips.

"Iris Galacia, I need your help."

"I'm just a tarot reader. My cards don't rescue people."

My mother screams and the angles of her face contort. She slams the table again. The usual rosy gold that fills her cheeks is now flaming red. She is asking who the hell this kid is. Why they broke her window. Why do they think they can just come into her private space like this? Who are they to invade this family? Get between her and her daughter?

"You're more than a tarot reader," they say. "And saving yourself still counts. That's what matters most."

Crows fly in and begin to swarm mother, pecking at her and attacking. She tries to wave them away, picking up stacks of paper and throwing them at the black birds of omens and blessings.

"We should get out of here." Marin chuckles and I find a smile growing on my lips too.

I try to get up, but I'm still stuck to the chair and I almost cry. Pressure builds behind my eyes and they start to water. Things begin to blur. Can I really save myself?

"You can—you already have."

I take a deep breath and plant my feet on the ground, and the next moment I'm at my mother's office door, trying the doorknob with Marin.

"It's locked!" My voice cracks and I glance back to my mother's desk where she is still fighting crows. They're hurting her. "Mother, give me the key!" I can still save her, too. We just need to let the crows out.

"You are not leaving!" Her words are still firm despite the chaos.

"But you're hurting. Let us out!"

"Letting my children leave me is the last thing I will do."

I turn back to Marin, but their hand is already grasping the doorknob, and it's only a moment later when it cracks and falls to the ground.

They open the door. It's dark.
"We're going to be okay."
And they push me through.

Iris gasped, and a bout of coughs attacked her chest. With a wheeze and her back shooting right up, it felt as if she had been drowning for an eternity before rising above the tension.

"Where's Marin?" she said to the darkness, her voice raspy. But there was no response.

The two doors, the tunnel, Myst, weapons, beasts, illusions. She had to find the others.

She checked her elbow and her legs for injuries, but they were gone. Gone, but not forgotten.

Her body rejuvenated, she stood to her feet as quickly as she could, ignoring the spin to her head. Myst may have been going through something similar, and she didn't know him well enough to know if he could do it on his own.

As she went forward, she found one of his rods, still glowing orange, but growing dimmer by the second. She picked it up, placing it between her arm and side, and reached for her cards.

Seven of Wands.

He was in trouble, and she needed to help. The sounds of beasts returned, but they were distant and failed to instil fear into her bones anymore.

Soon came the grunts of a familiar voice, followed by yelling.

Six of Wands Reversed. Ten of Wands.

Many wands. Myst was initially confident in his approach, but then began to feel overwhelmed. She had to make space for him to break free.

His figure entered her vision. This time he was close enough for her to see unfamiliar shadow people attacking him in return.

The second rod was discarded to the side, left behind in the rush. She picked it up, tapping the two against each other and weighing them. They weren't too heavy, but her arms weren't used to swinging any weapons around.

In any case, this was for her friend.

She ran into the fray, crossing the rods and making her stance wide above a shivering and kneeling Myst. A shadow had a weapon of their own, slashing her guard but not getting through. Its words were incoherent, but as she turned to look at Myst, his eyes held no recognition of her, but fear for the visions.

"Don't send him, please! Don't!" Myst wailed as he bent over and held his forehead to the ground, bowing to the shadow. "You can't make him."

In a swift move, the mirage stood up, forming into a man, withdrawing from combat but still as threatening. More menacing. Commanding.

The rods gave way and Iris fell to the ground. She reached towards her friend and placed her hand upon his curly hair, and the space suddenly changed.

The three of them were in a room, warm from a fireplace on the back wall, and filled with lavish armchairs, expensive paintings, and music floating in the air from a record player. Myst's knees were against a rug, but he had hardly entered the room from where he was placed. The door was open, but nothing was on the other side.

A large, decorated window filled the wall to the left of her, and she couldn't recognise the buildings in the distance.

Then there was the man. He looked like Myst, but much older, with a beard and greying hair. He wore clothes that were reminiscent of noble clothing from the gambling house, but with other embellishments, more refined. He also had large, tall caemi ears and a tail that laid low.

"If I don't send him, then I will send you in his place," the man bellowed.

"Uncle, you know father wants me to be a scholar. What of my studies? And what of Jinan's studies?" Myst continued to keep his head on the ground, not bearing to see eye-to-eye.

Iris smoothed her hands down his hair and towards his cheeks, trying to make him face her, to see past the illusions. When his head wouldn't budge, she gently slapped his arms, but they remained stiff in place. He was afraid of this uncle.

"An eldest boy not taking his place in the guard is already out of line, yet I still play your father's games. We cannot leave your family without a warrior. Your brother must go if you are to be a selfish fox."

"He cannot protect himself, uncle. I cannot be there for him."

"Do you not see the flaws in your arguments? If you do not go, he does. If he does not, then you shall. If his weakness will need your protection, then you both go, and you both will return honour to this family."

Iris grunted as she stood up, holding the left rod's end against her shoulder and the right one forward at neck height. As she approached Myst's uncle, she swung the right one, only for him to catch it with no hesitance or lag, his eyes snapping to her.

"Who is this?" He narrowed his eyes, then flung the rod backwards, causing Iris to fall.

She braced for impact, letting the rods clatter to the ground. She shouldn't have gone against someone who was physically larger and stronger than herself. What was she thinking?

"Iris?" Myst caught her in his arms, eyes widened and marks of tears on his cheeks that were previously hidden. "Why are you... how did you get in?"

"I've been here the whole time." She rubbed her head, allowing herself to relax slightly now that she had gotten his attention. "And this isn't real. We need to get out of here."

"I'm at home... how do you know where I live?" He frantically whipped around. And she couldn't see it, but perhaps his world was starting to fall apart. "And... and I haven't met you yet..."

"*Asadel*, get this trespasser off our property. She does not belong here," Myst's uncle spoke again. Asadel? Was that supposed to be referring to Myst?

"Uncle, she is my friend."

"Friend? A senti as well... what a disgrace."

Thumping interrupted the conversation, and she turned to see the previously open door closed. She froze, watching the wood shake under each thump until she heard a voice.

"I'm looking for Myst Carrash." Kalaya. Her voice was like a refreshing drink after travelling a dry desert.

"There is no Myst in the Carrash family. Only Asadel and Jinan." His uncle's booming voice bounced off the walls and Myst covered his ears, bending down again.

"Myst? I know you're in there. Have you packed? It's almost time to go." Kalaya continued to knock on the door, and the next thing Iris knew, small orange embers squeezed through the gap between the wood and the carpet floor.

With only her instincts in that moment, Iris ran towards the fireplace, which seemed counterintuitive when she thought about it, but the flames from the other side grew bigger and warmer.

"I can't do it, Kal!" Myst cried towards the door, holding his palms against his eyes. "I'd be leaving everything I've worked towards behind."

"Take what's important, Myst. I know you can."

The Six of Swords. A journey where one took what they cared about most and left the rest behind for calmer waters. They didn't have to be the one steering the boat. They only had to be the one to make the choice to get on.

Myst had to make the choice, for Kalaya could steer the boat.

Starting from where Iris stood, the room began to fall apart, breaking away piece by piece and then disappearing as if it had never been there. She hopped closer and closer to the door, preferring a burning room rather than the infinite void below.

As she grasped the doorframe for balance, shock and wonder for how she wasn't getting burnt took over her mind. Myst grabbed the door handle, looking at her with determination and newfound energy. *Take what's important.*

Then they opened the door.

Chapter 22
the high priestess

Ash fell and painted the grey concrete black as the door was shattered to pieces. At least Marin and Kalaya's door was intact.

Iris stared back into the darkness, the voices of Marin, Kalaya, and Myst comforting each other muffled in her ears. She had seen her family in there. Her siblings who she left behind, her mother who she went on this mission for. She would not fail.

Then she tuned back in, facing the others.

"It seemed like a good idea at the time," Marin said, a serious expression on their face, but she could see the twinkle in their eyes. "And it got you out, didn't it?"

"How about, try the doorknob next time?" Myst's voice was quiet, but stern. He was returning to his usual self.

"You know what happens when I do that."

Not a moment later, Myst turned to face Iris, then marched towards her, wrapped his arms around her and pulled her in for a hug.

"Thank Ter and Mian that you were there. I don't know what I would've done if…" He opted to bury his face in her shoulder rather than continuing.

Iris blinked, feeling the warmth coming from the caemi. She hadn't done much except for a bad attempt at fighting. But no matter, since they had all made it now. It turned out both corridors led them to the end.

She lifted her arms to return the embrace and rested her cheek against his chest. His heart was beating fast.

"Are you feeling okay?" she asked, pulling away to look at his face. Tear marks.

"I'm…" His teeth played with his bottom lip. "I didn't think that would happen again. A nightmare about… that."

She nodded. "I completely understand."

He smiled. It may have been difficult to explain this to others who didn't share the same experiences.

"I just thought that after a while it would… go away. That I wouldn't be bothered again. I suppose I'm still not strong enough." Myst looked down and stepped away.

"No." Kalaya placed a hand on his shoulder. "Getting past what we saw in the dark is not about strength."

"Then how do I make it stop?"

"Time, friends, new experiences, healing… I can't say for sure, but what I do know is that we don't have to be alone."

Iris remembered Marin crashing into her illusion and into her life. It didn't mean her life was suddenly perfect, but it was the beginning of facing her feelings and memories, and new experiences, too. What did this mean for her?

She let the thought stew in her mind as she turned her attention to the torches that suddenly lit around them in a circle. Marin cheered from beside a sconce, where they were holding up a tiny fire.

A few suits of metal and chainmail armour came into light, causing Iris to jump before realising no one was wearing them. The walls curved around them, long swords and shields uniformly decorating, ready to be taken to battle.

"Oh, finally." Marin sighed. "But how are we supposed to find an artefact here?"

They had seen enough of the room to understand there was nothing out of the ordinary, and none of the caemi had said anything about an aura yet. They were met with a dead end coming to this room, and Iris had a feeling none of them wanted to check the corridor for an artefact.

Though, by now, she knew a tarot card could sometimes reveal more than originally interpreted.

"There's something we aren't seeing. This isn't all there is to the armoury..." Iris walked to the back wall and placed a hand on it. She was tempted to slide her hand along it to see if anything would budge, but doing that would risk her hand getting cut by the swords.

"Remove the fourth sword," Kalaya stated, waving in the general direction of it.

"What?" Myst and Marin asked in obvious confusion, their voices overlapping.

At first, Iris shared the same feeling before picturing the Eight of Swords in her head. The image depicted three swords, then the blindfolded lady stuck in loose bandages before the rest of the swords followed to the right of her.

"Oh, you're saying the swords on the card are an example of this armoury's puzzle..." She carefully counted four swords along the wall. She reached up, trying to grab the sword by the hilt to remove it without hitting the sharp edge. But her arm was too short, and the sword fell right into her hands.

Iris shrieked, expecting a sharp pain to course through her hands, but there was nothing. The sword was cold and blunt.

"Iris! Wait—why are you so calm? A sword just fell on you!" Marin screamed. The others gathered around her to inspect the damage, and Marin quickly grabbed the sword and threw it aside to look at her hands. "There's no blood?"

Myst retrieved the sword and gently placed his palm along the metal, no reaction coming from him either. "It's fake, the sword isn't sharp at all."

"Another trick of the Eight of Swords." That smirk came over Kalaya's lips once again, causing Iris' thoughts to buffer. "A lack of options with no clear way out, only caused by our own limiting beliefs and over-thinking. This armoury is a fake-out, only here for looks to hide the real treasure."

"That's… a strange choice on the queen's side, considering she's made her people believe an assassination was attempted on her. What if something really happened, and they needed these?" Marin pondered, now inspecting the sword.

"It isn't for us to work out, luckily, but that doesn't explain how we're going to find the artefact. The sword didn't trigger anything, so we haven't achieved much."

Before any of them could continue, Iris felt a shudder of chilly wind, despite no way for such a draft to make its way this far into the tunnel. Goosebumps raised on her arms and a prickly feeling crawled along her back.

"Did you guys feel that?" Marin looked around, supposedly having felt the same as she did.

The others nodded, also curious about the strange sudden chill.

"My, is that a group of caemi I see… oh, a senti too?" A voice they didn't recognise emitted from the hidden darkness of the armoury.

Iris froze up upon hearing it, though Kalaya stayed by her and linked arms once again.

"Who's there?" Myst mustered the courage to call out, but they all knew that if anyone was here, it wasn't where they were standing, which meant…

A clatter from another part of the room sent their attention back towards the dark corridors, and this time, Marin was the one to check it out. A few of the swords had been knocked off their stands and shields spun around right by the doorways. "What in the name of the patrons… is there someone else in here with us?"

"Surely not, we can't see anyone!" Myst's voice was starting to waver at this point. The chills were returning, and the room was plunged into an incredible cold.

"Do not be afraid, little ones," the disembodied voice said once again. "What are you doing here? How did you get past the tunnels… No one comes down here, damn fake swords. What kind of armoury is this?"

Wait. "Were you the one who did that to us?" Iris found herself stepping forward. She hadn't even considered what Marin and Kalaya would've gone through, and she wanted to be there for all of them. "Show yourself!"

"Please, what do you expect when you delve into an unknown place in the dark with nothing but your thoughts? That was hardly my fault… well, maybe I did the atmospheric noises, but…"

Iris kept her mouth shut, letting the voice babble on about what it did. She couldn't tell if it was lying or not, and part of her disliked that it may have been right.

"A fake armoury." Kalaya's voice took over the room, the only one to respond to what the voice was really asking. "You're guarding something from us, what do you ask of us to reveal it?"

"Oh, what bravery from the little cat caemi. Oh, not you. You're little, but not you, blue one." The voice rambled on, making Marin's cheeks flush. "Purple one, how do you know I guard something?"

It took some thought, but upon recalling Kalaya's room, her light in the prison's darkness, and her current performance, Iris concluded this was a result of experience with spirit communication. It was one of the many aspects of witchcraft that was possible for anyone, but took time and practice to truly master and be a natural. Kalaya was a natural: the way she conducted herself, the way she spoke, the way she almost connected to this voice.

"We're in search of the artefact belonging to our king and queen residing in the lands of Syriphia. May we have your good favour to retrieve it?"

By now, Myst and Marin had calmed down. Iris figured they were used to this as the ones who usually worked with Kalaya, but perhaps the darkness and the situation itself caused them to be caught off guard.

"No," it answered rather quickly.

And the cards started to connect.

Four of Pentacles.

"It's mine, you cannot have it," he continued.

Possessiveness of material objects, wanting to guard it as signified by the man's positioning on the card, holding the pentacle tightly, and also guarding the others. This guarding spirit ignored anything around him, and the large town in the background did not interest him.

"It doesn't belong to you, yet you guard it. We want to return it to its rightful owners," Kalaya insisted.

Seven of Cups.

"You only want to take it for yourself. I cannot know your true intentions and you cannot dare to question my guardianship."

A card of being shrouded by illusion. While Iris could understand why a random group of caemi and senti coming to take an artefact would bring alarm to a guardian spirit, it was likely prone to illusion and unrealistic ideas of forever keeping the artefact in these forged tunnels. It was a card of building an image of an ideal future rather than a choice for the present moment.

Six of Cups.

"How about a compromise?" Kalaya suggested, a teasing inflection in her voice.

There wasn't a snappy response this time, as if the spirit was contemplating. From Iris' experience, compromises were rather useful when it came to a stubborn client. Sometimes they would refuse any message she would try to deliver, presenting their own opinion on the situation, which wasn't exactly constructive towards the reading. Usually, Iris worked on a compromise between both of their opinions, slightly biased towards her own, so the advice wouldn't go unused.

"Proceed," the spirit called.

The Six of Cups was a card she remembered from her reading with Mikael, but the context was important for each reading. It was why each tarot card had a meaning, but Iris had learnt the intuitive meaning, alongside the other cards, was more important in her job as a tarot reader.

In this situation, it could be interpreted as the spirit giving part of itself, such as the depiction of the young boy having all the flower cups on the card and handing one to the younger girl. If Kalaya was similarly imagining this, it was likely her idea was—

"Come with us. Let us take the artefact and come with us to make sure it stays safe. We need someone to look after it on our way back to Syriphia, after all." A smile spread across Kalaya's lips. It was a genuine request and a rather interesting one at that. They didn't know if this spirit could harm them, but Kalaya trusted it enough to offer this.

"What if you take me somewhere horrible? This tunnel is rather horrible already, so I don't know how it could get worse, but... you know what I mean!"

Iris found the personality of the spirit amusing. He was stubborn, but also susceptible to awkwardness.

"I can offer nothing but my word, spirit. But I wish for your trust. We will protect you and the artefact, and you can also protect it. If it is that important, we are willing to accompany and accommodate you." Kalaya placed a hand across her chest as a gesture of honour.

Silence followed, each one of the caemi and Iris holding their breaths awaiting an answer from the spirit. Iris only had hope for what would happen next, even though the wait felt longer than any of the previous answers.

It wasn't until they heard shifting bricks from a part of the wall that they realised something was happening. In the place of the fourth sword, an opening was created and revealed a pedestal. On top of the pedestal sat a large glowing aqua orb decorated with shiny golden metal in the shape of a tree, clasping the orb like a hand. *The artefact is real. They were telling the truth.*

The four of them stared at the mystical orb in awe, being careful not to approach it too closely before they got the approval of the spirit. Iris could see the ears of the caemi twitching in the presence of the orb and she wondered if they could feel anything in their chest because of it, too. At least, she assumed the aura was located by the heart, corresponding with the soul.

"I call it the sorbra." The spirit's voice came back. "Don't ask me why, that's just what it told me."

"What is it?" Iris was curious. It wasn't every day she came across a magical artefact belonging to royalty.

"I don't quite know, but I like to describe it as a magical battery. It contains magical power, I know that much. I also know you can't easily get it out, it mostly absorbs power—with the permission of the user, of course."

"Do I have permission from you to hold it?" Kalaya stepped forwards with her hands out. The spirit answered positively and the purple caemi was able to hold it within her two palms.

"How does it feel?" Myst asked, but didn't dare to touch it without permission.

"It's... as Spirit says, powerful. It's contained, but you can just feel it with your aura. I'd go so far to say Iris could probably feel it if she tried."

"So, are we going or not?" Spirit seemed much more excited about leaving now that they were on their way to making it out.

"Of course. Would you know a way out of here?" Tiredness was pulling at Myst's voice. Each one of them wanted to get out of this place as soon as possible.

"I sure do. It's through the sewers, though."

Marin let out a loud whine, though they all knew he could handle a little trip in the sewer tunnels—they were on their way home after all.

And so, with the artefact in hand, Kalaya rescued from prison, and the new addition of the guardian spirit, the group made their way through the nightmare corridor that was better with all of them together, the slippery tunnel, past the long winding staircase and into the sewers which admittedly smelled quite a bit, but were their path back to the surface.

It was before long when they emerged somewhere along a mountain-side, the view of an afternoon sky and setting sun on the horizon watching over the ever-bustling Kingdom of Excava.

Chapter 23
the lovers

It was the day after rescuing Kalaya and retrieving the artefact when Iris woke up in the late afternoon in the safety of the inn, more refreshed than ever during the past few weeks.

A comfortable bed after a tiring day of problem-solving and physical activity was a great combination and meant they lazed around for most of the day after the rescue. Having to get used to knowing Kalaya was back meant they didn't have much to do with themselves when they woke up, but that was more than welcome.

"Cup of tea?" Marin entered the room with a tray holding a pot and a few ceramic cups. A small stream of steam was emitting from the spout.

"Tea? I don't think I've had tea before." Iris stared at the pot and cups. Even with such a long sleep, she still experienced that just-woke-up fuzziness, rubbing her eyes to bring focus. "At home, we only have water and alcohol."

"Alcohol?!" Marin carefully placed the tray on the table before flailing their arms. "Your parents were giving you alcohol?"

Kalaya laughed from the other side of the table, which caused the words Iris was about to say to disappear for a moment and for her to stare at the caemi, though she turned back to Marin after realising what she was doing.

"I'll have you know I'm old enough to be drinking alcohol, and there's a bar in the gambling house." But for now, she was curious about what tea was like.

Marin picked up the pot and poured a cup for the three of them. "Try it. It's just for while we wait for Myst to get back with the food."

"Do I get tea as well?" A voice that had since become familiar to Iris came from the other side of the room. "Well, I can't drink tea, but I want some."

"Of course, Spirit," Kalaya replied with a smile, selecting an empty cup and pouring a bit of tea in it. She walked over to where the sorbra was sitting and placed the cup beside it.

Marin sat down and sunk into the chair, embracing the warmth of their tea. "This is incredible."

"The tea?" Iris asked, staring into the coloured liquid in her cup. She picked it up by the handle and brought it to her lips. She could taste a nice mix of citrus and spice, even if it was a bit bitter.

"Well, yes, but I mean—we did it. We've retrieved the artefact which we failed to do weeks ago. Once we get our small feast going, celebrate Kalaya's return and all that, we can finally return home!"

With that revelation, a rising joy caused the group to cheer, and even the guarding spirit seemed to emit a positive energy. But for some reason, Iris couldn't help but notice a sinking feeling in her chest, like something was stopping her from celebrating as much as the others did.

Returning home. It was a thought of hers when she had first left the Galacia Gambling House, thinking about how soon it would be before she went back to work and faced her mother with her earned riches.

She wondered what was happening while she was away in another city, across the sea. Did they miss her? How angry was her mother? Would her family understand she left to earn the money her mother demanded of her?

She didn't like the dreadful feeling in her stomach. It was her home, meaning she was supposed to be happy about going back. Even if it meant no more adventures, routine work, and no guarantee of seeing her friends again.

A knock at the door interrupted her thoughts and the conversation the others were having. Kalaya and Marin quickly hid their ears and tails, the shorter caemi going to the door to open it and see who it was.

"We're back with dinner!" Myst's voice filled the room and the smell of fresh bread, roasted meat, stews, rice, and a variety of vegetables made its way into the room.

Marin rushed up to grab a plate from Myst. "Thank the patrons—wait, we?"

"Hello everyone…" After clearing the doorway and placing the various plates of food on the table, Yori shuffled out from behind Myst with a small wave and carried some glasses for drinks.

"Yori! What are you doing here?" Iris was relieved to see the gardener once again. He had been a big help in the plan and she didn't want to leave him without saying thank you.

"Myst and I ran into each other at the market. I was getting some new trimmers and gloves. He told me you guys were having a bit of a celebration and invited me. I hope it's okay that I'm joining." Yori added a low bow as well.

Kalaya walked up to the gardener. "I don't think we've met before, but you're more than welcome to stay for the night."

"You're Kalaya." Yori's eyes widened. "I heard rumours about you being captured. You're the friend they were trying to save."

"That would be correct," Kalaya replied with a chuckle. "I deeply appreciate the help you offered to them. I don't know how things would've gone without your help."

Yori looked away shyly and went back to Myst, staying close by as he was serving up the feast. "I appreciate you're letting me stay. This food looks really good."

The group passed some plates of food around and dug in, the hunger from the past day or so catching up with them. While it was a meal of a few components—meat, grain and vegetables—it was delicious and filling, and a great meal for the group to talk with each other over.

Iris didn't recall the last time she had such a hearty meal surrounded by people she truly cared for. Her family didn't do dinners together anymore, there wasn't enough time and their schedules didn't work out well for that. Now that they were all old enough to figure out their dinner, they were left to eat in their own time and place.

She shook the thought off. It was time for celebration rather than thinking of what her family used to do. Being grateful for the meal and being in the company of her friends should be her focus.

"So, are you part of the orb, Spirit?" Marin asked in no particular direction, continuing their meal.

"No, the orb has its own spirit to it, even if it doesn't speak as I do. I used to hang around the library of the castle until I saw the orb being taken through a doorway. I followed it until they placed it in that fake armoury. I hadn't seen it before, but I knew I had to protect it."

"That's sweet." Kalaya wiped her mouth with a cloth before pushing her empty plate forward. "And that was delicious. Thank you for the meal, Myst."

"Only the best for you all. This meal is well deserved!" Myst lifted his glass and nodded to the group.

As Iris finished her meal, she took one of the glasses Yori brought in from the middle of the table and poured water into it, taking a refreshing drink. When she placed the glass down, Kalaya was standing next to her, causing her to jump a little and cough.

"Ah, Kalaya, sorry. I didn't expect you to be standing there." Iris smiled weakly as she regained her composure the best she could.

"Not to worry, Sybil. I was just wondering if you wanted to take a walk with me. There's something I want to show you before we have to go back to Syriphia."

A warm smile from the caemi captivated Iris, and she nodded. This is exactly what she wanted as well, to have some time to talk to someone else like her so she could learn something and feel that connection she had been missing for a lot of her lifetime.

"We'll be back later!" Kalaya called to the rest of the group as she and Iris walked up to the door, getting ready to leave. Right as the door opened, Kalaya quickly made her way across the hall to her room, emerging after a few moments with her violin case.

"Have fun!" Marin called from inside the room, his words slightly muffled from having all the food in their mouth.

And with that, Kalaya led the way with Iris following closely beside her, admiring the golden sky but noting it didn't nearly compare to the purple caemi's sparkling eyes.

"Close your eyes."

Kalaya had told her this as they approached a forest, and Iris was inclined to trust her. As she closed them, Kalaya took her hand and started leading forward through the forest, leaves crunching beneath her boots and the branches rustling in the wind.

Without sight, she could only take in the sound and smell of what was around her. She knew they were still walking in the forest by the pinewood wafting through her nostrils, and an almost vanilla scent in the air. She also heard the flapping and flying of a few birds overhead, and when she stumbled, her free hand caught onto a trunk that was rough, but not sharp.

She focused on the refreshing energy around her, the trees providing her with clear breathing and relaxation. Even just this guided walk through the forest was a beautiful experience.

"Take a big step here," Kalaya instructed, and she could hear her move some branches aside.

Iris did as she was told and found herself stepping onto more even ground.

"You can open your eyes now."

And that she did. While it was a bit darker now that the sun had set, the moonlight bathed the sandy ground below her. Before her was a large body of water with small ripples appearing and disappearing all across it. She didn't think water did that by itself, but it was pretty. It reminded her of the ocean, just on a smaller scale.

Around them was the forest, so it appeared they were standing in a clearing where a large pond was situated. It felt calming and like they were protected by the strong trees surrounding them.

"It's beautiful, isn't it? While staying in Excava Kingdom for our mission, I wanted to find a place to relax, connect with the natural spirits and also practice my violin." Kalaya was staring out at the water, also looking at the ripples.

"It is…" She joined Kalaya. "I've only met a handful of spirits in my time outside, but it does feel comforting to be here."

"It's nicer to be here with someone else, especially with someone who understands. While Marin and Myst are my best friends, they don't have the same connection to the natural world and magic in all senses as I do."

Kalaya crouched down and placed her violin case on the beach, then opened it. "Take a seat, I'll play you a song."

"A song? For me?" Iris was taken aback, but sat down as she was told. She looked up at Kalaya, who was illuminated by the moonlight, the silhouette of the caemi looking graceful with the violin placed under her chin.

"Mhm, a song to my saviour. The lovely Sybil, Iris Galacia."

Iris loved the way her name sounded with Kalaya's accented voice, but what came next was even more beautiful. As Kalaya placed her bow to the strings, a mystical sound emitted, and a song started to play from the small instrument, filling the night air around them. Iris was fascinated.

While violin music wasn't rare at the gambling house, hearing it in person by someone who was playing for her was an experience she couldn't describe in words.

Little orbs of light started appearing around them and from the water, hovering towards the sound of the violin. The lights began dancing, spinning around the purple caemi to the tune of the song. Kalaya also began to spin with the lights, almost like she was dancing with them.

Iris watched on with wonderful delight, eyes wide and chin in her hands. The warm feeling in her chest only grew, and she giggled at the show the caemi and lights were displaying, the song continuing on and filling her ears. It was like being a child again, watching something unfamiliar, yet wanting more of it.

In a gentle fall, the song slowed to a stop, and the lights remained dancing for a few moments only before floating back to the edge of the forest and into the water, the ripples returning. So, they were created by small spirits.

Kalaya sighed, taking a seat beside Iris and putting her violin back into the case safely. "It's been too long since I played my violin. I'm a little rusty."

"Rusty? But that was… amazing. I don't know what to say, I've never heard anything as wonderful as what you just played. I can't imagine what your playing would be like when it's not rusty," Iris rambled on before she noticed Kalaya staring at her, causing her to stop. It wasn't like her to ramble, her siblings told her it wasn't good for her image.

"I'm flattered, and I'm glad you liked the song. It's one I've been waiting to play for someone."

"Someone in particular?" She held her breath in anticipation.

"Oh, no. Just for someone I would come across and I would know if I wanted to play the song for them. That someone is you now, it seems." She gave Iris a wink, which sent blood rushing to her cheeks.

"I-I see, that's lovely." Iris couldn't control her smile. "So, what were the spirits doing? Was that part of your magic?"

"Not exactly. You see, Marin and Myst use their caemi magic to produce light. For me, I use a combination of the two magical arts. Witchcraft helps me to develop a connection to the spirits around us, such as those of water and earth, and my natural caemi magic helps me sustain enough energy to almost exchange it with them."

Iris recalled Kalaya mentioning this, but she wasn't very knowledgeable on the subject of combining both magics. "Can you elaborate more on what you were doing, then?"

"Some spirits love music. These spirits that reside in the forest are attracted to the sound of my violin. I found that out when I first played here and these balls of light came out of nowhere. With my caemi aura being present, it helps them stay visible and around me since they have a source to feed off.

Normally, with witchcraft, you will need to find another source of energy as a senti, or use your own, but that can drain you."

She was already learning so much from Kalaya, and she hoped to remember everything so she could write it down when they got back.

"You seem very in tune with spirits," Iris noted. "My witchcraft practice hasn't advanced very much, I just do divination at the moment."

"Well, it doesn't need to be flashy. It can be personalised and something that helps you feel fulfilled. For me, I like communing with spirits. For some, it may be too much to feel the presence of spirits constantly and have to listen to them. To each their own." She paused for a moment, letting out a soft hum. "Though for someone like you, I doubt you haven't encountered spirits before. Do you have any odd experiences you can note?"

Odd experiences weren't common for Iris, but there were two things she could recall even during her time at the gambling house.

"Between meeting Myst and Marin, I had a lot of run-ins with crows. I understand they can be an omen, but I haven't looked into it enough. Then there's also this strange thing that happens when I shuffle. I don't see it because I keep my eyes closed, but it feels like some sort of mist comes from my hands and surrounds the cards, beckoning the ones I need to the correct position."

"I imagine you ground and centre before each reading. It's almost like you meditate each day, but in small intervals."

Iris blinked. Kalaya was right. Was it a common practice for tarot readers? "I do that, yes. How does that relate to spirits?"

"Those who are spiritually attuned require meditation and grounding to keep themselves protected from the constant noise, but also to welcome the magic of spirits into their lives. The spirits are on your side when you do readings, and they accompany you unintentionally. It isn't a bad thing, you just need to ensure you don't get carried away by them," Kalaya spoke her words with confidence, then lifted her finger to the side of her nose. "The crows may have been a few messengers I came across."

So the birds did mean something, after all! "Of course, that makes a lot of sense." Iris nodded, though wasn't sure what being 'carried away' by the spirits meant. "Where did you learn this from?"

"Mostly self-taught, in secret. My family was never very accepting of it, as they were strong believers in caemi magic only. Noble families are like that sometimes, unfortunately."

"Noble?" The only person she suspected with a noble background was Myst, but she didn't know enough about him yet to make any accurate calls.

"Yes. Actually, Marin, Myst, and I are all from higher-class families. I suppose that's why Myst is the least open to my witchcraft despite how it helps. He is accepting, but sceptical because his family's status is higher than Marin's and mine."

That confirmed her suspicion, but opened more questions. "Why are you all guild questers then? Aren't those guilds better for people who are in need of the money rather than nobles with… noble duties?" She wasn't exactly sure what nobles did, but she did know they had enough money to comfortably gamble away at home.

Kalaya chuckled with a shrug. "The noble life gets boring. It's all about representing a status and working towards inheriting it. Then working on that with your future children. There isn't much fulfilment to sitting at home all day, waiting."

That was closer to her own experience than she expected it to be. While her own everyday life consisted of sitting at home all day, and working towards serving her family's business, was it boring? She found tarot to be fulfilling, but perhaps the constant stream of disconnected clients and some returning, but irritating ones, didn't exactly fit the description.

"So, you all chose to leave that behind to become guild questers?"

Iris looked across the pond and into the darkness of the forest. There wasn't much to see. Though for a moment, she believed she saw a flash of light from the spirits. She blinked and rubbed her eyes, looking out once again, and a quick flash went by. It was like a little game.

"It's deeper than I can explain in a few sentences, but a brief overview contains Marin feeling too restricted by that lifestyle while having other values. I wanted to do something more with witchcraft than hide it all the time from my family. Myst is a bit more connected to his noble side, keeping some of the values, but he still has a strong drive against nobles treating the lower class as just that, lower."

"Huh, that explains the Yori situation," Iris recalled.

"The Yori situation?"

"Well, he seemed to have a deep interest in the gardener when he mentioned the royals not bothering to know his name. Since then, Myst has been paying close attention to him and even asked him out."

Kalaya laughed. It sounded beautiful. "He can be like that sometimes. A bit aloof until something catches his attention. But that's how you know the interest is genuine."

That was an accurate reading of what Myst was like. It didn't stop her from wanting to get to know him more so their friendship could improve. Myst reminded her of her older brothers when they were younger.

"Tell me about yourself," Kalaya said, still looking at the pond.

"What would you like to know?" Even after talking to Marin about herself previously, it was still strange to be asked about. Her clients had a base level of understanding about who she was, not even knowing her name. They didn't need to know it.

"Anything. What do you do outside of saving young ladies from castles?" Kalaya gave Iris a cheeky look.

Iris smiled, though the question reminded her of home. It still confused her that she felt so sad about going home. She understood sadness was a feeling when having to leave something she enjoyed, but there was also fear mixed with what she was experiencing. Almost like she feared being met with what was home, even if she completed her task.

"Every day, I wake up and get ready for work. I wear a nice dress with my blue cloak. I also wear white gloves to complete the look. I take my favourite deck from my bedside table and go downstairs to my booth, where I perform readings. Then my work starts."

"And when does it end?"

"At the end of the day, then I have my evening meal. Then there's paperwork. Sometimes, there are meetings. I occasionally have to attend disciplinary meetings where my mother—I mean my boss—disciplines my poor performance. It keeps me thinking about improvement. Which is a good thing."

Her voice began to waver, and she could feel sniffles coming up. Before long, her eyes started to well and her sight of the pond before her became blurry through the tears. Why was she feeling this way? This was supposed to be her life as a businesswoman.

"It's supposed to be good, right?" Iris pleaded quietly, not expecting an answer as it had always been like.

"No, that's horrible," Kalaya said in a stern voice, sending a sudden jolt through Iris like something was stabbing her right in the heart. Horrible? What did that mean?

"What you're describing is... not normal," Kalaya continued. "Your mother never lets you out?"

She shook her head, quiet whimpers coming from her. "Why would I ever need to leave? Work is all I have, and it's always been that way."

"It's not like you're working right now. Work isn't all you have, you also have Marin, Myst, and me now. I suppose Yori and Spirit count as well."

"But the business…"

"Shouldn't be your concern. If you're working somewhere where it's all you do and your mother even has to yell at you, that's just wrong. It's not good for you." Kalaya shuffled closer to Iris and wrapped her arm around her, guiding Iris to rest her head on her shoulder.

"Then what am I supposed to do? I can't just leave my mother and siblings like that."

"That is… exactly what you do. I'm sorry, not to make your thinking sound stupid." Kalaya paused. "I mean, in situations like this, you need to think about yourself first. You're an adult now and look at you, you don't go outside, but you've been out here for a few weeks just fine."

Kalaya was right on that front. Even with leaving for the first time with a stranger, she found herself fed every day, a place to sleep each night, and a friend to talk to and have adventures with each and every day she was gone from home. It was what she had at home, but miles better and it made her a lot happier.

"There's a difference between running away from problems you can solve and running away because confrontation will only hurt you more. It's about separating yourself from what drains you."

"I do enjoy doing this over going to work every day… it's so tiring." Iris let herself relax into Kalaya's shoulder and closed her eyes. Her mind was always working so quickly to keep up with the bustling gambling house, but that wasn't needed if she wasn't there.

"Your siblings are stuck in that situation, but they will be able to leave when they are old enough. It's good to care for them, but you can't always put them before you. Perhaps one day you can go back to talk to them, instead of going back forever."

Iris took a few breaths and imagined going back to the gambling house after moving out without them knowing, having gone to build her own life outside of Vestirr. It was peaceful, until an image of her mother appeared in the vision, causing her to jump.

"What's wrong?" Kalaya jumped as well, but returned to her position after a second.

"My mother, she... scares me." Iris had never said that out loud. It felt wrong to say that, but she also knew she wasn't lying.

"Ah, that tends to happen if she's constantly yelling at you and putting you down. Unfortunately, motivation can be fear and she is the fear in what drives you. At least when it comes to your business."

Kalaya provided her a voice she had been missing this entire time, reasoning and logic she failed to come to as the one experiencing what she did with her family dynamic. It was refreshing to have another perspective, but also a bit scary to come to realise all of this.

"She's one of the reasons I went on this adventure in the first place. I was afraid of what would happen if I didn't have the money she wanted by the time she wanted it, and I knew my business wasn't good enough to earn that much for her. I needed another way to get more money and Marin helped with that."

Kalaya shrugged. "You won't need to give that money to her if you don't go back. You can just keep it."

This earned a weak laugh from Iris. "And then what?"

"And then you make your dreams come true. Marin, Myst, and I are still working on it, but look at us. We get to travel the world, wear whatever we want, meet whoever we want, and just enjoy life. Do you have a dream?"

The answer was yes, but no. For a few years after discovering tarot, she had a dream to share her knowledge and skill with the world, being able to read for different people who were truly interested in the power of tarot and wanted to learn about it. Though, after constantly being told it was impossible by her mother and siblings, she pushed the dream away and left it locked in a box to never open again.

Until this moment.

"I like the idea of travelling the world." Iris looked up at the sky, billions of sparkling stars overtaking the darkness. She wondered how the stars looked from different parts of the world. Even then, she was only used to the stars she could see outside her bedroom window. "I want to read for different people, not just drunk, smoky, rich people who throw away their lives for money."

She found that quite hypocritical of herself, living up until now for the money so she could contribute to her mother's business. Though, she could change that if she wanted, right?

"You can travel the world if you want. I mean, it's easier said than done, of course. I just wanted to offer a new view. Something different from what you've always known. In the end, it's your choice about where you go next."

"I do appreciate the alternate view. I haven't had that until I met you and the others."

Iris shifted, and Kalaya placed her arm around Iris' waist instead, pulling her close. It was like a warm snug blanket despite the breezy summer's night.

"Tomorrow, Marin, Myst, and I return to Syriphia, and you are set to choose where to go next," Kalaya whispered.

Iris stayed silent, still mulling over the entire conversation they just had and the suggestions that came with it. It was no easy choice, and one she would have to sleep on before making her decision. She only had one night, in any case.

The purple cat caemi lifted her head and turned to Iris, her wide purple eyes still sparkly as ever, comparable to the night sky above them. A few spirits made themselves visible and danced around the two.

"We haven't known each other for long," Kalaya stated, breaking eye contact to look away. "But I'm going to miss you, Iris Galacia."

Chapter 24
the World

The docks hadn't changed in how busy and crowded they were as Kalaya, Myst, Marin, Yori, and Iris gathered in one of the ports, suitcases placed together, though Iris' sitting away from the others. She didn't want to mix her luggage with the others if they were going to be on different ships.

Bells were ringing from the clock tower, marking the hours of the morning and adding to the bustling noise of the port. There were ships docking up and people loading cargo, stalls still ever busy trying to sell their produce. Unfortunately, the absence of caemi was still evident on the way here, but her experience with the others made her wonder if there were any in disguise, like her friends.

Iris yawned. She had tried her best to sleep soundly last night in preparation for the trip ahead back to Vestirr, but the conversation she had with Kalaya kept her up for a few hours. Even now, it was still running through her head, her mind attempting to divide everything into pros and cons for what choice she would make.

No matter what, she humoured the thought of staying with the group, but the fear of what her family would think was lingering. Perhaps it would be easier to just go home, as she had been telling herself this whole time.

Myst walked up to her and held out his hand for a handshake. Iris went to take it, only to be caught by surprise in a hug that he pulled her into. "Iris, thank you. I'm not sure if we would be standing here right now with Kalaya if it weren't for you. I'm sorry for any doubts I had and... the trouble I caused."

Iris stood frozen for a moment before lowering her arms to hug Myst back. While Myst had caused a bit of trouble, they worked through it, and there was only growth to come. "I had been wondering about you since I did that reading. I'm glad that mystery could be solved."

"Quite the odd situation, wasn't it?" Myst chuckled and let Iris go, bringing a hand to his eye and wiping it.

Now it was Kalaya's turn. The purple cat caemi, though in disguise like the others, stepped forward and hugged Iris, except she added a small kiss on her cheek as she let go, causing Iris to bring a hand to where her face heated.

"You've been a great help, and someone had to keep these two together while I was in prison." Kalaya playfully elbowed Myst, who rolled his eyes. "I wasn't lying when I said you were my saviour. I owe you for my freedom, and you helped us complete the mission we were sent to do."

Kalaya patted the bag she was carrying, reaffirming the orb was safely sitting in it, ready to be taken back. They had also told Spirit beforehand that it couldn't come out and talk in public, so Iris said her goodbyes with Spirit back at the inn.

She watched on as Yori and Myst said their goodbyes, though Myst confirmed he would return for the gardener so they could continue to go out. It was a sweet gesture to watch until Marin barrelled into Iris with open arms and held her tightly, whining and crying like a mess. She quickly caught herself, as not to send them both into the ocean, and held Marin just as tightly, this time attempting to hug them back instead of only head patting them.

"Iris! I'm going to miss you so much, I will always remember you," Marin somehow managed to say between loud sobs, causing some people around them to turn.

Iris nervously ran her hand through their hair. "Hey come on, it's okay. I'll remember you too, you've been an amazing friend."

The short caemi only continued to sob into Iris as they held her tightly. "Do you have to go?"

She didn't know how to answer that, knowing she wanted to stay, but feeling like she needed to go home where her family would be expecting her. It didn't stop her from wanting a sign, though. Something to tell her what the right choice was despite knowing the opinions of the others.

It was as if the universe was listening when she felt a hand on her shoulder and turned around to see Taelyn and Nora standing behind her.

"Hey sis, what's going on?" Her brother gave her a gentle smile she hadn't seen in years. Her mind flashed to the regret filled conversation she imagined in the tunnels, but the way he stood before her now... she didn't have to be afraid.

"Taelyn, Nora. I'm just saying goodbye to the others." Before she had met Marin, she only said goodbye to clients that she didn't care about. Why did the first time it mattered hurt so much?

"Goodbye? Where are you going?" Nora asked, looking to the others who were tearing up, and Marin, who was still hiding their face in Iris' shirt.

"Home... I'm sure mother is expecting me. Aren't you going home now as well?" She looked at Taelyn curiously, but he seemed to gaze away with an awkward look. Usually, he was much more confident when talking to Iris.

"Ah well, you see... I'm staying here." Her brother scratched the back of his neck.

"Wait, what? Here in Excava?" Iris expected her brother to be the last person to leave the Galacia Gambling House as the one to inherit it.

"I've found what I wanted here." He turned to Nora with a smile, and she smiled back, taking his hand. "I've been wanting to stay with Nora for... a long while now, only being able to be with her through letters sent over the sea and waiting weeks to get a response. I'm finally here, and I'm going to stay."

"What about the business?" Iris insisted, not knowing if she was insisting on behalf of her mother or to receive confirmation that her brother was truly considering not returning home.

Taelyn let go of Nora's hand and placed both of them on Iris' shoulders. She was used to seeing a disappointed look on her brother's face when it came to these gestures, but that gentle look remained.

"Listen, Iris. I know I haven't been the best brother. I know I've always put the business in front of everything. Always thinking about the future of the business, but never my own. It was only money, clients, and paperwork." He sighed, as if to take a moment to find the right words. He had never been the one to reveal his thoughts like this to his siblings. "I'm choosing to step away from that now, I have my own life and our mother doesn't have that much power over us anymore. You have no one to convince but yourself now. You have the chance to do the same as I, with these people."

Taelyn gestured behind her, and she turned to see the group watching the two of them speak patiently. They gave her small smiles of encouragement and gestured back to her brother as if saying to take his advice. "I don't know them, but they seem to care a lot. You have a choice, Iris. You can decide how this ends."

Iris stood still for a moment, and it clicked: this was the confirmation she was seeking. If her eldest brother, who had always been about the business, was choosing to stay with who he loved instead of returning to a life of boredom and working in someone else's image, then there was nothing stopping her from following her dreams and desires to stay with the group she had grown to be friends with.

Iris opened her arms and hugged her brother, and he hugged back. "Thank you, Taelyn." She also turned to Nora as she let go. "I'm sure you will look after him well."

After Nora gave her a look of approval, Iris turned back to the group and sprinted towards them, this time being the one to send Marin toppling over and stumbling on the dock. Fortunately, Myst and Kalaya were able to stop the two of them from being sent off the platform.

Iris laughed, wrapping her arms around Marin and hugging them tightly, even shaking them in excitement. Marin didn't seem to oppose, cheering in response to the affection with the others joining in.

"So, Marin." Iris smiled widely.

"Yes, Iris?" Marin arched an eyebrow, giving her a curious look.

"Think you can get one of your connections to take us to Syriphia?"

She wouldn't need her cards to tell her how this ended.

Acknowledgements

It takes a village to raise a child. In this case, the child is TELL ME HOW IT ENDS.

I'd first like to thank my team who helped me bring this book to life. This includes my beta readers: The Final Librarian, Elion, Mushroom and Lydia who provided excellent feedback for me to consider. Then my editor, B.K Ntouris who spotted everything I didn't and also taught me new things about grammar. Then my cover designer, Alex Patrascu who I knew was going to be my cover designer before I decided to indie-publish. The cover is simply… beautiful and breathtaking. If I showed this cover to my younger self, they would explode. Then my character artist, Happon, whose art style I fell in love with at first sight and knew it was made for my characters.

Turning to indie publishing from holding onto that traditional publishing idea for so long means I need to thank all the indie authors that inspired me and have supported me along the way: Phoenix Ning, Margherita Scialla, Beau Van Dalen, SJ Whitby, Freydis Moon, TN Vitus, Rafael Nicolas, Kellen Graves, Sierra Elmore, Aimee Donnellan, Jay Leigh, Alex M. Nájera, L.E Harper, Ivana L. Truglio and L.L Hunter.

Next is my family, so my mum for always supporting my dreams, my dad who used to ask me what I was writing on the family computer when I was little, Uncle Ping for sharing my love for tarot and being supportive, and my siblings Kathleen, Theodore and Patrizia for their interest in what I do and wanting a copy of my book even if you don't read it.

Thank you to my partner, Zak. You put up with me pointing to the book section in every shop and telling you that my book will be there one day. Also, thanks for being proud of me.

I'd like to thank my best friends: Saiza, Faye and Lisa for all our trips to the bookshop in the city and for your undying hype for books and me. Your friendship means a lot.

To all the tarot readers and witches I've learnt from over the years. Your insights and expertise were invaluable.

To Words Alike, my wonderful writing Discord server that I also love like a child.

To the Twitter writing community that has always welcomed me.

To my ARC readers and Street Team who were incredibly supportive of my launch.

To all the voices that have been quieted by traditional institutions. To historically under-represented voices. This is our time to shine.

Thank you, reader, for picking this book and giving it a chance. You're making a dream come true.

If you enjoyed Tell Me How It Ends

Consider leaving an honest review! Your impression of the novel can help another reader find their next read and supports the author.

Sign up for my newsletter at quintonli.com/subscribe

You will be notified of new releases, events, pre-orders and other exclusives!

What's next for the Chaos in the Cards series?

Stay tuned for WHEN BOHEMIANS VOYAGE (Book 2 of the Chaos in the Cards series) where we follow Iris, Marin, Myst and Kalaya to the lands of Syriphia.

Author Bio

Quinton Li (they/them) is a Melbourne-based non-binary novelist, poet, and fiction editor. With a love for fortune-telling, angelic beings, and the human condition, it's no wonder many of their works across fiction and poetry touch on these subjects. Alongside these themes, they strongly resonate with queer and Asian diaspora works and believe art can change a perspective or enhance it.

let's connect:

Website: www.quintonli.com

Twitter & Tiktok: @itsquinnli

Instagram & Facebook: @quintonlieditorial

CPSIA information can be obtained
at www.ICGtesting.com
Printed in the USA
LVHW051226230623
750516LV00012B/119